THE CASE OF THE MISSING CORPSE

By Joan Sanger

M. EVANS
Lanham • New York • Boulder • Toronto • Plymouth, UK

Evans

imprint of The Rowman & Littlefield Publishing Group, Inc.
1 Forbes Boulevard, Suite 200, Lanham, Maryland 20706
://www.rlpgtrade.com

Thornbury Road, Plymouth PL6 7PP, United Kingdom

ributed by National Book Network

rary of Congress Cataloging-in-Publication Data Available

N 13: 978-1-59077-481-6 (pbk: alk. paper)

™

The paper used in this publication meets the minimum requirements of American
ional Standard for Information Sciences—Permanence of Paper for Printed Library
erials, ANSI/NISO Z39.48-1992.

ted in the United States of America

To

BERT

MY BEST OLD "PARTNER
IN CRIME"

CONTENTS

PART ONE: NEW YORK

PART TWO: HAVANA

Contents

PART THREE: POINTS UNKNOWN

PART ONE

New York

Chapter I

EXIT—A SPORTSMAN!

DISTINCT in the recollection of every reader of New York dailies is the sensation caused early last Winter by the disappearance of Stephen P. Wyndham, internationally known sportsman and last in line of one of the oldest and wealthiest of Manhattan families.

Of course, you recall the case. For days, every newspaper ran columns on the Wyndham mystery, conspicuously spreading the latest news of his extraordinary disappearance directly on the front page, in the very midst of international dispatches, of news of the then-momentous Supreme Court decisions or the latest outbreaks among gangsters and racketeers.

The headlines stared at you over your coffee each morning.

INTERNATIONAL SPORTSMAN MISSING FOR MONTHS

MILLIONAIRE DISAPPEARS FROM HAVANA HOTEL

POLICE SUSPECT KIDNAPPING IN WYNDHAM CASE

CUBAN MYSTERY DEEPENS

The case deserved the importance given to it. It was arresting! It was challenging! It was as weirdly mysterious as the tropical night during which it had happened. But there it was, an absurd threat to one's own sense of security—that in this day and age a man of international reputation and established position, seemingly too easy-going for an enemy, an ambition, or even a modern complex, had apparently made his exit and without a clue.

The public interest in the case was cataclysmic. Every clubroom in New York was rife with gossip.

"Peculiar thing—this Wyndham disappearance."

"Damned queer. My boy used to know him at Yale."

"What was he like?"

"H'm . . . the best of the Wyndhams, if you know what I mean."

"Well, that doesn't say so much. Always were a funny lot despite their wealth. But this young Stephen?"

"Oh, some woman, no doubt. Strange that so long a time has been allowed to elapse without anything being said. . . . It's nearly ten months since his actual disappearance you know!"

"Why, I was told that he . . ."

During those days every strap-hanger in the subway still had his theory. At rush hour, Wyndham enjoyed a sort of retroactive celebrity, never achieved in all the days of his brilliant polo at Meadowbrook, or his yachting glory at Newport.

"Ten to one the guy wanted to blow out!"

"G'wan. With all that dough. Naw!"

"Er . . . my wife was saying at breakfast he may have been taken for ransom, you know."

"Perhaps, and done away with later for safety. There's enough of that sort of thing these days."

"Moider, dats wat I says, and we ain't goin' 'ter know why."

Looking back now on the grim and puzzling array of facts as one by one they came to light, facts that were to lead their mocking trail all the way from a sedate Murray Hill mansion to a lonely, tropical waterfront, facts that were to touch a depth of human treachery, a pitch of human passion, an extreme of human necessity undreamed of, you realize how futile any advance theory of young Wyndham's disappearance inevitably must have proven.

However, those first weeks were weeks of optimism. During that time tens of thousands of police circulars, bearing Wyndham's good-looking, clean-shaven likeness, were broadcast to every headquarters in the United States and every foreign capital as well.

MISSING SINCE FEBRUARY 13TH
STEPHEN PRENTISS WYNDHAM

Born in the United States. Age, 34 years, height 5 feet 11 inches, athletic build; hair, dark brown; complexion, ruddy and considerably tanned; grey-blue eyes, regular teeth, excellent physical and mental condition. Scar on right forearm from recent polo fracture. Last seen at the Hotel Sevilla Biltmore, Havana, Cuba, on the night of February 13th. Communicate with Chief Inspector Police Department, 18th Division (Missing Persons Bureau), New York City. Spring 1-3100.

The police, to do them justice, made superb efforts in the matter. They raced hither and thither after every available clue. They interviewed each acquaintance who had evolved a hypothesis, each crank who claimed to have information (and there were legions of these!), each chorus girl who dreamed, because of orchids once sent by the young millionaire, that here, at last, lay a chance for publicity.

For once, at headquarters, they were tireless. They were indefatigable. But after turbulent weeks of excitement, where were they? Except for some superficial information as to the history and habits of the departed, all duly published in the Sunday supplements during that time (God knows I should remember these, having edited no less than three myself!), young Wyndham's disappearance remained as baffling and inexplicable as on that memorable December day when Miss Isabella Wyndham had first called headquarters and solicited public help in trying to discover what had happened to her brother.

This particular phase of affairs is imprinted with peculiar vividness on my mind for about this time came an abrupt unexpected development in the case which stumped us completely around the office, and left me so savagely out of humor that even Peter Alcott commented on it at lunch.

I say *even* Peter Alcott, as a sort of measure. Alcott had been running a daily sports column for some time on the *Globe,* and his unvarying nonchalance had become a byword with all the men on the staff. Nothing ever fazed Pete Alcott, and, likewise, nothing ever seemed to evoke from him more than the most ephemeral flicker of interest. All this on the surface, of course! I'd watched him a dozen times, in sheer amazement. At the ringside at prize fights, at football clashes, at final show-downs in golf and tennis tourneys. In every case Alcott had hazarded an advance opinion in print as to the final outcome of the match. His professional judgment was at stake. But throughout the event, no matter which way the tide was running, there was always that same unruffled cabbage-like calm that nothing apparently could disturb. To tell the truth, at such times, I was never fully convinced that Pete really saw what was happening at all. But at the end, when he stretched his long legs and shoved his fedora down a little tighter on his head, he would laconically show me the error of my ways.

"Thought you'd lost your fifty when the Kid landed that upper right?" . . . or . . .

"When Taylor tied that score . . ." or whatever it happened to be.

"Bet your life, I did!"

Then he'd smile his lazy, good-humored smile and the next day his column would prove beyond question that not only had he been aware of every passing play that I and the gallery had taken in, but of a score of other details, that all the rest of the crowd had missed. There was no chance signal, no contestant's quickened breathing, no shift in the direction of a breeze, be it ever so slight, that escaped his Argus-eyed attention. His sporting sense was uncanny—but that's beside the point! The point is I was out of humor at the new development in the Wyndham case, and Pete had commented on it.

It happened we were snatching our usual cornflakes and coffee at a nearby lunch room, known to every man on the staff for its creeping indigestions and its galloping ptomaines. We'd taken to dropping in at the place together for months now—in fact, ever since Alcott had first come to the *Globe*. In glum silence I sat munching away at my cereal and at last I drew my coffee closer.

"Say, can't you bring this dishwater hot for once?" I snapped at the little blonde waitress who was fixing her hair nearby.

Good-naturedly Alcott pushed his cup across the table toward me.

"Try mine. It's scalding."

"No, let her get it!"

We relapsed into silence. In due time the waitress brought me hot coffee, gave the sugar bowl a friendly shove in my direction and departed. I glanced down at my spoon, remarking acidly, "Jesus, some time a clean spoon is rather to be chosen than . . . er . . . a clean name. Just an old proverb from the Portuguese! Did you ever see the like?"

Viciously I rubbed my spoon on my paper napkin while Alcott grinned across at me. "What's the matter with you today? Good God! You're insufferable!"

With the morose air of a man forced to be generous, I began to explain.

"I'm up a tree you almighty sporting writers don't have to climb. Jesus! Get this! Space all saved for the latest on this Wyndham case. Half an hour ago Billy Farrel 'phones over from Police Headquarters that they've clamped the lid down. Absolute instructions to give no more information out. Not one damned word more! Why? God knows! I can't make head or tail of it. Pretty, isn't it?"

"Sounds lousy. What are you going to do?"

"Damned if I know. The public's all het up and panting for Wyndham news. There's been nothing like it in years. Now, this new jam at Headquarters."

"Funny." Alcott took a few drags on his cigarette in silence. "Of course, there must be a private agency working on the case!"

"Hell, suppose there is!"

"Why not get at them!"

"Oh, you colossus of inspiration, you brain trust, you. . . ." I was overcome for words. "What do you think I did when Billy Farrel called us up? Sit down on my goddamned spine? We've been in touch with every agency in town. We've tried every known ruse and a few original ones. Nothing doing! We're deadlocked . . . deadlocked . . . get that!"

Alcott blew three perfect rings of smoke ceilingward, while I sat there glowering across at his battered, worn countenance, at the eternal disorder of his great shock of prematurely grey hair, at the unvarying complacence of his deep grey-blue eyes, and wondered inwardly what it was that I always liked so immeasurably about the fellow anyhow. Suddenly, he leaned forward.

"You know, I've got a crazy sort of an idea!" He stamped his cigarette out before proceeding. "Yep, it might work, but it won't help your next edition!"

"Oh, I can take care of that! What's your hunch?"

For answer, he dug into his vest pocket and exhumed an old python skin cigarette case—a rather remarkable case as I look back on it now, and cer-

tainly one that was to act as our passport far beyond
the bounds of conventional experience.

"That's the hunch," he said, as he laid it quietly on
the table.

"Aw, can the comedy!"

"I'm serious. That case once belonged to Stephen
Prentiss Wyndham!"

I picked it up and examined it with new interest.
Alcott enjoyed my surprise.

"Intrinsic value, zero, I'd say. Ordinary type, made
from the skin of a python or some other little jungle
pet that Wyndham picked up on one of his African
hunts. But regardless of the raw material, that case
might be worth a hell of a lot to the *New York Globe*
right now!"

I turned the case over critically.

"Well, for Christ's sake! If you can tell me how we
can spin two columns a day out of the fact that a dead
or missing millionaire happened to give the *Globe*
sporting writer a leather cigarette case, which, if I
know my young Wyndham, he might just as well
have given to any one of a dozen lousy reporters, after
any one of a dozen events . . ." I paused for breath.

Alcott smiled in good humor. "Keep your shirt on.
You're absolutely correct about every fact but one.
I'm really not after my picture in the paper, old man.
It only struck me that this little souvenir, if handled
properly, might possibly get us a private look-in on
Miss Isabella Wyndham." He paused. "Anyhow, if
you wait while I 'phone the office, I'll help you try!"

I was on my feet in a flash. "Say, you old stiff,
where you been all my life? I'll 'phone the office. You

settle the check. God, who'd have thought you had it in you?"

Twenty-eight minutes later we had hurdled through the traffic to Madison Avenue and 34th Street and were mounting the brownstone steps of the dignified old Wyndham mansion.

Chapter II

AN ECCENTRIC OLD LADY
TALKS

I FREELY confess that as I stood in the vestibule of
the gaunt four-storied Wyndham residence, and
listened to the peal of the doorbell as it reverberated
through the vast solitude of the great place, I was conscious of a lurking excitement in my blood that I had
not known in all the days since I had traded the
adventurous lot of a cub reporter for the none-too-
certain dignity of an office chair.

Even Alcott looked a trifle flushed with expectancy,
though, of course, being Alcott, he made no comment. Nor did our sense of adventure derive wholly
from the fact that here we stood—two young newspaper men, bent on forcing our way straight to the
center of the most sensational mystery in years! After
all, for that we had worked out a careful strategy in
the taxi, en route, and we were content to take our
chances.

No, something of my feeling was ascribable to the
venerable Wyndham manor itself and to the curiously formidable atmosphere that enshrouded the
place. I studied the brownstone pile before me, trying
to analyze what it was in the combination of ordinary
stone and mortar that thus had the power of affecting
me. Around the mansion New York surged and

pulsed, beating its way to its sedate doors, clanging and roaring past! Haughty, unheeding, defiant, the old house drew its dark blinds and let Manhattan whirl on its way, determined to stand just as it had in all the eighty-odd years since old Prentiss Wyndham, first puffed with his stupendous coup in northwestern railroads, had decided to build himself a dwelling that would be at once the outward sign and symbol of his achievement. Dark and forbidding, the Madison Avenue house had risen. Dark and forbidding, it stood its ground, a strange, incongruous gesture against the perpetual chance and mutability of the great metropolis. The thought flashed through my mind that the ancients erred very understandably in attributing to certain inanimate objects a spirit of their own. This house now—but Alcott was cutting in.

"Don't look so blooming sober, or we'll never get by!"

I gave a chuckle of amusement and in an instant the hard-boiled newspaper man once more was uppermost. That is, on the surface, of course! (And there, incidentally, stands a popular delusion that should be laid before I die. Hard-boiled gentlemen of the press! Of all the romantically minded, credulous hearted, empty handed saps that I've encountered in the years I've been gathering no moss—*you!* But I can't deal adequately with you now! The mood of this incredible case is too much upon me.)

I took out a cigarette!

"Y'know, there's a story around the office that this plot alone is assessed for three million dollars and the old lady won't sell because her cat takes the sun on the side terrace."

Alcott was making a heroic effort to adjust his outrageous muffler, but he shrugged.

"More likely she doesn't want to leave the family skeletons alone in the old closets. And still more likely, it's just sheer laziness!"

He paused abruptly, and a second later even I heard the sound of footsteps that he had caught so promptly from within. Almost immediately the door swung open and a butler, who resembled nothing so much as a well-nourished ferret, stood eyeing us with somber questioning.

"Is Miss Wyndham at home?" Alcott did the talking.

At Alcott's easy presumption, the man looked genuinely taken back.

"Miss Wyndham is at home to no one except by appointment, and she gave word of none today."

His tone was haughty—very haughty—for surely the worst snobs in the world are the servants of the wealthy, the waiters at the Ritz, and the *vendeuses* in fashionable shops the world over. I think the fellow would have closed the door in our faces but Alcott detained him.

"Just a moment. It happens we've come here especially to see Miss Wyndham, and it's quite important we should."

Something in his manner of speaking arrested the closing door, and while the butler stood wavering, Alcott reached swiftly into his pocket, drew forth his pen and pad, and hastily scrawled off a note. Once finished, he tore the page off, gave a pleasant nod to the perplexed servant and handed the note to me.

"Can anyone make it out, d'you think?"

I deciphered with effort.

My dear Miss Wyndham:

You will recognize the accompanying cigarette case as one that once belonged to your brother, and will find time, I hope, to greet in its present owner a sincerely interested friend. Certain aspects of his peculiar disappearance have made it imperative that I get into communication with you at once. I await your instructions.

Peter Alcott
New York Globe.

Dubiously, I turned the note over to the butler. "It'll do, providing Miss Wyndham is a cuneiform specialist!"

Alcott gave him the python-skin cigarette case, and at the same time, slipped him a bill, I think. Anyhow, the butler was his man.

"It's rather blustery today. Maybe you would like to step inside!"

We needed no urging, and with alacrity, followed him into the corridor. Through the sepulchral gloom of the place, I glanced at the great reception rooms that opened on either side, feeling vaguely oppressed by the general odor of mustiness and the too-heavy opulence of all I saw. Somber portraits, in massive gold frames, lined the walls. Priceless brocades and tapestries, statuary and porcelains crowded the rooms. "Just the loot of a half dozen fat receiverships," thought I to myself, to dull the edge of any possible awe.

We seated ourselves in the hallway and prepared to wait. For a while the pervasive hush of the great house was broken only by the butler's retreating footsteps and the lonely tick of the grandfather's clock on the distant stair.

"Holy Mike! What a tomb!" I said by way of breaking the depressing silence. "I may need jack but y'couldn't pay me to live in this joint!"

"Nor me. That's straight!"

"Then it's settled what we say when we're invited."

We both laughed in high spirits, but suddenly Alcott left off.

"Who's there?" a startled voice at the end of the corridor was asking. Silence. "I say, who's there?"

Following the direction of the sound I was amazed to see a woman of perhaps sixty or upwards eyeing us intently from the remote end of the dark corridor.

We rose as she approached us. A large Maltese cat was ambling familiarly at her side.

"I hope we didn't alarm you," Alcott said politely for she seemed distinctly ill-at-ease. Through the half shadows of the hallway she bent a curious intent scrutiny upon Alcott as he spoke. Then as though reassured for the moment by his grey hairs, his shabby clothes or whatever she thought she saw, she shook her head.

"Oh! no!" she said with strained nervous dignity. "My butler is new. He isn't supposed to admit strangers. And just now—your voice and laughter . . ." She broke off suddenly. "Ah, this house is full of ghosts!" She passed her hands over her eyes as though she would wipe out some recollection. Then abruptly she changed the subject.

"Cooper said you wished to see me?"

She glanced from one of us to the other, dubiously. Alcott bowed. "The note was mine, Miss Wyndham." He said easily. Then he noticed her questioning glance at me. "I've taken the liberty of bringing a very good friend, who happens to be as interested in your brother's case as I, myself. Mr. John Ellis!"

While Alcott spoke, I noticed she peered again at him with a peculiar intentness, then turned and coldly examined me. Even in the half light of the hallway I was struck by her chill blue eyes, by the sharp angularity of her features and the faded hair that was drawn back so tightly that I wondered inwardly if she employed a monkey wrench instead of a comb in the process of arranging it.

"My seeing you is a great exception to my rules." She gave an uncertain glance toward the drawing room on the right as though debating a momentous step. "Perhaps we can talk more comfortably in here."

She rustled into the darkened room ahead of us—a curious, ineffectual little figure in her rusty black dress, with its old-fashioned high-boned collar and its long, tight sleeves—strangely out of place against her background of pomp and circumstance.

At her gesture, we seated ourselves on chairs that once (alas!) might have been regenerating to the spirit but which now certainly seemed a trifle hard on the flesh. No apology was made for the drawn blinds, and no light was turned on. As my eyes with difficulty peered through the half-light of the room,

I observed with interest that there was no electric button anywhere about to have been pressed. Progress at the Wyndham mansion, at least regarding illumination, seemed to have stopped short a good many years before with the installation of the very ornate gas fixtures that hung from the ceiling. I caught Alcott's glance searching the room. Miss Wyndham also was looking sharply at him.

"May I ask how you happened to know my brother?"

"I met him in Miami a couple of winters ago. It was natural that we should have run into each other. You see, your brother was pretty well known in the sporting world and I've been covering sporting events for a long time."

Well, I thought to myself, that was garnishing the facts up rather royally. Back a few months, before Pete Alcott had first come to the *Globe,* I knew he had been a first rate sports writer on a second rate newspaper in a third rate Florida town, but as he talked to Miss Wyndham he made this sound most impressive and after all, the details were none of her affair.

"Your brother was wonderful to me at the time. I've never forgotten and I never will."

Miss Wyndham's thin, pallid lips tightened perceptibly.

"Stephen seems to have been well enough liked, and by all kinds! It only makes this terrible affair all the more difficult to explain."

Alcott was silent a moment.

"You and he didn't get on so well together, did you? You'll pardon my asking!"

But quite obviously Miss Wyndham did not pardon the question. She flushed to the roots of her hair and her cold blue eyes looked at us with boundless contempt. By some spiritual electricity peculiar between many human beings and their favorites, the cat caught her mood and his back arched tensely.

"Perhaps you'll do better to state the purpose of your call."

Alcott was undismayed.

"I thought I had. I'm deeply interested in this queer mix-up, Miss Wyndham. Just now there's an impasse at Police Headquarters. On your authority, they state no further information is to be released. Is that true?"

"And what concern is that of yours?"

Alcott was good humored.

"Well none—perhaps. However, I've already indicated my interest in your brother and my connection with the *Globe!*"

"So . . . that's it!"

Miss Wyndham rose to her feet and pulled the bell cord vigorously. Her voice shook with emotion as she spoke, and that confounded cat of hers actually began bristling in sympathy.

"I thought I did wrong in breaking my established rule, but your note, together with his cigarette case . . . !" She broke off abruptly. "Let it be understood, I have nothing to say for your cheap scandal-mongering press. It's the first time in years I've admitted a stranger to this house. It will be the last. My man will show you to the door. Here, Jeremiah!" (This last to the cat, who humbly slunk after her to the door.) We had risen to our feet. Now Alcott bowed.

"As you wish! But one thing I may as well state directly. If you refuse to cooperate with us now when we need you, Miss Wyndham, we shan't hesitate to give your personal sentiments in this matter a little airing in the press."

Miss Wyndham's nostrils dilated nervously and her thin lips set. There was a moment of tense inner struggle. Then she turned to Alcott coldly.

"I don't know what my brother has told you and what he has not. He and I have never been congenial and good reason why. For years I've had to sit by and watch his spendthrift habits and his wastrel ways. Since he was a child, I've seen him turn his back on every counsel my dear father had given him. Yesterday, when I spoke to Headquarters, I vainly hoped to put a stop to this public pillorying but it seems you newspapers must have your Roman holiday. You can print what you like about me." Her voice grew strident with excitement. "As I say, print what you like!"

Alcott watched her outburst with quizzical eyes. As she concluded, he smiled.

"Bravo! What do you say to our including a little feature about the will!"

In all the course of a varied reportorial experience, and that is including a good deal, I don't believe I ever witnessed a more abrupt metamorphosis than that which now occurred. At Alcott's words, every vestige of color drained from Miss Wyndham's face. Her dry lips moved in a futile effort at speech. A hunted look crept into her eyes. From outraged dig-

nity and pride, and all the gesture of the grand manner, she shrank at one stroke into a pitiable terrified
old woman who, with a trembling hand, gestured to
us to be reseated.

"It seems you know more about us Wyndhams
than I deemed possible."

She spoke in a low tone, forcing the words out as
though each one cost her a supreme effort. In the
doorway her butler appeared in answer to her earlier
summons, but he might have been a wraith for all
the notice she paid him. It was Alcott who indicated
to her that the man was waiting, and even then, she
only motioned him listlessly away, without once taking her eyes from us.

"Nothing must be said of the will just now—surely
you understand that. Promise me there will be no
word of it and I in turn . . . I'll help you in any
way I can."

To me there has always been something revolting
in abject fear. I turned aside, no longer able to witness her acute distress, as she sat on her magnificent
Louis Quinze chair, twisting and untwisting her
hands. Fortunately, Alcott did not share my squeam-
ishness, and he traded on her emotion to good advantage.

"That's only common sense, Miss Wyndham. I had
a hunch even before this snarl at Headquarters today
that neither the Police nor the Press were informed
of *all* that pertained to this inscrutable business.
What I really want to know . . . er . . . *who is?*"

Miss Wyndham turned her frozen eyes full upon
Alcott. Again the low strained tone.

"And if I tell you . . . can I rely on you to see

that there will be no publicity for me? Nothing that
Stephen may have told you? Nothing whatever, you
understand?"

Alcott nodded reassuringly.

"You have my word. Insofar as I can shield you
from publicity, I will, Miss Wyndham."

I stepped on Alcott's foot to remind him as un-
gently as possible of the vested interests of the *New
York Globe,* but the man was impervious.

"You can trust my friend as well."

She swallowed in a kind of relief, then pointed
unsteadily to the bell cord on the wall.

"Ring that please!"

With my recent annoyance at Alcott still un-
abated, I gave the tapestry bell-pull a wrench that
nearly brought it down and almost immediately the
ferret-faced butler appeared at the door.

"Bring my writing portfolio from the desk on the
top floor."

The man obediently vanished, and Miss Wyndham
turned back to us, apprehension still in her eyes.

"Every document and letter that has been brought
to light in this entire affair is in the possession of Mr.
Elihu Stone, my family attorney."

Alcott raised his eyebrows.

"By which I infer you have made some private
effort, aside from the Police?"

"Yes! Yes! Mr. Stone has called in two of the ablest
detective agencies in the city . . . with injunctions,
of course, for absolute secrecy."

Of that secrecy certainly no one was more acutely
aware than I. I thought of my morning of futile
inquiry and tried to control the sudden surge of ela-

tion which I felt. However, Alcott, with immobile countenance, steadily continued his barrage of questions.

"Would you mind telling me when you last heard from your brother?"

"I had a card from him last February from Havana." Her voice was low.

"Nothing since then?"

"No . . . not a word."

"That was over ten months ago. Weren't you in any way concerned by the . . . er . . . prolonged silence?"

"No. I was used to it. The occasions when I heard from Stephen were the exceptions, not those when I didn't." She said this harshly, her eyes looking colder than ever. "To me he was always very thoughtless and inconsiderate. I've hardly seen him in years."

"Indeed?"

"Yes, once I was even a year and a half without a communication from him, while he was off on some absurd hunting expedition in Africa or the Punjab . . . or maybe it was Tibet, I don't remember which. But anyhow, I long ago gave up worrying about Stephen."

Alcott smiled slightly.

"Then may I ask just what prompted you to get in touch with Police Headquarters a few weeks ago?"

Miss Wyndham darted an uncertain look at us. "My lawyer, Mr. Stone, suggested it."

I put in quickly. "Was Mr. Stone your brother's lawyer, too?"

"No. He didn't even know Stephen. But it hap-

pened there were some financial difficulties down-
town."

"Can you be more exact?"

"Yes, the brokerage firm with which my brother
deals was in urgent need of communicating with him.
It had something to do with his account, I believe,
but alas, I don't fully understand these matters. They
had tried to reach Stephen at the Racquet Club,
where he is in the habit of staying when he is in the
city. He was not there. All inquiries were referred to
one of his friends, a Mr. Ford. It developed that Mr.
Ford was not in the city. Then, gentlemen, I was
called. Needless to say I was deeply shocked. I turned
to Mr. Stone for advice. He called in professional
help, but even that availed nothing. In despair we
turned to the Police."

Alcott nodded. "Most of that ties up very neatly
with the reports that already have been made public.
Can't you tell us anything more, Miss Wyndham?"

Miss Wyndham looked sharply at us. "I must leave
the rest to Mr. Stone to impart."

We lapsed into silence. God only knows what secret
influence we followed in so doing but its effect on
Miss Wyndham was curious to observe. Her cat had
been rubbing its grey fur against her ankle, gazing
up at her with its narrowed agate eyes. Now she
pushed him away restlessly. Some unaccountable impulse to avoid our silence took possession of her, driving her to talk with uneasy volubility.

"This tragedy is frightful, of course—but it was
only to be expected. He who will sow the wind must
expect to reap the whirlwind. The Bible tells us

that, but there are not many who read its pages these days. And certainly *not Stephen!*"

She clasped and unclasped her waxy yellow hands, while her mouth set grimly.

"I only thank God that my poor father never lived to witness this. He used to think everything that Stephen did was perfect. Perfect! H'm! The very fact that the boy took after his mother was enough to account for that, and after *she* died my father was never in this house enough to know what Stephen was like. Some absurd sentimentality about her. She was his second wife, you know! . . . I wonder why Cooper takes so long?"

She got up abruptly, walked to the doorway and then turned back, hands still clenching and unclenching.

"Don't suppose I'm sending you to Mr. Stone because I have anything to fear from what my brother may have told you. Oh, no! It's only that I see you know so much, you might as well know more. And I have your promise about that will—your solemn promise." She fidgeted about in her chair. "What can be keeping Cooper so long."

"He's been gone only four minutes by your mantel-clock. You're overly nervous, Miss Wyndham!"

Cooper's entrance at that moment prevented her reply. Miss Wyndham took the portfolio from him, opened it and peering hard through the dim light of the room, hastily penned a note. She rose, as she handed it to Alcott.

"That will suffice to introduce you to Mr. Stone."

I looked at my watch and roughly computed the

time it would take us to reach the William Street address which I noted on the envelope.

"Would you mind phoning him that Mr. Alcott and I are on our way?" I asked.

She stared at me with wide-eyed incredulity.

"You know about the will . . . and yet you don't know there is no telephone in this house?"

Diplomatically Alcott interposed. "But, of course, we know, Miss Wyndham! Mr. Ellis spoke from—er, force of habit. Our thanks and good afternoon!"

I felt Alcott pull me swiftly toward the door.

A few minutes later a chill East River gale was blowing in our faces. We hailed a passing taxi and Alcott gave the driver Mr. Stone's address. By some strange impulse I turned for one last glance at the Wyndham mansion. At the front window I saw Miss Wyndham, her white face pressed against the pane, peering down at us with cold, frightened eyes.

Chapter III

THE OFFICIAL REPORT
IS ALTERED

AND now that we've a chance, you big stiff—
what the devil *is* this mystery about the Wyndham will?"

When I shot this question at Alcott, we were sitting
in the outer office of Stone, Granger and Reed
awaiting the convenience of Mr. Elihu Stone. The
reception room had been empty when we arrived;
nonetheless, a seemingly omnipotent office boy, after
taking our letter and bearing it off to parts unknown,
returned to inform us it would be some time until
Mr. Stone could see us. Indifferently, Alcott had
shrugged and slumped into the first chair. I had followed suit, none too sorry for the opportunity to talk.

"And when you finish telling me that, you can explain why in hell, you didn't let me in on all this
before!" I was all set for "inside stuff" and it was
with some surprise that I saw Alcott grinning at me
sheepishly.

"Say, are you kidding me or am I kidding you?"

"What d'you mean?"

"Only that at this particular point, you'll have to
think up your own explanation of Miss Wyndham's
fool conduct. I'm afraid I can't help you out just
now, old punk."

"Can't or won't!" I said testily.

I stopped short in order to recall to mind every detail of his conversation with Miss Wyndham. Carefully, painstakingly, I went over the entire scene, trying in the name of cold logic, to correlate it with what he had just said. In retrospect, all the eccentricity and suggestibility of Miss Wyndham's behavior stood out in clear relief; but still there remained Alcott's own definite innuendo about the will and even before that, his apt thrust about the strained relationship of sister and brother. My face must have shown my complete bewilderment for Alcott began to laugh.

"Oh, come off, Ellis! You'll be making me sound as didactic as a would-be Sherlock Holmes."

"What in hell do you think I'm aiming at, you big bum!" I said seriously.

"Oh, anything to oblige you. Only the trouble is that certain things just won't bear analysis, you know." But I shook my head with an energy that drove him on.

"Say! Haven't you ever had your favorite picked in a horse race, your money placed, when suddenly the horses are led out and in a flash, for no conscious reason at all, you decide to play a sudden hunch?"

"No," I said bluntly. "I never go to the races. And as for what you call a hunch, I see that simply as an easy way of explaining what one's too goddamned lazy to think out."

Alcott laughed indulgently. "Good Lord! As a kid I began to suspect Sherlock Holmes the moment he lapsed into his first analytical monologue. Now, I'm beginning to think his friend, Watson, must have driven him into rattling off those bogus explanations. Just the same, you ought to try the hunch system, yourself. Really! I recommend it highly."

"Keep your damn fool hunches. I'll stick to logic!" We subsided for a few moments into silence. I knew Alcott too well to hope for anything further from him. At such moments he was about as unapproachable as some mystic on an inaccessible mountain peak. At some future date, with a few stiff drinks to the good, he might expand—but that distant prospect did not simplify my problem of getting two columns of news for the next edition. Consequently, I thought fast and furiously.

"The chances are you took your pot shot at a strained relationship between Stephen Wyndham and that sister of his because you saw her face freeze over at the first mention of his name. Now that I think of it, I even got that myself!"

Alcott grinned. "Anyhow, I see you were too smart to swallow the story about Wyndham having made a confidant of ye small town sports writer. *That*, of course, wasn't true." He laughed in immense, though solitary, enjoyment.

What a fellow! With infinite reluctance I denied myself the pleasure of giving him a friendly jab in his already once broken nose. With a sudden burst of understanding, I perceived how Pete Alcott could have come by any of the half dozen scars which up until now I'd been so generously attributing to unheralded heroism in the great War. However, his ridicule, no matter how annoying, wasn't going to deter me.

"As for your hitting so *aptly* upon that will——"

I got no further. Alcott's hands went up in a gesture of mock surrender!

"All right. Have it your own way." He paused a moment, and his eyes were twinkling. "For years, you see, I've been noticing that all of our best families are a little touchy on the subject of wills. Anyhow, four out of five of 'em. When I was a kid, I remember planning, if ever I got in a jam with a boss who was big enough, I'd step up to him and say in a low aside precisely what I tried on Miss Wyndham today. With her, the formula worked like a charm." He paused self-consciously. "For the love of Mike! Don't you think 'fool hunch' sounded better than all that?"

I never got a chance to answer him. The office boy came in at that juncture.

"Mr. Stone will see you *now*."

We followed him back to the most office-like of offices, where Mr. Stone rose stiffly to greet us. A chalky-faced, grey-haired individual he was, who looked as though he had worried his way to the top of his profession. I noted at a glance that the letter from Miss Wyndham lay opened on the desk before him, and I could tell from his overclose scrutiny of us as we entered that he had been somewhat surprised by its contents. Formalities exchanged, and once seated, he picked up the letter and bestirred himself to talk.

"H'm! As you doubtless know, Miss Wyndham instructs me to present you with what data have been gathered in connection with her brother's disappearance."

"That was the understanding!" said Alcott.

"As her counsel, I must say her decision seems to

me most ill-advised, but I assume she has her reasons for so acting."

"Very good ones!" Alcott spoke tersely and to the point.

Mr. Stone rose to his feet deliberately.

"Well, it's all most contrary to her usual procedure. H'm, most contrary."

He walked up and down the office for a moment, surveying us dubiously and from his look I knew that any effort we might make to be disarming would only be love's labor lost.

"May I inquire what your connection with Miss Wyndham may be?"

Alcott spoke with dignity. "I thought her letter would be sufficient introduction."

"H'm, of course!"

Mr. Stone walked around his desk to a metal box which stood on the far side.

"It is all most irregular, you know. Most irregular!"

He shook his head so doubtfully that it was with genuine relief that I saw him turn the key in the box and raise the lid. A few official looking documents, a bundle of notes, most of them on pink stationery, one or two business letters and telegrams lay within. There was also a round, flat medallion in finely wrought gold. It looked so innocent and oddly out of place that I picked it up and turned it over. On one face minutely engraved were the initials "C. S." Without even looking up I knew Mr. Stone was watching me intently. Then he began talking:

"This comprises about *all* we have been able to

learn of poor young Wyndham. You'll not find it very helpful I'm afraid."

He drew forth two sheafs of typed paper and extended them to us with a cynical shrug.

"These are the reports to date from the James A. Buchanan Agency. These are from Hoyles'. Are you familiar with either?"

"With both!" I said drily. I took the Buchanan files and handed the other across for Pete's surveillance. I've no idea how long I'd sat there thumbing through page after page of unimportant notations when I was suddenly aware of Alcott elbowing me none too gently. I looked up in surprise. With a finger to his lips for silence, he indicated Mr. Stone, who at that moment was standing looking out of the window, his back to us. Swiftly Pete pushed a pencilled note under my eyes.

Last page missing from this report. Think you can reach it from waste basket on left. Large foolscap page with pink margin line. Corner showing.

As quietly as possible I drew forth the page indicated.

It was practically blank. At the top, was the page number. Lower down, a single line! I looked at Alcott quizzically. By way of answer he indicated a typed paragraph in the Hoyle report which he had been reading.

"And last," the report read, "it has been definitely ascertained that there was a poker crowd in Stephen Wyndham's rooms at the Hotel Sevilla Biltmore on February 13th, at or about the hour that, according to all present indications, marked his last known appearance. The personnel of this party seems to have been as follows:

BARTON DUNLAP	NEW YORK CITY
JOSÉ SANCHEZ	HAVANA
SANFRED LAMAR	NEW YORK CITY
CALVIN WATTS	BALTIMORE, MARYLAND
PHILIP BRADY	RESIDENCE UNKNOWN
GEORGE MEENAN	NEW YORK CITY

I read down the list, recognizing some few of these names, wondering slightly at a few of the others. As I concluded, Alcott slipped the page that had been so singularly treated back into its proper place and I read with amazement the line that had been intended to conclude the report.

"An eighth player seems to have been Mr. Charles Elihu Stone of New York, though this has not been checked as yet, due to Mr. Stone's continued absence from the City."

Chapter IV

"THE DEAD MAN'S CHEST"

ALCOTT broke the silence.

"Hope you don't mind if we camp here, Mr. Stone. This box begins to look like a regular mine of information."

Mr. Stone shrugged for answer. "Help yourself! At seven, however, I must leave you. I have an appointment at my Club."

I pushed my memo book toward Alcott.

"Get a copy of that poker list," I begged him *sotto voce*. Then aloud, "How did you manage to get hold of the names of the crowd in Wyndham's rooms?"

"Through Mr. Wyndham's friend, Mr. Ford. His radio communications should be there." Stone indicated the box and Alcott dug them out without delay.

"H'm. All sent from aboard a yacht. . . . 'Seven Seas' Longitude W.92°, Latitude S.3°. . . ." Alcott knit his forehead as he glanced through the dispatches. "I notice Ford states he will be cruising around the Galapagos Islands for the week. Interesting corner, that!"

He broke off abruptly and turned his attention to the flesh tinted parcel of letters, opening one after another idly.

"And just how did you come by these?"

The question was addressed quietly and for once the old lawyer answered as though off guard.

"Those letters were found in the dead man's safe deposit box."

Alcott raised his eyebrows. "The dead man's box?"

Mr. Stone spoke testily. "We may as well face the facts it seems to me. Months have passed without word."

Alcott smiled. "Yes, but no corpse has been found as yet . . . at least, none that we've heard of. But perhaps you . . ."

Mr. Stone interrupted angrily. "No! no! Of course not. However, after weeks of search when no clues of any kind were revealed, I obtained a court permit to open Mr. Wyndham's vault in the hope of finding something that might give us a lead. This was done yesterday morning in the presence of a member of the family and an officer of the bank."

Alcott nodded in a non-committal fashion but I was agog.

"What else did you find in er—your dead man's chest?"

Stone looked at me with annoyance.

"Very little of interest. It was about the usual rich man's box—with the exception of—er—that bundle of letters."

"Letters, aha!" I said facetiously, but my tone sounded as out of place as a jazz band at a funeral. "Let's have a look."

Meditatively, Alcott tossed a handful over to me. "Since you're all set for taking notes," he said with a smile, "you'll want a few on these, Johnny. 'Lolita Caros' is signed to the formal ones. 'Lola' as the letters grow warmer. All are written from Havana. All point to an affair. . . . I'd say of the sizzly sort. All except this one are dated at least a year before Stephen Wyndham's disappearance. From the postmark on this last it seems to have been written only a short time before young Stephen shot the works." Alcott tapped the desk thoughtfully with the note.

Overcome by curiosity, I took it from him. Round, unformed handwriting sprawled over two pages.

DEAREST STEVE: I saw your friend, Mr. Ford, yesterday and he say to me that you are coming here in two, maybe three weeks more. My happiness it is so great, if this is true. I do like you tell me about José, but what the use? I do not love him. I never, never can.

I have read your letters so many times over since you go away. You love me a little when you wrote those letters. You will again, *querido mio.*

I count the days these two, three weeks. Then maybe I am in your arms again, and again I know what real kisses once more can mean.

Lola.

"Whew," I whistled softly as I finished, making a gesture as though to fan away the semi-tropical heat waves that engulfed me. My efforts were wasted. Alcott had his head bent over a business letter, and Mr. Stone was once more gazing, with that ever slight expression of worry, out of the window at the fantastic skyline of lower Manhattan, that stood out so majestically just then against the frosty stars of early dusk.

"Say, what have you got there?" I had caught the glint of suppressed interest in Alcott's eyes.

He looked up nonchalant as always. "This is a copy of a letter from Wyndham to his brokerage firm, Manning and Wilson. It's dated last January, and instructs them to extend to his friend, Ford, unlimited power-of-attorney to buy and sell, to deposit or withdraw funds from his—Wyndham's—account. It may be important. It may not be. It's hard to say."

"Who the devil is this guy Ford? This is the third time we've bumped into his name."

"Hugh D. Ford," Alcott read out from the letter, his tone matter-of-fact, as always. "He does occasional political articles for the better magazines, I think."

He looked toward Mr. Stone for confirmation. Stone nodded, but nodded hesitantly, as though he were doing a rash thing indeed, to thus express himself without special writ from the Supreme Court.

"Not *the* red-headed Hugh Ford who married the steel king's daughter some six weeks ago?" I asked in interest.

Again Stone bowed agreement.

"Jesus!" I said aloud, thinking inwardly that this Wyndham case was getting to be a sort of social register for old Manhattan. Yes, I knew all about Hugh D. Ford! A few weeks before the Wyndham case had broken, Ford's elopement with Kay Devereaux, the wealthiest gal in the country, had furnished what then was thought a pretty good feature. Somehow, and no one knew how, that couple had managed to dodge the usual Mendelssohn and orange blossoms, get themselves a license and a wedding ring without the press even getting a look-in at the show. Of course, I remembered Hugh D. Ford. Red-headed, red hot young political commentator! Perversely, I even remembered a headline that almost slipped by at the time, "RED FORD WINS FORTUNE."

Then I was off on a new line. "By the way, Mr. Stone, you mentioned a will having been found in Mr. Wyndham's box. Are you acquainted with the terms?"

"Slightly. A member of my firm drew it."

"Can you give us a general idea of the contents?"

"The bulk of his estate, real and personal, passes to his sister, Miss Isabella Wyndham, in the event of his dying without wife or issue."

"I see. Then, from a financial standpoint, Miss Wyndham stands to profit very substantially from young Wyndham's death?"

Mr. Stone nodded, and with an air of long suffering, he began making a neat stack of the letters we had scattered about the desk.

"Lucky break for her!" I burst out impulsively. "Especially since the feeling between those two doesn't seem to have been exactly clubby."

Mr. Stone made a deprecating gesture.

"It wasn't a case of sentiment; it was a case of law. The terms of young Stephen's will were laid down by the conditions under which he had inherited from his father."

"I see. And do the same conditions hold with regard to Miss Isabella's will?"

"Er—only in a slight measure." He spoke with professional restraint, and again I felt, looming behind him, a whole life-time of conservatism and caution. However, if I was supposed to have been silenced, I wasn't.

"Pretty queer, the whole business!" I remarked, acidly. "Especially since from what I've found, the old man doted so on his son, Stephen."

Mr. Stone spread his hands in a gesture of mute acknowledgment of all the profound irrationality of the Universe.

"I've every confidence that Miss Wyndham will prove a faithful steward of the family wealth."

"Just why?" I shot the remark out so suddenly, that Mr. Stone flushed and bit his lips.

"I see no necessity to explain myself," he remarked coldly.

Well, I couldn't blame him. There we sat; Alcott, looking for all the world like a high class bum, his slouch fedora on the back of his head, his walk-up-a-flight suit unpressed, I would have been willing to bet, for over two weeks, while I—well, maybe I looked a shade better, but I wasn't too confident about that. Anyhow, to Mr. Stone, we were two strangers, in from nowhere, who, armed with a letter from a client, proceeded to interrogate, to demand, to cross-examine, until I couldn't wonder at his very evident annoyance.

But to all of this Alcott seemed just about as cheerfully unperceptive as a steam roller.

"Since you prefer not answering on that . . ."

But Mr. Stone's mood underwent a swift change. "I resented the manner, not the substance, of your—er—friend's question. My confidence in Miss Wyndham happens to be based upon years of acquaintance during which time I have observed her interests have always been of a most worthy nature. In fact, I happen to know that a substantial part of her fortune has been pledged quite recently to the up-keep of a certain Chinese mission."

"A Chinese mission? Indeed!" Alcott paused thoughtfully. "Now, a few questions about this letter of Wyndham's to his broker. I see nothing here as to what's been happening on that score."

Mr. Stone looked sharply at us. "I hesitate to speak on that matter, not because of any lack of confidence in you, gentlemen, but because certain facts in that direction are so—er—er—peculiar, so very peculiar that I think it would be wiser to await more definite information before expressing myself."

"By which we infer Mr. Ford has exercised his power-of-attorney rather freely."

"I imply nothing," Mr. Stone said hotly.

A knock at the door prevented our rejoinder. The omnipotent office boy opened the door, ever so slightly, and thrust his head in.

"Beg pardon, sir. Your nephew, Mr. Charles, is outside."

"Tell him to wait."

The door closed. Alcott rose abruptly, giving me a signal to do likewise. There was of necessity a few moments' delay, while I attempted to restore the box to something of the order in which we had found it. And it was then that I noticed for the first time that the small gold medallion with the monogram "C. S." had disappeared.

"Mr. Stone," I started hotly, but Alcott shot me a restraining glance and I modulated my voice. "We've taken enough of your time, sir, but there's one thing I'd like to say before we leave. If you've been altogether frank with us, you have nothing to fear from your confidence. If you haven't—well, we're connected with what we—er—playfully call—the press! Good evening."

Mr. Stone drew himself up stiffly.

"Good evening."

A few moments later, I brushed past a heavy-set, moon-faced chap lounging by the door of the waiting room. His myopic eyes encountered mine in bewilderment.

"Mr. Charles Elihu Stone," I said to Alcott as we shot down in the elevator. "And whatever *you* want to do, old man, I don't expect to budge from this building until little old Charlie does, too."

"Had a hunch you'd feel that way." Alcott smiled. "But take a tip from me, old punk! Don't forget about that missing gold medallion!"

Chapter V

A CURIOUS WITNESS

PETE left me at the main entrance of the building. "If I weren't up to my neck at the office I'd stick with you." He caught sight of the clock outside the Bank across the way. "Great guns, forty minutes late now and two interviews promised! S'long."

"Thanks. You've seen me out of the rough, anyhow!"

As I said this, Alcott, hurried though he was, pulled up sharply, and stared at me. For a brief moment there flickered into his eyes a look of uncertainty, incredulity, and unbelief. Then he slapped me on the shoulder.

"Good God! My frank advice to you would be to get this whole Wyndham business off the front page, and turn your talents loose on something else. You've picked a tough nut and a damned queer one. That's my private hunch, Ellis!"

"Sez you!" I laughed.

I hated like the devil parting company with him just then. He'd brought my first lucky break in days. Thoughtfully, I watched his long, lank figure cut through the traffic and dive into a cab.

Left to my own devices, I got in touch with the office, smoked two cigarettes, and never once took my eyes from the main doorway.

Darkness settled down in genuine earnest. Offices emptied themselves of their workers. Thousands—well, maybe it was only hundreds, but it seemed like thousands—strode and pushed, bustled and dragged through the door that I was watching. I scanned each face. No Charles Elihu Stone.

"Is there another exit to this building?" I asked the elevator starter, after about an hour.

"Shure now and there is!"

But I never learned where it was. At precisely that moment, Mr. Stone and his nephew stepped off the elevator. Their faces were set and serious. Looking at the younger man this second time, I was struck again by his expression of moon-faced insouciance and wondered at it, since it contradicted so oddly the obvious intelligence of his eyes. I had an impression it came from his too-rounded chin. I wasn't certain.

On the blustery street corner, Charles took a hasty leave of his uncle and began threading his way through the crowd.

I was close upon his heels. We swung down the subway stairs at Chambers Street and, in due time, were pushed and pummelled into a Van Cortlandt express. Sandwiched together in the surging rush-hour crowd, I could feel young Charles breathing against me and could study, at close range, that amazing combination of weakness and strength in his face. But I bided my time. At 96th Street, the human cargo loosened up a bit and I found a seat. Charles Stone could have done likewise, but, instead, he stood staring absently through his thick, double-lens glasses at the posts that rushed by in the darkness outside.

At 116th Street the doors had nearly closed when, with a sudden start, he recollected himself and sprang forward. Had I not been sitting just by the exit, I could never have followed in time. However, out after him I swung, and, keeping a comfortable four feet in the rear, trailed him up to the street.

"Just a minute, Mr. Stone!"

Unheeding, he hurried on. Up the broad sweep of steps by the old Columbia University Library, three steps at a time! Across the bleak wintry campus, our hurrying footsteps resounding through the quiet evening. Abruptly he turned off into one of the buildings on the side!

"Mr. Stone!" This time he wheeled around and inspected me curiously through his thick, double-lens glasses.

"I rather thought you were following me," he said, in a quiet, almost purring tone.

"What the devil did you think I was doing?" I asked pleasantly. "Walking for my health? No, it's really important that we talk."

"Important? And to whom?" As Stone spoke, his mouth expanded out and out, accordion-like, into an incredibly broad smile.

"Perhaps to us both." I introduced myself and explained the seriousness of my mission. All the while he was fumbling for his watch.

"Sorry, but a professor I know is giving a lecture just now. It's one that I specially want to hear. Of course, if you care to, stick around—"

I stuck. I stuck what I think was the most abstruse lecture ever given on Chinese Philosophy and Comparative Religions. I stuck for another half hour after class while young Charles and a keen-eyed professor argued obscure Chinese imagery. I stuck until a faint but certain suspicion began to dawn that young Mr. Stone was trying to wear me out. Outside on Amsterdam Avenue busses rumbled by, machines honked, a city surged. Oblivious to the world, Charles talked away, in soft sibilant tones.

"I've always felt there are a couple of definite stages in all criticism, whether of these ancient Chinese religions or anything else. If you try to see them as the serious inductive systems of mature minds, they outrage your reason. If you treat them sympathetically, as poetry, you begin to like them. After all, religion's not much more anyhow than human experience interpreted by human imagination."

The keen-eyed professor studied Stone's face in surprise.

"And how can you correlate this viewpoint with your choice of vocation?"

I tried to reckon how long this could possibly keep up.

"Oh! Consistency is the bugbear of petty minds," Charles was quoting grandly. "If you drive me to it I'll explain it by saying that to me the Christian myth seems the most poetic and beautiful of them all."

Puzzled, the keen-eyed professor persisted.

"With that viewpoint, my young friend, I can't quite picture *you* as a missionary to China."

As though electrified, I sat up and took notice. At the mention of his future vocation, young Stone had dropped his eyes uncomfortably.

"I've loved Canton ever since I was a boy," he answered slowly. "Anyhow, I've been uncertain lately whether or not I'd stick to being a missionary." Suddenly his voice sank lower. "Though, at that, I guess I won't roam very far from the Mission."

The professor answered, I never knew what.

In my mind a sinister sequence of ideas had taken form, linking themselves together, fairly bowling me over with their impact. The elder Stone had mentioned some large donation of Miss Wyndham's to a Chinese mission. Of course! And now that I thought of it, this fact lent a curious significance both to young Stone's statement and to the old lawyer's effort to keep his nephew's name from the case.

Abruptly I stood up. Making as much noise as possible, I started as though for the door. It was wasted effort. In a high, rather excited voice, young Stone was arguing away, his myopic eyes bright with enthusiasm.

But regardless, I broke in.

"Beg pardon, Mr. Stone!"

A trifle irritably Charles spun toward me; then suddenly he expanded into that broad vacuous smile. "Oh, of course! I'd almost forgotten! I'll be right there!" He turned and bade the professor "Good night." Then crossed to me and again looked at his watch.

I anticipated him. "Yep, I'm starving, too. Can we get food anywhere around here?"

"Sorry, I'm meeting a friend for dinner."

"Oh, I see. Then we might as well jump to the point!"

"Of course." He smiled, and at that smile of his, I grew grave.

"I happen to know you were in the crowd at Stephen P. Wyndham's rooms in Havana—on the night of his—what shall I call it?—murder, disappearance, what?"

"Murder, I'd say!" Charles spoke quietly but I noticed that his smile flickered out. "How did you know I was there?"

"That's my business. Er—why haven't you come forward and told your story to the police?"

"I returned exactly three days ago from Pekin!"

"I see. Still, if you were informed of any events . . . ?"

"There were others much better informed. I had been with Stephen Wyndham only fifteen minutes when the major events of that strange night transpired. . . ."

"Were you and Wyndham friends?"

"In a way. I've known him off and on ever since I was a kid. He was older, of course, but the families were acquainted. And Steve Wyndham was an awfully likable sort."

"On the surface it seems so!" I said cynically.

"What do you mean?" Charles eyed me with curiosity.

I shrugged.

"At just what time this evening do you expect to finish up?"

"Oh, at about twelve or shortly after."

"I'll come by your place."

Charles looked me over dubiously, then broke again into that broad wholesale smile. "Better not.

I might be late, and my mother—er—really she wouldn't know what to make of anyone calling at that hour!"

"Say. Are you trying to dodge me?" The fellow seemed the strangest admixture of masculine intelligence and feminine perversity that I'd ever encountered.

"Of course not! Where shall I meet you?"

On sudden inspiration, I gave him Pete Alcott's number on West 44th Street.

"Thanks! At twelve I'll see you."

That settled, Stone turned abruptly aside, and heedless of the waiting elevator, bolted down the broad stairs and out into the night.

Chapter VI

A NOTE OF WARNING

AFTER I'd let Charles Stone go, I cursed myself roundly for being a fool. Disconsolately I grabbed a bite of supper and dropped by at Alcott's place to spill my troubles.

"That Stone guy will never show up," I said mournfully to Alcott as I finished telling him of the encounter. "It's good hard jack to stale boloney on that." For consolation I poured myself a drink.

"Want to bet?"

But I didn't want to bet. I didn't want to talk. I didn't even want to drink. Disgruntled, I flung myself down on Alcott's red plush sofa, the Wyndham case still churning in my head, and stared moodily across at the opposite wall where hung a peculiarly horrible reproduction of "Venice by Moonlight." I think it was oil paint on black velvet. Anyhow, it was awful.

"God, what a lousy place this is!" I said irritably. "How can you go it?" I looked around at the imitation mahogany secretary, at the shoddy torn portieres, at the dismal court outside, and thought absently of all the decent small-town fellows who are sucked up yearly into the great metropolis and into holes like this.

"Oh, it's a cheap sublet and it answers." Pete yawned.

"Well, every man to his taste." I poured another drink and made a wry face at that velvety "Venice by Moonlight."

"Say, don't think for a minute that's the touch of my fine Italian hand." Alcott laughed self-consciously.

But of that particular atrocity he was exonerated before he had spoken. Obviously, none of the tawdry pictures or hangings, knick-knacks or books bore Pete's personal stamp—whatever that might have been, and the Lord alone knew that! All I held him responsible for was occupying such premises.

And that was enough.

"Well, it's lousy anyhow!" I took another drink. "You ought to move over with us boys!"

"Oh, this suits me O.K."

"There you win. No one will ever enter either you or the joint in a beauty contest." I must have been getting an edge on. I could have kicked myself after I'd spoken. It's one thing to imply to a fellow that he looks like a chimpanzee when he's just plain ugly. But with Alcott, well—he went in for homeliness on a fancy scale. And although, in all the time I'd known him, I'd never heard him make one single comment on the subject, nevertheless, any half-wit could have told he was sensitive, if by nothing else than the way he'd trained his mustache in an effort to cover the scar above his mouth.

"Oh, this Wyndham case is eating into me, I guess!" I said apologetically while I poured another drink.

"Don't let it. I'm turning in!"

"What do you mean?"

"It's getting late and every now and then I have to work for my living." He laughed and stretched to his feet.

"Stop your kidding!"

"I'm serious. Furthermore, you'll only freeze your missionary up if we make a camp meeting of his visit."

"Oh, *he's* not going to show up." I looked gloomily at my watch, certain in the knowledge that if it rested with me I would have fired any reporter on the paper who would have bungled a lead the way I had this one.

"Oh, I rather think he *will,* and *promptly.*" Alcott was nonchalant as always. He commenced unbuttoning his shirt to the tune of "The Ladies" which I suddenly started whistling and about three notes off key.

> "I've taken my fun where I've found it;
> I've rogued an' I've ranged in my time."

Alcott looked over at me in amusement. "Not so down in the mouth as you were, eh?"

"What makes you think that?"

"Nothing much. Only I've noticed you always trot out that tune whenever you think things are going your way."

I left off abruptly. "Well, this once you're wrong!" But at that, he really wasn't. At his optimism, I'd felt a resurge of my own. However, Alcott gave me no chance to continue my refrain.

"See how you feel after this!" He had dug from his coat pocket a letter which he now tossed over to me. "That sweet little note was waiting for me when I got back to the office."

The handwriting looked curiously familiar. In another moment I realized why.

Mr. Peter Alcott
New York Globe
New York City.

Dear Sir:

Despite your pledge to respect my privacy, I feel it a duty to advise you. Bad fortune pursues those who meddle needlessly in Wyndham matters. It is a kind of family curse. Heed it or not. I have warned you.

Isabella Wyndham.

"The crumby old hag!" I said with a grin. "She wants to make sure we don't rattle the old family skeletons."

Alcott looked at me narrowly. "Sure you don't feel as though you want to give up?"

"You crazy punk," I burst out in high amusement. "Look here! We'll keep her letter for a good luck charm."

I stuck the letter in my pocket. Yet ridiculous though it seems, I felt no further impulse to whistle that evening. I lit a cigarette instead.

It was a bit later when Alcott paused at his bedroom door before turning in and said gravely, "By the way, did you ever learn the Morse Code?"

"Sure! Why?"

"Oh, nothing in particular. Only if you should

happen to hear any peculiar sounds tonight, don't by any chance think it's rats!"

I was to remember Alcott's words just a half hour later when I was sitting opposite that keen overly soft face of Charles Stone and listening to what I think was the strangest narrative I ever heard. Of course, Stone was smiling as usual. For that matter, he was smiling when he came in.

Chapter VII

THE NIGHT OF
FEBRUARY 13TH

IT must be recorded, to Charles Stone's credit and to my everlasting surprise, he arrived promptly, and because our appointment was not exactly early, we proceeded without much ado to the matter at hand.

In fact Stone edged toward the subject before he even removed his ulster. "Punctuality's supposed to be the thief of time, I know," he began self-consciously, "but I wouldn't have been late tonight even at the risk of a worse charge than that. D'you know, all evening I've been trying to figure out just why you feel the special need of talking to me."

"Er—maybe you'd rather talk the matter out with the police?" I said succinctly. He shrugged and laid his hat and coat aside. I liked his cool indifference.

"Oh! That's entirely up to you. However, since I'm here, we may as well get it over with."

He sat down on the far side of the room by the radiator, explaining that it had turned bitter cold outside. I offered him a drink. He poured himself a stiff one, and drank it down without a chaser.

I explained to him, by way of a start, how necessary a link his story was. Stone sat forward and began to talk in a caressing sing-song voice. "I really wish

I could tell you more about the whole ghastly mix-up than I'm able to. I think I mentioned before that I was very late in arriving at Wyndham's hotel on the night of the thirteenth. I remember it was raining cats and dogs and by the time I got to Wyndham's rooms it was already half past eleven. I remember the time distinctly because I'd noticed the clock in the hotel lobby when I stopped to enquire for the number of his suite."

He paused abruptly and glanced toward Alcott's prize bottle of Scotch. "Er—may I?"

At my nod he poured himself another drink.

Suddenly I caught the sharp tattoo of Pete Alcott's pencil busy already against the thin wall that divided his bedroom from the room in which we were sitting. I glanced uneasily at Stone. Then I rejoiced in the stroke of good fortune which had impelled him to seat himself on the far side of the room. At the moment he was sipping his Scotch totally oblivious to the sound. "And if he does hear it," I argued to myself, "I can always blame it on the noisy radiator." Meanwhile I decoded Alcott's raps without difficulty.

"Ask Stone why in hell he happened to go to Wyndham's rooms at all."

I put the question somewhat more civilly to Stone. But even so, I noticed his color mount. He gave an embarrassed laugh and interrupted his narrative. "I went there because—oh, well, it's rather difficult to explain! You see, I have an insatiable curiosity about life, and even though I half expect to be a missionary when I finish at the University, I get a little fed up on the fruits of the tree of knowledge every now and then. I want the tang of experience, knowledge of men, some understanding of the things that make the wheels of life go round. You understand me, I'm sure.

"For some inexplicable reason Steve Wyndham always represented the acme of those things to me. It wasn't simply a matter of his wealth and my comparative obscurity. It went deeper. He had a *savoir faire* that I lacked and which, from the time I was a kid at school and first saw him after he'd made the football team at Yale, I longed with all the passionate idolatry of eleven to emulate. That's straight. I don't think Wyndham even faintly guessed my—er—profound admiration."

Stone smiled. "To him, I was just the son of a preacher, who happened to be the friend of a sister," —his smile broadened, "who had somehow managed to make herself particularly objectionable to him. Not a very good introduction to be sure, but despite it he was always pleasant to me just as he was to every one.

"Well, last winter I broke down from overwork at College and through Miss Wyndham's generosity I was sent on a vacation to Havana for my health. On the fatal thirteenth, down on La Playa beach, I ran into Wyndham with a friend of his—a red-headed fellow named Hugh D. Ford. He told me that he was having a poker crowd that night in his rooms and I should come. I knew perfectly well there would be a mixed crowd and high stakes and drinking and all that. You ask why did I go? I went because, as I implied before, I don't believe in taking myself too seriously."

He drained the whiskey and soda at his side and

smiled. "You know, I've a theory if Adam had known how to laugh, the whole story of Paradise might have been different."

"I see," I said vaguely, devoutly hoping that Alcott's perception would prove a little better than mine, "And now, on with your story!"

"Well, as I was saying, Wyndham's room was crowded when I got there, and it seemed doubly so because the place wasn't large and the air was thick with the smell of cigars and drink. I wasn't sorry to see that the Venetian blind at the window was drawn and closed, for I was quite wet and chilly from out of doors and the rain was still coming down in torrents. As I entered, Steve stopped long enough to say 'Hello,' then he went on playing his hand. I pulled a chair up and looked on.

"The crowd was using money instead of chips, and the size of the pile in the centre of the table was a tidy sum. Anyhow, it represented a darn sight more than I'd used at the University in all my three years there. It made my missionary blood rise, and the coolness of those men only exasperated me further. Steve especially. He had just raised the pot and there was not a flicker or a muscle to indicate any tension. He simply didn't care. I remember thinking how especially well set-up he looked just then, immaculately groomed as always, his face bronzed and hardened from exposure, his keen blue eyes smiling dangerously and radiating the same electric quality of vitality and well-being that he'd had as a youngster. I recall thinking to myself half enviously, 'Steve's surely had all the breaks if any one has!'

"That was about half past eleven. I never said that again, I can tell you.

"When the hand was over Steve wanted me to take his place, but on my wallet, I couldn't, although I didn't explain why. Steve kept insisting, with that singular lack of imagination that's so characteristic of fellows who've never seen the other side. 'Oh, come on! I've got to clear out of here at twelve anyhow. You'll just keep the ranks from thinning.' Steve indicated a small, overnight bag that stood just behind him. I remember one of the men looking up and saying, 'What do you mean—got to clear out at twelve? We're just warming up!'

"Steve laughed. 'I'd meant to explain before. I've got to quit tonight at twelve. Have to, really! You men can keep right on until morning if you want. Along about that time Red ought to be breezing in to keep an eye on you!' He glanced toward the adjoining room which I gathered was occupied by Hugh Ford. That was the red-headed fellow I mentioned before. He was known to the crowd as 'Red.'

"There was a general protest. 'Yeah. But who'll feed the kitty if you leave us all alone?'

"Someone said glumly: 'Ford won't, that's sure! He's always three jumps ahead of every nickel he can make on his next ten articles.'

"Steve laughed. 'Pick another victim. At twelve I'll just up and out! I'm giving due warning now.'

"He interrupted himself to introduce me to the crowd. As I recall it, there was a very decent looking movie director by the name of Brady, a heavy set Cuban planter by the name of Sanchez, there was also Judge Lamar, whom I'd met previously through my uncle but never liked, and Barton Dunlap and Calvin Watts whom I also knew. These last two men were old friends of Steve's, acquaintances that dated back to prep-school days. I guess Steve saw something in them. One thing sure, I never could. There was also a heavy-set, coarse-looking fellow, whose name has completely slipped me. I hated his bloated face. Nonetheless, he stood out particularly because he had so little to say. Just played along, you know, with a rather aloof cynical manner that aroused my interest, because it went so oddly with his very ordinary exterior. I think the man was from New York. Anyhow, he seemed to know all the works around here. Night clubs, politicians, Broadway—the whole show."

"Would you know his name if you heard it?" I broke in, remembering the list I'd gotten hold of that afternoon.

"Perhaps."

"How does Meenan sound? George Meenan?" I asked deliberately.

Stone shook his head. "Can't say for sure. You know all this is over ten months old. If you said George Washington I'd tell you that name sounded sort of familiar, too." At his little joke Stone broke again into that incredibly broad grin of his and, as always, I found myself irritated by its sheer irrelevance.

"Well?" I said drily.

"Well, Steve poured me a drink which I took and Lamar offered me a smoke which I turned down. That's my one shining virtue, you see. Then every one settled back to the game. This Cuban fellow,

Sanchez, was just starting a new deal when the telephone rang. Watts, who was sitting nearest the telephone, got up, for a wonder, and answered it. After a moment, he turned to Steve. 'Some one wants you,' and I remember he smiled significantly at Wyndham as he answered it.

"Wyndham took the receiver. I got the distinct impression he was talking to a girl. I also got the impression that Sanchez, for some queer reason, was ruffled by the call. He was sitting just next to me, you see, so it was easy enough for me to observe him. At first he just laid down the pack of cards. Then he began turning around and around on his chair, like a corkscrew. Suddenly, he got up, and puffing furiously at his cigar, he walked up and down the room, glowering at Wyndham.

"For the life of me I couldn't decide just why Sanchez acted so. Even though we heard only one side of the conversation, it was obvious Wyndham didn't consider it at all important."

"Just a minute," I broke in. "Do you recall any of that conversation? It all helps, you know."

Stone thought for a minute. "It's hard, you know, after this lapse of time, but according to my best recollection, the whole thing ran like this. 'Yes, this is Steve Wyndham!' Silence on our side. Then Steve saying, 'Thanks, but it's impossible.' Another silence. 'No, it's really impossible. Please understand!' Pause. 'I'm sorry but I have guests now.' Pause. 'No, I'm busy after 12 tonight.' A long pause. Then firmly, 'No, I'm sorry, but I've told you that before. Suppose we let matters rest.'

"That was about all. Pretty soon Steve said good-bye and hung up."

"I see. Now, go ahead."

"Well, as Steve turned back toward the table Sanchez strode over in front of him. 'That was Lolita,' the Cuban said tensely and I noticed his face was twitching with excitement. Suddenly he struck out blindly at Steve. I never saw anything happen so quickly! But even so, it wasn't hard for Steve to ward off his thrust.

" 'Don't be an idiot!' He laughed and that was about the worst thing he could have done.

"Sanchez flung his cigar aside and started for Steve in earnest. He hit out wildly. In blind rage. His face had gone white and his eyes were narrowed to two flames of hate. A couple of the men sprang up and tried to hold him back. I think it was Lamar and Dunlap, but I'm not sure. Anyhow, Wyndham just waved them back. He was like that, you know. As I remember, he didn't even bother to take the cigarette from his mouth, or relax the slight smile which Sanchez' first outbreak had occasioned. He didn't have to. His body was hard—in wonderful condition. Anyone could see that. And though Sanchez struck out with a fury that looked like sheer anguish in its desire, Steve warded off his blows as easily as though it was all child's play. It would have worn out anyone else but him, I'm sure. After a little, Watts grabbed hold of Sanchez and swung him around.

" 'Are you out of your mind, Sanchez? If you were listening at all, you must have heard Steve tell whomever that was that he wasn't going to see her.'

"For the space of a few seconds, Sanchez stared stupidly at Watts, then ran his hand across his head. He looked awfully foolish. He must have felt worse.

"Steve came over to him and put his arm across his back in a friendly way.

" 'No hard feeling, Sanchez. Let's get on with that deal!'

"Sanchez wiped his forehead and went back to the table. Steve sat down in his place. Everybody tried to act as though nothing had happened, with the result that there was a lot of wisecracking and artificial gaiety for a few minutes, during which time Sanchez picked up the pack of cards and dealt. I noticed his hands were shaking and that he was biting his lower lip in a nervous, highly excitable way. But for five or ten minutes everything went as sweetly as a congregational meeting. Then, just as this fellow, whose name I've forgotten, was raising everyone's bid, *it happened!*"

Stone's voice was low and tense, and he moistened his lips with his whiskey and soda before proceeding.

"I say *it happened,* and yet to save my life, I can't tell you *what.* All I know is that suddenly, without apparent rhyme or reason the electric lights in the room went dead, and since I think I mentioned before that the Venetian blind was drawn, we were left in pitch darkness. Well, of course, that dampened nobody's spirits. We all thought something had gone wrong with the current, and in a moment or so it would right itself. Every one started kidding or singing 'Where was Moses when the light went out?' and stuff like that. I heard somebody groan and some

one laughingly echo it and then say mournfully, 'It
would be my luck just when I held a royal flush!'

"Somebody got up. Somebody's chair went over.
Somebody opened the hall door and said, 'Well, I'm
a son-of-a-gun if it isn't as black as the ace of spades
out here, too!' Somebody suggested we send downstairs for candles or a lamp, or, at very least, the hotel
management. Somebody went out. Anyhow there was
the sound of a door opening and closing, though
which door I couldn't have said. Somebody began
fumbling with his automatic lighter, but as usual,
the blamed thing wouldn't work. I reached out for
the box of matches I'd seen everyone using in the
middle of the table, but in the darkness, I couldn't
find the box; instead I encountered someone's hand
and suddenly Watt's voice said humorously, 'Hey,
we'd better guard the kitty!'

"At that, the lone automatic lighter flickered on at
last and shed feebly over the center of the table. The
men made jokes about the fact that the money was
still there, and of course, laughed a lot at all their
own nonsense. I looked again for the box of matches,
but I had no better luck in finding it than I'd had
before. I heard some one moving about the room,
but I couldn't have said *whom*. Out in the corridor
there was the sound of doors opening and closing and
of some few of the people who happened to be in
their rooms, enquiring in English and Spanish, and
everything else, what the trouble was. My own idea
was that there'd been a short circuit that must have
killed the lights in our section of the hotel only, for
through the hall door the sound of the orchestra
could still be heard drifting up from the lounge

downstairs. Then out of the darkness, one of the hotel attendants came in with lamps and suggested that they might help until the house electrician could locate the cause of the trouble.

"As I say, the lamps arrived suddenly and in the brief instant when everyone was blinking in their sudden glare my attention was riveted by the flash of a steel blade in Sanchez' hand. It was the blade of an extraordinarily long pocket knife and as he swiftly closed it and thrust it into his pockets, his eyes met mine in a look that at once arrested and disturbed me. You've heard of being chilled at a glance? Literally, I broke out in goose flesh. Why? This must seem crazy, I know! But you see, out of the eyes of that respectable looking Cuban planter I caught a depth of abysmal brutality such as I had never before seen. It was really uncanny. God! Like looking into some inferno of evil!"

Charles Stone paused in his narrative and for once his singular smile was conspicuous by its absence. Then he went on in his sing-song voice.

"What was stranger still was that I kept my mouth shut, when I knew at that moment I shouldn't have." Stone swallowed hard. It was easy to see he was overwrought for his hand shook as he picked up his highball glass.

However, in the interim of Stone's silence, I became acutely aware of the rap-tapping of Alcott's pencil against the nearby wall and in sudden dismay I realized that the sound had been going on all the while I had sat absorbed and listening. Now I caught the measure of Alcott's irritation in the sharp precision with which he was rapping away, and decoding, as swiftly as I could, I put his question to Stone as though it were my own.

"About how much time do you think passed from the minute the lights went out until the hotel attendant brought the lamps?"

Stone looked thoughtful for a moment.

"It's hard to say. Roughly speaking, about ten minutes, or a little longer."

"In complete darkness?" Alcott tapped out again, and again I put his question so that Stone never once suspected the by-play.

"No, I'd say it was only four or five minutes 'til that automatic lighter was burning there in the center of the table, but up until then the room was in complete darkness." Stone sipped his drink in silence. All zest seemed to have gone out of him.

"I don't want to hurry you unnecessarily, but a few moments ago you said you felt you had kept quiet when you knew you shouldn't. What made you feel so?" I asked in interest.

"Because," Stone looked at me fixedly through his thick double lens glasses and his countenance assumed a stony rigidity, "when I recovered sufficiently to look around the circle, Stephen Wyndham's chair was vacant and Steve himself had vanished as completely as though the earth had yawned open and engulfed him. Since that hour, as you know, he has not been seen or heard from again!"

I gave a very poor imitation of a blasé newspaperman. I was prepared for exactly this revelation and yet Stone's bald statement of the fact struck home.

It was in a sort of subconscious way that I remember catching the sound of Alcott's rapping.

"Could you say surely that during the period of darkness Sanchez had moved from his place by you?"

"No! That was it! I couldn't be sure!"

There was something in the way Stone said this that struck me as strange. It might have been that the question had given him a prop to support his own indecisive line of conduct. But there was something —I couldn't quite analyze what.

"Did any one happen to notice just what time it was?" I asked in interest.

"Yes. It was five minutes past twelve. That I noticed myself."

"H'm!" I said drily. "Didn't I understand you to say Wyndham had announced that he would be leaving at twelve?"

Stone nodded. "I know that's just what most of the fellows contended when Red Ford and Watts said that they thought the whole episode sounded *devilish* unlike him!"

"Hold on!" I said, remembering the list of players I had in my note book. "You don't mean *Ford!* He wasn't in on the game, was he?"

"No, he wasn't. But by a funny coincidence, I happened to run into him in the corridor about this time. You see, I'd gone outside for a breath of air for my head was swimming. Anyhow, when we went back into the room the crowd was still speculating about Wyndham's disappearance."

"H'm. Were the lights on by then?"

"Well, I'm not sure. But I'd say yes. You see, the

entire difficulty was only a question of a burned-out fuse. In fifteen or twenty minutes, at most, we had all the light we wanted."

"Well, go ahead! You were saying Watts and this Red Ford thought the whole episode peculiar?"

"Yes. Watts seemed very much nonplussed by the whole thing, although he didn't say much. He just kept repeating with a sort of aggravating persistence that he thought it was damned funny of Steve to walk out in the dark without so much as a goodnight. Then the rest of the gang began kidding the life out of him, pointing out that Wyndham had previously announced his intention of leaving, and after all, what did Watts want? Tears and a declamatory recitation of 'Fare thee well and if forever?' Watts began to feel the absurdity of his position, I guess, for at length he took refuge in the fact that he'd thought he'd heard someone at Steve's end of the table, give a pretty good imitation of a groan. In this, Judge Lamar agreed, whereupon Dunlap and Brady promptly claimed the honor of having groaned, too. And since everyone knew they were quite idiotic enough to have done it, that ended that. To tell the truth, there had been so much horse play and nonsense, it did seem silly to take any of it very seriously. And yet, with it all, I couldn't help glancing dubiously at Sanchez every now and then."

"What was his attitude through all of this?"

"Oh, he was very quiet. Didn't have much to say one way or the other. Only once, when I'd been looking at him rather searchingly, he pointed out, not to me but to the group, that Steve's hat and overnight bag were gone, and added almost insolently, I thought, that all this speculation seemed to him much ado about nothing."

"Closets?" I caught Alcott rapping.

"Did you think of looking in any of the closets?" I improvised quickly.

"Oh, yes! Ford thought of it because, you see, he wasn't so readily convinced. There was only one closet in the room in which we were sitting, but when Ford tried to open it he found it locked."

"Wasn't that peculiar?"

"Ford didn't seem to think so. He said Wyndham kept all his trick fishing rods and golf sticks and such stuff locked up in there. According to Ford, Steve was as temperamental about his paraphernalia as a couple of prima donnas, on opening night."

"H'm, how about the money on the table? Was that O.K.?"

"I think it was O.K. Anyhow, nothing was said about it. However, there was one thing that Ford thought very peculiar."

"What was that?" I inquired with interest.

"The simple fact that the door which led to his bedroom was locked."

"And what was so strange about that?"

"Oh, Ford seemed very much surprised at this because, as he explained, this particular door was always kept open."

At this point, I proferred my memo pad and fountain pen to Stone, for I was in bad need of a diagram. Without any hesitation, the young man sketched in a rough plan of the suite that Wyndham and Ford had occupied. I append a copy of this drawing herewith.

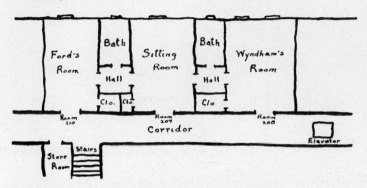

"You see," Stone said as he finished, "Ford explained that he and Wyndham used the room in which we were sitting—that is, room 209—as a sort of ante room and always entered their respective bedrooms from there instead of from the main corridor."

"Was Ford certain that he had not locked the door earlier that evening?"

"Oh, yes. Ford seemed positive about that. In fact, at first he wasn't sure how he was going to get into his room at all because as he explained it, most of the time the key to his hall door was sticking *inside* the lock. Anyhow, together with Watts, he went out into the hall to summon an attendant and a few moments later we heard a click at the lock of the door that led from his room to the sitting room and were surprised to see Ford and Watts come smilingly in. All their anxiety about Wyndham had been set completely at rest for, on Ford's bureau, they'd found a brief note of goodbye from Steve, explaining that something had arisen necessitating his hasty departure and appending a short memo of instructions of what Ford should do with his stuff if by any chance he should be away longer than a week. So that was all, or should have been all, except—"

"What about the locked door?" Alcott was tapping so persistently that I had to put his question if for no other reason than to silence him.

"Oh, the door. They all joshed Ford about that, saying knowingly that there had been rumors that he was sort of up 'in the air,' these days and now they knew it. I remember Judge Lamar announcing with a side glance that he'd seen in the evening paper that Kay Devereaux . . . I think that was the name the Judge mentioned . . ."

"Yes it was. Go on."

"Anyhow this Devereaux girl had flown down that day from Palm Beach. I remember Ford got as red as a lobster. He made a grand-stand play at nonchalance, but it wasn't very effective. Just the same, he kept insisting that these particulars did not alter the fact that when he had gone out that afternoon his hall door was locked and the door to the sitting room was open. However, once having discovered there was a girl in the case no one took his protests very seriously. That is no one. . . . but myself."

"And why did you?"

"Because of one peculiar fact. A short while later, when the crowd was breaking up, every one reaching for their hats, settling up their accounts, and all that stuff, I noticed on the floor near the chair, where Steve Wyndham had been sitting, the butt end of one of his—Steve's—Russian cigarettes.

"That doesn't sound like much, does it? All right. Listen. I stooped to pick up that stub because I thought I saw it still smoking. In this it happened I was wrong, but in so doing, I noticed to my surprise that the butt end was off, *bitten clean through*. Do you understand me? I didn't need the stain of blood which I now saw, to convince me that in some undreamed of moment of tension Steve's teeth had met on that cigarette. A train of unutterable thoughts whirled through my head, paralyzing me, turning me into stone. When at last I raised my eyes from that tell-tale stub, it was only to encounter the chill gaze of Señor Sanchez.

" 'Pardon me,' he said, with studied politeness. 'I believe you have picked up my cigarette.' Automatically, I handed the stub to him. Somehow, I never knew how, I managed to bid the others goodnight. Then, completely u. nerved, acting as though I were in a dream, I turned and fled from that chamber of mystery.

"The very next day I sailed for home."

Chapter VIII

A PACT IS SEALED

AS Stone concluded his narrative there was a brief silence. The young man looked as though he would like to be off. In my mind a stream of thought was flowing. "You're a plausible youth, Charles Stone, but can I believe you? You've had plenty of time to invent a good story; how much of it will bear checking? Moreover, why did a fellow with your particular tastes ever elect to be a missionary? You're not the type, Parson Stone, not the type! What is your association with that strange Wyndham sister? . . . H'm yes . . . and that recent huge bequest to a Chinese mission?" Suddenly, the pale face and wide, frightened eyes of Miss Isabella rose to my mind and I restrained an involuntary shudder. Aloud, I asked: "By the way, do you happen to know any reason for Miss Wyndham's intense dislike of her brother?"

Stone shrugged. "Just a case of temperament I'd say. Miss Isabella's all Puritan. Steve was Cavalier! Also there was a gap of nearly thirty years in their ages. If, to all of that, you add the inevitable antagonism that must have been aroused by the Senior Wyndham's preference for Steve, you have the whole psychological picture, as I see it. Anyhow, whatever the reasons, it was so marked that I don't think Stephen went home six times after prep-school."

I nodded sagely, but I wasn't convinced.

"There's nothing more specific that you could tell me?"

"No."

"Do you know of any unusual circumstances that might have surrounded the will of Wyndham Senior?"

Stone looked thoughtful for a moment and shook his head. "Nothing." Then he added as upon second thought, "Except perhaps that when the old gentleman bequeathed the Madison Avenue home to Miss Isabella there was a special codicil that the place had to be preserved exactly as it was at the time of his second wife's death, not a stick nor a stone to be altered. Beautiful sentiment and all that, but the result is that there isn't a modern convenience in the place, not even an electric light! I'd call that somewhat unusual, wouldn't you?"

"You're damned right. Is there anything else?"

"Nothing of which I know."

It was then that I shot my bolt.

"Perhaps you could tell me something of a small gold medallion, minutely engraved with Wyndham's initials and—er—yours?"

At the mention of the medallion, I thought Stone started, but I could not have said surely. One thing was certain, however. From that instant the young fellow's manner changed abruptly from one of open frankness to one of hostile reserve.

"I've never seen the piece you describe," he said with annoyance. "And since I've told you about all I can in this matter, I'm sure you won't mind if I move along. It's getting late." He rose to his feet and shouldered into his ulster.

"I'll bother you for your address—just in case of emergency," I said with a yawn.

"Of course." He wrote his number down in a small, precise hand.

"Good night!"

"Good night, and thanks for your help."

The door closed and I made a long distance dive for the telephone that I knew stood in the next room. In my haste I nearly upset Pete who, arrayed in pajamas of passionate orange, was stalking up and down the floor.

"What's the hurry?"

"I think we'll still make the last edition. And Holy God! What a scoop! What a scoop!" I executed a restrained Highland fling and dialed the office as quickly as I could. All the discouragement of the early afternoon had fallen from me. I believed I'd just succeeded in getting the city editor on the telephone when, without the least warning, Alcott crossed over to me and deliberately clicked down on our connection.

"What's the idea? You big baboon!" I exploded in wrath.

"I think you're crazy!" he said, quiet as always and looking straight at me. "Look here! If you want to ruin every chance you have of getting anywhere on this case, just come out in the next edition with the few good leads you've got. Smear them all over the front page! Give every half-baked reporter in town and every well-meaning but clumsy member of the police force a chance to bungle them before you get a bit further." He shook his head disconsolately. "Good Lord! people like yourself are the most dangerously explosive material in the world! You ought to have a guardian appointed—really."

There was a sharp common sense to what Alcott was saying that made me pause. Turning the matter over, I saw how incontestably true it was that, if I published the information we had just run down, it would only turn the case into a sort of reportorial "free-for-all" in which the *New York Globe* would come off no better than the next paper, and, possibly, not even as well. Furthermore, in the interest of the Wyndham case itself, the wide publicity and muddled outcry consequent upon any fresh newspaper publicity might only retard the ultimate solution by keeping the guilty party or parties informed of the direction of public interest and effort, thus giving them ample opportunity to cover their tracks or to escape. Of this sort of thing, certainly, there had been enough public instances of late to serve as a warning. The longer I considered the facts the sounder Alcott's advice looked. At last I meekly hung up the 'phone and turned to him.

"Damn it. There goes one of the best stories I ever broke. Stone *was* a knockout, you know."

"H'm! Couldn't help but be!" Alcott laughed. "Consider the latitude of his interests. God and the devil, soft living and hard liquor!" He glanced dejectedly through the doorway toward his empty bottle of Scotch. "Yes, he had breadth of viewpoint, your young Parson Stone. You certainly ought to cultivate him a bit!"

"What did you make of his story?"

Alcott took a few puffs on his cigarette before answering. "A rather brilliant compound of truth and genius and just good old-fashioned lying, I'd say!"

This coincided exactly with my own earlier misgivings, but Alcott's pontifical statement of the fact drove me to energetic dissent. "Well, the boy impressed me for all my original prejudice!"

I said this with especial vehemence hoping to goad Alcott to loquacity. The ruse worked. He came over and patted me soothingly on the back. "Keep on, some day I'll write your memoirs and call them, 'Gullible's Travels.' Good old Ellis!"

"Aw, shut up."

But I was amused. "One thing did strike me phoney. That mountain of evidence he piled up against Sanchez."

Alcott shrugged. "All of which may have been true, y'know!"

"Sez you! And where did you think the lying commenced?"

Pete broke into laughter. "Hang around a little while. We might see!"

"Oh, be funny, why don't you?"

"I was never more serious, I assure you!"

I shot a look at Alcott and knew I need not have doubted the fact. He was sitting close by me on the edge of the table, where the telephone stood. His long legs dangled loosely over the side, and his glance strayed absently out the window. I studied his face, noticing with interest that the furrows in his forehead were graven deeper that I ever remembered, and that there was a peculiar grim determination in the set of his jaw.

"This case is getting you the way it has all the rest of us around the office. Look out, Alcott."

"Oh, well, I've an alibi. For years I've been interested in Wyndham's career, you know. After all, that gives a fellow a sort of personal feeling. . . ."

The phone cut in raucously and Alcott picked it up. For the space of a few minutes I heard him in low-voiced conversation. Then he hung up, and very nonchalantly handed me a slip of paper on which I'd watched him swiftly jotting down some message.

"You asked me where Stone's lying commenced. Take a look at that!"

I took the paper from his outstretched hand.

"And in case you want to know," he drawled in his usual lazy way, "that radio was sent five minutes ago to the *New York Globe* from aboard the good yacht 'Seven Seas' cruising, as you learned this afternoon, around the Galapagos."

My eye raced across the message. It read:

AT NO TIME WAS STONE INVITED TO HOTEL ROOMS BY WYNDHAM OR MYSELF. CAN'T SUGGEST REASON FOR HIS PRESENCE. IF MY RETURN WILL HELP INVESTIGATION RADIO AT ONCE.   FORD.

"Your fool hunches are getting better and better!" I burst out as I finished. "When did you think of communicating with Ford?"

"As soon as Stone finished that most interesting explanation of his presence, and I'd had time to figure that it wasn't quite so late down there where Ford is."

I looked my amazement. "But how in hell did you manage it?"

Alcott nodded across to the closet. "Took the phone in there, shut the door and let the *New York Globe* attend to the rest. And while I was at it," Alcott looked sheepish, "I took a few other liberties, too."

"What now?" I gasped.

"Well, seeing you were up to your neck on this Stone lead, I've started Billy Farrel running around, presumably on your authority, trying to get you a line on all those men who were in on that fatal little poker party at the Sevilla Biltmore. I told him to hunt down every blamed thing he could get. Past, present and future. You've simply got to beat those detective agencies to it, you know, if you're going to get anywhere on this case. Farrel hasn't an idea what's up, of course. And we mustn't let him. All he knows is that he's to get all the information he can and meet you in the city room at twelve o'clock tomorrow morning. Also, a little while ago I phoned my own assistant—yes, all of this from the closet over there—and started him checking up steamship passages and little things like that, on our sporty Parson Stone. It's not that I don't believe the general outline of his story. I do. But I thought the invented portions, if we can find them, would prove much more interesting food for contemplation." Suddenly, Alcott paused self-consciously. "Say, Ellis, I hope you don't mind my barging in as I've done!"

"Mind? M. Constantius God! Right now, you're the one person I want to stick around." This came from the bottom of my heart (wherever that metaphoric spot may be) but I proceeded to look so put out at my own spontaneity that Alcott confronted me squarely.

"Really mean that?" he asked quietly.

"Aw, I never go in for Valentines!"

He lit a fresh cigarette with the butt end of his old one and strode to the window. For a while he smoked in silence meditatively contemplating a fat old lady across the court who was disrobing for bed.

"If I was dead sure you meant that . . ." he began at length. Then he broke off and turned abruptly to his typewriter. For the space of a few minutes his keys clicked soberly. Then having pounded out whatever it was he wanted, he brandished aloft the paper and its carbon and crossed to me. His eyes were twinkling with amusement. "I thought we'd just put it down in writing!" he said with a laugh.

I looked at the paper in surprise and read:

It is agreed that John Dwight Ellis, party of the first part, and Peter Alcott, party of the second part, do hereby pledge themselves, insofar as compatible with their respective responsibilities, to work jointly toward a solution of the Stephen P. Wyndham case, until such a time as both shall decide this mystery has been adequately cleared, or, failing that, until such a time as it shall seem, according to the best judgment of both parties, that the case is entirely impossible of solution; in either of which events all credit, reward and emolument deriving therefrom is hereby waived by Peter Alcott.

I looked up with a grin. "This all looks like just so much gravy to me. Of course, 'it ain't just! it ain't fair!' but where the hell's my fountain pen?"

I rummaged through my pockets for my pen, feeling all the while a tingle of immense elation such as I hadn't known since the days when as a bare-legged, dirty-faced, utterly disreputable small town boy, I'd slunk off to forbidden places, to swear magnificent loyalties and plan impossible escapades, with all the most disreputable youth in the neighborhood. Some philosopher has defined life as a long search for a friend, but, to my way of thinking, he's wrong. Alongside a genuine comrade-in-adventure, all mere friendships pale to anaemic twaddle. I located my fountain pen on the table in the other room and strode back to Alcott to find him once more glancing his document over.

"I'm going to add another clause!" he looked up to announce. "You don't have to sign it if you don't want, but if I'm going to roll up my sleeves and get to work on this case, I want a safety break against that sweet impulsive nature you showed a while ago." He nodded toward the telephone, but I wasn't to be insulted. Just then, with every square inch of me, I was feeling the pull of the lurid enigmatic adventure on which we were embarking. Meanwhile, Alcott, unruffled as always, scribbled away at his postscript.

It is further agreed that in pursuance of the above stated ends, neither party to this contract shall at any time give or cause to be given newspaper publicity of any sort, kind or description without the express consent of the other.

In high jubilee, I signed the covenant feeling a surge of confidence that had been unknown to me for weeks. In some metaphysical way it derived from the quiet set determination of Alcott. Good old Alcott! Yes, I still feel that way about you in spite of all that has transpired since that momentous night.

When everything was duly sealed, signed and delivered, I turned back in genuine earnest to my note book.

"There are a few things here we've *got* to find out, Pete." I mused aloud, making rapid fire notes on the last page of the little memo book while I talked.

"1. What is the mystery of that Wyndham will?

"2. Of what is Miss Wyndham so apprehensive?

"3. Why did lawyer Stone try to conceal the fact that his nephew was present at the time of Wyndham's murder, disappearance or what you will?

"4. Why does a fellow like Charles Stone elect to be a missionary?

"5. What was the actual reason for Charles' visit to the Sevilla Biltmore on the night of February 13th?

"6. What has this Red Ford done with the power of attorney entrusted to him by Wyndham?

"7. What is the explanation of that mangled cigarette which Stone found on the floor?"

As stated before, I talked aloud as I wrote. Now, as I finished my last question, Alcott yawned sleepily.

"You'll be a smart little boy if you find out the answers to all those questions!"

"Hell, I've got to!"

"Then don't forget that missing gold medallion."

In another minute Alcott was gently snoring.

Chapter IX

THE CHECK-UP

BEFORE nine o'clock of the following morning, I was down on Wall Street at the offices of Manning & Wilson, brokers. In my pocket was a letter of personal introduction to Mr. Thomas Manning, which upon sudden inspiration I had procured from a friend. If I had my own private misgivings on the probability of finding Manning in at this hour, they were promptly dissipated. Mr. Manning proved to be one of those quietly electric individuals, who despite greying air and rugged countenance, manages to toss off a market letter before breakfast, transactions in some fifty thousand shares before lunch, and at least four cocktails before dinner. In short order I found myself shaking hands with him and pouring into his ears the story of my mission.

"You put me in a very awkward position," he said with quiet directness as I concluded. "You have been correctly informed as to Mr. Wyndham's account with us, also as to the unlimited power of attorney which he entrusted to his friend, Mr. Ford. However, transactions of this kind are in their very nature confidential. A broker cannot reveal. . . ."

"I understand all that, sir!" I burst out impetuously. "But this is not an ordinary case. It's a red-hot emergency! Every item of information relating to

Stephen P. Wyndham's affairs is urgently needed if we are to avoid coming to a dead end in this investigation! If you have Wyndham's interests genuinely at heart. . . ." How I managed it I'll never know. I got a few moments alone with him. I unloosed a veritable Niagara of eloquence. I argued, I persuaded, I cajoled, with what I thought was little success. Then, suddenly, Mr. Manning broke into a smile.

"Young man, I may as well thank the Lord I'm not a woman and have done with it!"

He rang for his secretary.

Fifteen minutes later, from a corner cigar store, I phoned Alcott at his desk.

"Get this! It's hot stuff. On July twentieth last, Hugh Ford drew twenty-five thousand dollars from Wyndham's account. No explanations offered. He repeated the same performance in September. Again no explanation. How does that sound?"

"Not exactly bashful," I heard Pete's voice. Then silence for a moment at the other end of the wire. "Did Manning offer any comment on Ford?"

"Yeah! Said he was a charming fellow."

"H'm! He ought to be!"

We were both too keyed up to talk any longer. On my side I was experiencing a sudden overwhelming impulse to see my young acquaintance of last night once again.

"Why," I asked myself, "when Parson Stone was tarring up the boys in on that little party in Havana, did he so conspicuously neglect to blacken Ford along with the rest?" Against Ford there wasn't a word that I could recall. It struck me as queer, but then everything in connection with the case disagreed so completely with all traditional receipts for investigation, clue or inquiry that I paid scant heed to that. However, as it still lacked two hours to my appointment at the office, I gave rein to my curiosity.

I located Charles Stone's apartment in a very dingy walk-up on East 93rd Street. As the door of the third floor rear was opened, I caught signs of great disorder. An empty trunk stood near the door, a welter of things about it. Whether its presence represented Stone's recent arrival or a hurriedly planned departure, I didn't have time to decide. A dour looking matron of middle years was glancing at me questioningly. Something in the mould of her face and her carriage made me gamble on my salutation.

"Mrs. Stone, I think?"

"Yes! What do you wish?" She spoke in a dull, sullen tone.

"Could I see your son, if he is at home?"

At this moment Charles himself, stepped quietly into the foyer. He was wearing some sort of oriental lounge robe. It made him look curiously foreign. As he recognized me, an expression of annoyance crossed his face, but immediately his broad smile replaced it.

"Ah! So you want to see me again?" he said in that soft purring tone.

He led me into a small private study, where I stopped short in sheer amazement. Walls hung in soft old mandarin silks, a low settee, two carved teakwood chairs, a lacquered screen, a single blue Ming jar where the light that came through the carved wooden fretwork fell in broken patterns upon it. That was all. But in crossing that threshold I felt as though I'd crossed the China Sea.

I looked at young Stone in mild bewilderment. "I see you carry China with you."

"Yes, in more senses than one!" The remark slipped out before he was aware of it and for the moment he looked strangely ill at ease.

"I'm afraid I've interrupted you!"

I nodded apologetically toward the open packing case which I noticed in the corner. An array of books and papers were strewn about it on the floor.

Instead of answering, Charles merely shrugged with frigid reserve.

I began deliberately. "On thinking over our conversation of last night, there were a few loose ends that bothered me. Can you tell me anything about this fellow Red—I mean—Hugh Ford?"

Stone looked at me superciliously. Then he broke suddenly into that incredibly broad smile of his. "Mr. Ellis, I don't know you from Adam, but I'll give you a piece of gratuitous advice. What you're doing is no use. You're only holding an intellectual inquest over a dead and hopeless situation. Whatever could have been done about Steve Wyndham should have been undertaken nearly a year ago. The fault is mine that it wasn't. At this stage. . . ." he shrugged, "I've a conviction you're only wasting your time and my own."

"Nevertheless," I persisted, "I'd like to know anything you can tell me of Hugh Ford."

Stone wasn't to be thawed. "Why don't you ask some of the others?" He glanced toward his packing cases.

"After all, I knew Red *only slightly.* As for his friendship with Wyndham, that dated back to his senior year at Yale, I think."

"Ford's not from New York, I gather?"

"No. I think he's from the middle west. I'm not sure. He's not the sort that talks much about the 'ole folks at home.' "

"Not so well off, you'd say!"

"Not from what I've heard. It's always been a puzzle to me how Red himself made out."

"I've understood he writes rather saleable stuff for political magazines."

Stone shrugged. "Oh, he's clever enough that way." He said this so sarcastically that I knew, in an instant, that it was only oversight that had saved Ford from the general mud-slinging, the night before. "What he makes from writing wouldn't yield pin money in the crowd he hangs out with."

I smiled. "Well, some fellows have the luck you know. Anyhow, money troubles are over for him now, or ought to be! He married the rich George Devereaux's daughter last month."

"So my uncle informed me. That was the girl whom I told you Red was going with at the time of Steve's tragedy." Again Stone's glance strayed restlessly toward his packing cases. "Is there anything further you wish to know?"

"Oh, plenty! But I'll wait for another time!"

"As you wish!" Stone saw me to the door. His manner was unbending and reserved throughout.

As I walked down the ill-lit stairway I asked myself a dozen times, why my mention of the small gold medallion on the night before had so perceptibly altered the boy's manner. Then as I neared the second landing all speculation suddenly ceased for coming up the stairway toward me, in the half light of the hallway, I recognized the ample proportions and ferret-like eyes of Miss Wyndham's unique butler, Cooper.

"Good morning!"

"Good morning, sir!" He blinked at me in surprise. As the man came closer, I caught sight of a letter which he was carrying in his hand. The sight of that letter was my undoing. I hatched a quick plan.

A few moments later when Cooper was righting himself from his regrettable but (alas!) quite unavoidable fall and trudging off to rescue from the first landing a letter that he quite naturally assumed to be his own, I hastily opened and read the missive which Miss Wyndham had evidently penned to Charles Stone in the greatest of haste.

Come to me at once upon receipt of this. One terrible thought has been obsessing me since yesterday. Your uncle tells me that you too have been questioned. For God's sake come quickly.

Isabella Wyndham.

Re-sealing the letter as best I could, I tossed it over the banister to Cooper. "Say, I think our letters have gotten mixed!"

The man looked up sharply in my direction, handed me my letter in passing and said not another word.

It took me what seemed an interminable time to get to the office. As a matter of actual fact, I arrived there twenty minutes before the appointed time. I routed Pete Alcott out of what has so reverentially come to be called "conference." He looked absurdly tired out for a man whom I had left snoring the night before but he didn't act so. In the hubbub of the City Room I told him of my strange encounter with Cooper. When I finished, he gravely shook his head at me.

"Ellis, at heart you're really a law-abiding citizen, despite your profession. Now, with me, I get a positive itching in my feet at the mere thought of that interview!"

"What could I have done. . . . ?" I began, but Pete only raised his eyebrows and when at length he spoke, it was not to answer my question.

"By the way, I've had a few lines of inquiry out on Stone and strangely enough, the boy's story seems to check. That is, everything ties up except the erroneous impression he chose to give of having been invited to the Sevilla Biltmore by Wyndham and Ford. It seems on February fourteenth of last year, a Charles Elihu Stone actually sailed from Havana on the 'S.S. Carribean.' That would be the day following that fatal little party, just as he told us. Of course, this might well have been a dummy sailing but I've a hunch that it wasn't.

"Also, ten days ago one Charles Elihu Stone entered the Port of San Francisco on the 'Empress of the East,' having been away from his native shores nearly ten months. That lends corroboration to the boy's statement that he had been home only a few days prior to talking to you. An interview with your acquaintance in the Department of Philosophy elicits the information that the youth is an extraordinary combination of brilliance, ego and perhaps a dash of present day decadence. Professor Porter thinks I'm a distant relative, interested in the boy's education. He spoke freely, despite his evident affection for the youth. But with it all. . . ." I didn't hear the finish. The rattle of typewriters about drowned Alcott's voice. I moved closer.

Alcott looked pensively across the City Room as he proceeded at his point. "Stone simmers down to a few all-important questions. One, you've already written down in that damned memo book of yours, Ellis. One, we shan't even mention for some time. But the other, you'll be scribbling down in there so soon, that I'll save you the trouble right now!"

I handed over my trusty little black book. Under my last question, I saw Alcott write boldly, "What took Stone to the Orient and kept him there ten months at this particular stage of his career?"

Alcott smiled as he closed the book. "When we find that out, believe me, we'll have gone a long way toward learning why Parson Stone forced his presence on that peculiar little poker party at the Sevilla Biltmore."

It was then that I asked the question that had been pounding in my brain since the previous afternoon. "Alcott," I said very quietly, "do you think it's possible that for reasons unknown, Charles Stone himself is mixed in this Wyndham mess?"

Alcott shook his head in perplexity and his face looked graver than I ever remembered it. "At this point, all we know for certain is that someone in that.

room that night was, and I'd add, fiendishly so. What we've still got to find out is, *WHO!*"

I longed to pursue the subject, but just then I saw Billy Farrel swinging across the City Room.

Billy Farrel was a good little scout. He had come down to the *Globe* straight from the academic shelter of the School of Journalism, and a more hard-working, conscientious, painstaking youngster never wore down his shoe leather and pocketed his twenty-five per week. Certainly, in all my recent difficulties there had been ample opportunity to judge his mettle. However, as he joined us, I knew by the way he was screwing up his round freckled face that everything was not going to his entire satisfaction.

"Say, where'd you rake up that bunch of names you handed out last evening," he flung at Alcott by way of salutation.

"Why?" Alcott asked soothingly.

"Nothing, except I've had a devil of a time getting results!" A prodigious yawn escaped him. "That gets charged to loss of sleep," Farrel said with a grin. "And this next. . . ." he reached over and picked up the phone. "This gets charged to a cautious Dutch ancestor." He laughed nervously. Then to the girl at the switchboard we heard him announce, "Say, if anyone shows up around the paper asking for William Farrel, Jr., tell them I just dropped dead of old age, or that I've gone to the Isle of Wight for my health. That goes for everyone! Get me, Madge?"

"Say, what's up?"

Instead of answering, Farrel mopped his forehead and thrust a filing card toward us. There, neatly printed, I recognized the list of the men in the poker crowd at the Sevilla Biltmore. Barton Dunlap, Jose Sanchez, Sanfred Lamar, Calvin Watts, Phillip Brady, George Meenan. Alongside some were a series of orderly notations. A few of the names were scratched.

Billy shook his head over those. "If you were real sports you'd have bought me a round trip ticket to Havana. Half of your list happens to be down there."

"Or in Kingdom Come or Hollywood," Alcott interpolated quietly.

"How d'you know that?" Farrel asked in surprise.

"Oh, I did a little research myself last night."

Quite by accident a few feet from where we were seated, a chair went over and at the sound, Billy jumped up as though it had been a shot.

"What's eating you, Farrel?" Pete asked, looking at him sharply.

He shook his head. "I've put my foot in it, I'm afraid. Which reminds me, if by any chance you should happen to see a broad-shouldered fellow with silver rimmed glasses and a malacca cane approaching slowly on horseback, give me a high sign and let me run! And now. . . ."

Alcott spoke in all good humor. "Let's get back to that list!"

Farrel bobbed his head. "Sure. About this Phillip Brady. Well, he gave me the least trouble of all. You told me he was a movie director and with a start like that I called every studio in town for a line on him. At the Fine Art, they told me Phillip Brady's under contract with them on the West coast where, at present, he's directing a super-picture called, 'The Female of the Species.' They also told me he was a Californian by birth, that he's roamed the four corners of the world, that he's hunted big game in Africa and that all mail addressed to the New York office would be promptly forwarded to him. I think the blooming idiots thought I was a movie fan. Anyhow, I banged up in disgust."

Farrel's stubby finger progressed to the next name.

"Now for this George Meenan. There's something phoney there all right! I don't know whether you are wise to it or not but *that guy was found dead in his apartment exactly three days ago."*

"What?" both Alcott and I let out simultaneously.

"Yeah. I ran into a swell story but I'm not sure where to start on it."

"Don't be so damned particular—just get going!"

"It turns out this Meenan guy was some sort of big political shot, though this is the first I'd ever heard of him. One of these back-stage powers, y'know."

Suddenly and with peculiar clarity there came to my mind the description young Stone had given of Meenan at the Havana poker party. "A heavy set coarse looking fellow . . . an aloof manner that went so oddly with his . . . bloated face . . . seemed to know all the works . . . night clubs, politicians, Broadway, the whole show."

"Get on with the story," Alcott was saying quietly.

"There isn't so much to get on with, that's the kick. But up at 79th Street and Broadway—where this Meenan had his apartment, there's plenty of talk going around. It seems the fellow lived alone, entertained as though he was lousy with jack, drove a high-powered speed car and up to three days ago gave no indication of anything but the best of health.

Then what have we got? A valet who comes in after his evening off to discover the old boy dead at his desk. A search that reveals absolutely no evidence of violence, bloodshed, robbery or anything out of the way. An elevator boy who states that Meenan had come in earlier that evening with an unknown gentleman; that he had later sent downstairs for ice, his refrigerator being out of repair, and that Meenan's unknown visitor had left before the valet's return. That's every blooming thing there is to date and no amount of enquiry has uncovered even the identity of the unknown visitor."

I grinned. "Tst! Tst! Not even a calling card!"

But Farrel was in dead earnest. "Bet your life *not*, or maybe I wouldn't be here. The only thing that sounded half-way promising was some talk the elevator boy claimed he had overheard."

"What was that?" Alcott asked quickly.

"Oh, just something this unknown guy let out, not counting on being heard, I guess."

"Go on. Don't be so bashful."

"It wasn't so much, now that I think of it." Billy scratched his head. "Simply that he was leaving for Havana some time this week."

"Can't arrest a man for that."

Billy Farrel shook his head. "I know it," he said slowly. "But I can't help feeling there's something rotten in Denmark. Without a peep from anybody Meenan's death is officially set down to heart failure, the undertaker calls and there's a nice quiet funeral. At which point I've a notion a good many people in this old burg heave a big sigh of relief. A rip-snorting political scandal wouldn't be exactly relished just now, not after all those nasty rumors last year about some of the big shots playing hand and glove with the racketeers."

I smiled. "Shades of the Schmidt crowd again!"

"Aw. I'm not kidding! The point is your George Meenan is dead, either of natural causes or—'what have you?'"

Alcott looked grave. "Well, Billy, I think I'll set his death down to—'what have you?'"

I glanced at Alcott with interest. "Good God! Do you think it possible there's a connection between this so-called heart failure and—"

But Alcott cut me off. "I'm not thinking anything, just yet. All I say is I don't like it and I won't forget it. Now Farrel, what about those others?"

Farrel's stubby finger advanced resolutely down the list.

"Well, this Dunlap. . . ."

But from Farrel himself we never learned anything about Barton Dunlap. Abruptly, the boy broke off, his mouth half open, his eyes fixed on the doorway.

"What's the matter Billy?"

But Billy stood transfixed. If, as science tells us, all life began in hot water, Billy looked, at this particular moment, as though he'd waded straight back again, and into the hottest part. Following the direction of his glance, I turned to the door of the City Room. There stood our managing editor and, talking vehemently at his side, I noticed a huge, though well-built chap with silver rimmed glasses and a light malacca cane.

To my untutored viewpoint, the fellow seemed quite unnecessarily well turned out. His blond hair glistened with good care, his complexion was clear and ruddy. None the less, the impact of his ultra fashionable clothing, his well-matched tie and shirt and handkerchief, his carefully folded gloves and overcoat, his fresh carnation, oddly enough served to prejudice me against him. I wondered at my prejudice. More especially, I wondered at Billy Farrel's.

Alcott was whispering in my ear. "Mr. Barton Dunlap, unless I'm very much mistaken!"

Farrel overheard him and forced a smile. "You're on! S'long boys! Here's the card with all the dope. I'll be seeing you later!"

The last word reached us from over Farrel's shoulder. A moment later, he had disappeared jauntily through the opposite door of the City Room.

Not a move in the entire situation escaped Alcott. Before I had even recovered from Farrel's headlong rush, Pete noted the newcomer was inclining his head somewhat vigorously in my direction. He caught the Chief's look of mingled bewilderment and doubt. Suddenly, with all his usual indolent ease, Alcott stooped and picked up my noon edition which had fallen to the floor. Then *sotto voce:* "Looks to me like you're in for the fireworks, old punk! D'you mind if I stick by?"

With seeming indifference, he spread the paper open to the sporting section and seated himself on the next desk.

As usual, he wasn't far wrong in his surmise. I was in for fireworks, all right. Pin-wheels, sparklers and skyrockets! And, in a few seconds more, they had started.

Chapter X

AN IRATE CALLER

THE first firecracker came from my chief, Tim Gerraghty.

"Ellis!" he exploded, as he crossed toward me, the well dressed stranger appendaged to his side. "Who was that talking to you a few minutes ago?"

I gestured mutely to the top of Pete's head, which showed an inch or two above his all-absorbing sporting section.

"No!" the stranger flared. "We mean that younger chap and I've an idea you know it!" Despite the stridency of his tone, I caught the slight suggestion of Cambridge in his speech.

"Oh," I said innocently. "That was just one of our cub reporters. Anything wrong?"

"Wrong?" the fellow snapped angrily. "I should say so!" For a moment he tried withering me with one of these "less-than-the-dust" glances. But I don't wither easily. "A fine pass we've come to when a man's privacy can be invaded and violated by every lowdown reporter from the press! Really!" He pronounced the last word "rilly" but there was no trace of four o'clock teas in the way his right hand tightened over his cane. His blond face flushed with anger. "That young ass went out that door. I saw him!" And having delivered himself of that, the stranger turned and strutted across the city room, his head up, his stick gripped in silent fury. Our one stroke of luck was that the place was fairly empty at this hour. It would have been too good a show for the boys.

I looked at Gerraghty and fairly bristled with interrogatives. That the Chief was in a hole I could see. His lips were pressed sternly together.

"That's young Barton Dunlap!" he shot out significantly. Then sizz bang! "You men have gotten me in a damned fine mess. It looks like there'll be the deuce to pay!"

The tone more than the remark struck home. In all my years around the old news factory, it was my first genuine flare-up with the chief. And though I was far too deeply involved in this Wyndham tangle to count any minor consequences, still I'd have given a great deal to have avoided this encounter. Gerraghty happened to be one of those rare men who have a way with them. There wasn't a man on the staff who didn't feel it as I did.

"What's the difficulty?" I asked in genuine sympathy.

The chief nodded off toward Dunlap's retreating figure. "It so happens that fellow's grandfather is one of the part owners of this paper!"

"Still I don't quite see. . . ."

"H'm. One of our boys was reported snooping around Mr. Dunlap's club last evening, asking a good many personal questions. And to make matters worse, a couple of hours ago, at what seems to have been—er—a most inopportune time, this same enterprising young man forced his way into Mr. Dunlap's apartment." (Just like Billy Farrel, I smiled to myself.)

Gerraghty was proceeding drily. "The first I knew of the matter was when young Dunlap burst into my office, hurling imprecations at the press in general and threatening a local shake-up here!" Gerraghty paused. There was an embarrassing silence. I felt the pinch of my own indirect responsibility.

"If you'll leave it to me, sir, there's just a chance— a slim one I'll admit—but I might be able to handle the situation."

The chief shot a swift, appraising look in my direction. "We couldn't be much worse off, that's sure! You know where to find me!" He turned on his heel and was gone.

Three seconds later I caught up to Dunlap. "That reporter you're after, won't be back for a while!"

Barton Dunlap turned around arrogantly and glared at me. I hadn't realized how much simpler the whole situation looked with his scowl turned the other way. I started gamely. I tried good fellowship. It was all a total loss. The man's attitude was oddly disconcerting.

"Er—isn't it Mark Twain or somebody who advises for emergencies like this, when you can't explain matters, just deny them?" I asked at length.

"H'm, try it!" Dunlap snapped.

"Oh, I'm not going to, and you're not either," I said, with impeccable good humor. "Instead of even pretending to deny things, I thought we'd both reverse the adage and explain 'em!"

"Explain!" Dunlap went off into sparks. "As

though any explanation could alter the indignity to which I've been subjected!"

I looked the firebrand over coolly and came to the point. "You were a very good friend of Stephen P. Wyndham, I believe."

"What's that to do with this?" he asked haughtily.

"A great deal, Mr. Dunlap. Since you didn't come forward and tell what occurred in the Sevilla Biltmore on February 13th, we've been driven to going after you!"

For a moment Barton Dunlap studied my face in what seemed to be frank surprise. "Are you trying to say that the espionage to which I've been subjected was supposed to be conducted in the interests of the Wyndham case?"

"Exactly! Though it's not widely known as yet."

"Well! Well! *That* does make a whale of a difference!" He emphasized his point with a rap of his malacca cane. "Who's handling this matter for your paper?"

"I am." I introduced myself. There was a sudden right-about-face in his attitude.

"I've been enormously put out, y'know—still I wouldn't want to hamper you in any way."

"No one's going to, Mr. Dunlap. We mean to get to the bottom of this matter!"

"Well, I've wanted to cooperate from the beginning, don't y'know!"

It was my turn to be sarcastic.

"So it seems, if you'll pardon my saying it. That's why Wyndham's been out of the picture for over ten months now without the slightest hue or cry being raised by any of his friends. That's why. . . ."

Dunlap flushed to the roots of his hair and glancing around, he interrupted me quickly.

"Isn't there some place other than this corridor where we can talk?"

I nodded toward my desk in the City Room and headed back that way, glad for the pretext to have Alcott within earshot once again.

"This is somewhat better!" Dunlap drawled as he sat down and I noticed with suppressed amusement that the fellow seemed to strut even when he was seated.

"You really must get a few things straight. However, I'm not to be quoted."

I tried to ease his mind on that point but for a seemingly endless instant the issue looked dubious. Then abruptly, Mr. Dunlap put down his overcoat and hat, and verbally, took the plunge.

"Y'see, until the newspapers first broke with this Wyndham story, it never once occurred to me or, for that matter, to any one of the men who knew Wyndham well that there was anything amiss in this entire matter, don't y'know."

"That listens well!" I said, with a skeptical smile. "However, I wouldn't let my grandmother's poodle leave a room and remain unheard of for over ten months without troubling myself somewhat more than you gentlemen have done in your friend's case!"

Dunlap met my eyes with a quizzical smile. "Perhaps your grandmother's poodle isn't as habituated to frequent excursions as we knew Stephen Wyndham to be. Wyndham and I have been acquainted since

boyhood, don't y'know, and this wasn't the first time
that he pulled off something like this!"

He said this with a frankness that was completely
disarming.

"No?" I found myself saying.

Dunlap lit a cigarette and unbent to the point of
actual loquacity.

"Decidedly *no!* Up at Hotchkiss they still talk
about the rumpus he stirred up in the third form
there. For some five weeks or so, he had the school
authorities almost on their heads, while the local
police were scouring about the countryside, looking
for him. And where do you suppose Wyndham was
all the while? Off Montauk Point on a fishing trip
with the former captain of his father's yacht. He
hadn't troubled to confide in any of us for fear we
might talk a trifle too much!" Dunlap gave a short
reminiscent laugh while I looked all the incredulity
I didn't care to voice.

"Oh, you think that's rather peculiar?" Dunlap
eyed me with tolerant amusement. "Well, you
wouldn't have thought twice about the matter if
you'd known Wyndham as we did. From the time of
his father's death, he was rather his own master,
y'know. No rein or check of any kind. To be sure,
there was his older sister, but somehow he never
seemed to care a rap for her. As for the old Wyndham mansion, it gave him the hibbie-jibbies, so he
rarely if ever went home."

"H'm. So you imply that Wyndham's friends had
grown accustomed to these absences!"

"After a while, yes. But it took training, you see.
There was one occasion, a year or so after college, as

I recall it, when he wandered off from a hunting expedition returning from Africa, turned right about face and went off on a crazy nine months' trek into the Punjab, along with some Tom, Dick or Harry who had chanced across his path. That was Wyndham all over. He never troubled with much ceremony. You simply had to take him or leave him as you felt disposed. Most of his friends took him, of course, and were jolly well glad to!" Dunlap paused. "But you see, it was this past impulsiveness that led us all so far astray this time."

"Yes," I let out suddenly. "Whoever plotted Wyndham's end calculated on that!"

Dunlap looked at me sharply and folded his gloves into careful creases. "Oh, I rather doubt that. It would narrow the range of the guilty down to someone who knew Wyndham fairly well. And that's too utterly unspeakable!"

"But not unthinkable!" I remarked unwisely.

Dunlap looked at me with a flash of anger in his eye. "I'm not sure what you're driving at, young fellow. But speaking for myself, I rather feel as though I've about done everything I can in this matter."

"I'm sure you do!" It was absurd how I let the fellow irritate me.

Dunlap rose to his feet and reached for his coat and hat. Then, just as he was on the point of departure, he got an attack of galloping common sense and turned superciliously to me.

"To be sure I didn't call in the press, as you, perhaps, would have liked me to, but get this straight! As soon as I was convinced that Mr. Wyndham *had*

met with foul play, I went directly to the one person
who had authority to act in this matter, told exactly
what I knew of the facts, placed myself in readiness
to be of whatever service I could."

I looked at the man with new-born interest. "To
whom did you go?"

"To Miss Isabella Wyndham, of course."

The telephone ringing at my elbow saved the day.
It was Gerraghty.

"How are you making out?"

"I think everything's O.K. chief!"

Suddenly from over the top of the sporting page I
saw Alcott give me a little wink. It was so swift I
wasn't sure I'd seen aright and when a moment later,
he seemed utterly engrossed in making notes on the
margin of his paper I was doubly uncertain. Nonetheless, I stalled for time.

"Wait a minute, Mr. Gerraghty. Maybe Mr. Dunlap will speak to you himself." I handed the phone
over to my caller and stepping between him and
Alcott, I screened as well as I could the passage of
the scribbled message which I felt ought to be coming my way.

I wasn't a moment too soon. Dunlap's talk with
Gerraghty did not take long.

"Your managing editor is a nice chap!"

"Oh, we all second that around here."

Dunlap reached for his stick.

"Mr. Dunlap, before you go, I want to apologize."
The words came hard. I was taking my cue from Alcott. "When I spoke, I hadn't realized that you had
tried to help in this matter at all. For reasons I don't

understand, Miss Wyndham and her lawyer omitted all mention of your visit."

"That's deucedly odd!"

"Worse than odd, for we're in bad need of a little first aid around here. The fact is, we've had one version of what occurred in Stephen Wyndham's rooms on the night of February thirteenth. It would help enormously if you would tell me how far that story coincides with your own recollections of that most peculiar occasion!" I looked directly into Dunlap's watery blue eyes.

Dunlap gave an embarrassed laugh. "I'd like awfully to help you, don't y'know! But the fact is that night at Wyndham's, I'm afraid I was rather—er—in my cups!"

"The entire evening?"

"Yes. I had enough of an edge on to completely discredit me as a reliable witness."

However, I wasn't to be put off. Without revealing my source of information I repeated young Stone's story to him, omitting all mention of the knife that had been seen in Sanchez's hand and all reference to the blood-stained cigarette.

Dunlap listened with what seemed rapt attention. At the conclusion, he nodded. "That's just about the straight of the thing, don't y'know! Even I recall most of that!"

"Do you think you could draw me a diagram of the positions of the men at the table that night?"

Dunlap raised his eyebrows. "Do tell me, what *can* be the use of that?"

I wondered myself. The question had come to me on the scribbled memorandum from Alcott.

"Just a roving fancy!" I smiled and pushed my pad and pencil a fraction of an inch closer to him.

Reluctantly Dunlap replaced his imported camel's hair coat and Bond Street hat and took up the pad and pencil I offered.

"Really now!" he said, as after a moment's thought he began to diagram the position of the men at the poker party. "This makes me feel miles off in all my own conjectures, don't y'know!"

"How so?"

"I was convinced that someone from the *outside* had entered the room during the period of darkness, or that Wyndham himself had walked out to meet his death!" he said pointedly.

"What made you think that?"

"Oh, nothing much. Only I've an indistinct impression don't y'know, of the connecting door to Ford's room having been opened in the dark!"

I looked at Dunlap searchingly. "But you said you were pretty tight and remembered practically nothing."

"Nevertheless, I had a definite impression of Ford's door being opened, don't y'know. Wyndham and I were sitting at that end."

"You were seated just next to Wyndham?"

"I think that's what I've indicated, isn't it?" This was said with but thinly veiled sarcasm, but I paid no heed.

"Aside from the opening of Ford's door, did you hear anything else suspicious during that interval of darkness?"

Dunlap smiled. "Really, I was half asleep, don't y'know. Even the events you described to me a while ago seemed as though they were taking place a hundred miles away."

I glanced with curiosity at the diagram which he had placed before me and which is herewith reproduced:

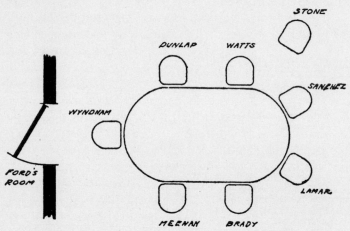

Dunlap watched me reflectively. Then abruptly he seemed taken with a bright idea.

"Oh, I say. The man for you to talk to is Meenan. He was sitting on the other side of Wyndham, don't y'know."

"H'm. I'd like to talk with Meenan. Only, unfortunately, *he's dead!*"

"You don't mean it." Dunlap broke out in what seemed genuine surprise. "Why that fellow seemed to have the constitution of an ox!" He shook his head reminiscently. "He and I were matching drinks that very night."

I looked Dunlap in the eye. "Nonetheless, he died

three days ago and under, what to some, seem rather peculiar conditions."

"Oh, I say now. You don't connect him and the Wyndham murder, do you?"

"I don't connect him with anything just now. But to some, it's got an ugly look."

I started a new line.

"Were you sober enough to gather any impression of young Charles Stone when he came in?"

"I'm afraid not. Anyhow, I've never liked that chap and if I told you that I've a hazy impression that he seemed fidgety and uncomfortable throughout that evening, I wouldn't know how much was prejudice and how much good Bacardi Rum!"

"Then let's forget Stone! Do you know of any motive that any one of the six men there that night might have had for doing away with Wyndham?"

Dunlap wrinkled up his forehead. "I can't help you out a bit, really. You see, Wyndham and I had drifted somewhat apart these last ten years. On my side *marriage* and a temporary residence abroad. On his, these everlasting expeditions and his passionate prepossession with polo and boating and all that, don't y'know. Last season down south was the most I'd seen of him in years. And then that was due only to the pull of old times. No real intimacy left, y'know."

I nodded and started anew.

"Man to man, what did you think of Jose Sanchez' insane outbreak in the room that night?"

Dunlap shrugged. "Sanchez knew, like everyone else, that Wyndham had once—er—looked out for

La Caros." He paused. "By the way, have you ever seen that girl?"

I shook my head.

"She's superb, really!"

I gathered I was talking to a connoisseur. The tone he used was just about the same one might employ in describing a particularly good brand of sherry or a well-prepared roast.

"But Lola as the motive for the murder! Really now!" Dunlap smiled with tolerant amusement. "It just hadn't occurred to me, y'know! Wyndham's affair with her was over and done with, having run its own volatile little course all the way from Rio where it started one warm night, to New York where it ended one chilly day. But all this you doubtless know. Anyhow, you asked about Sanchez' outbreak? My own belief is that it was nothing more than a temporary irritation or just bad digestion. Jealousy's a rather overrated emotion, don't y'know!"

I raised my eyebrows in interest, but did not contradict.

"One thing more. Were you smoking during the evening?"

"Yes, I think so. Why do you ask?"

Why? Why indeed! It was another of Alcott's damn fool questions. "Oh, nothing particular! There's just one important point more. You said that when you were finally convinced that Wyndham had met with foul play you went directly to Miss Isabella Wyndham. What convinced you that Wyndham had met with foul play?"

"Because," Dunlap hesitated a flicker of a moment, then abruptly his jaw set in a hard line of decision.

"Because lately I've learned that a person who had every reason to expect to see Wyndham on the morning of February fourteenth neither saw him nor, in fact, received any word from him from that day on. As I told you, Stephen Wyndham was harum-scarum in general . . . but an omission of this kind was completely out of character!"

"Was this person he was to see—a woman?"

Again Dunlap hesitated and folded his gloves into careful creases. "I really don't like to answer on that, y'know!"

"Was the woman in Havana?" I persisted.

"No, Pinar del Rio." He flushed. "You know, you're deucedly clever the way you worm things out of me."

But somehow I had a notion that I wasn't as clever as Dunlap would have me believe. Nevertheless, the interview terminated with a fanfare of good will. I thanked Mr. Dunlap for his time and effort. I received profuse assurances of his willingness to cooperate at any time.

When he was gone I turned to Alcott.

"That stuffed shirt of Pompousness is going to be pressed into service a damned sight more often than he knows!"

"I wouldn't rely too much on that!" Alcott said, with a twinkle in his eye.

He handed over Farrel's card, pointing to the last line. But I started at the top.

Barton Dunlap. Penthouse, 405 East 57th Street. (Over this, in Farrel's writing, was a marginal note. *Adjoining penthouse empty*.) Studied law. Never practices. Member of all socially important clubs. High stepper. Temporarily short on funds and long on women. Vanity show girl in lead just now. Saw her in his apartment this A.M. Not bad looking. Divorced by wife, Carol Sutherland Dunlap in Paris last summer. Granddad supplies family funds. Dunlap off for Cuba this afternoon.

"Off for Cuba!" I said in a disgruntled tone. Then I sat up. "Jesus, that's a queer coincidence."

Alcott absently nodded and lighted a cigarette. One of the men from his office came up.

"Mr. Alcott, you're wanted on the phone. The party says it's urgent."

Pete looked up nonchalantly. "Have the call switched here."

He picked up my phone. I heard every word he said. "Yes. This is Alcott speaking . . . Who? . . . Oh yes, Mr. Stone. We got her warning but it makes no difference . . . (Pause) No, it's impossible for me to see her today. . . . Yes, quite impossible. . . . Why? Because in less than two hours time, Mr. Ellis and I are leaving for Havana."

PART TWO

Havana

Chapter XI

"X MARKS THE SPOT"

HOW we ever got off on the Florida Special that afternoon, I'll never quite know. We ran dizzy circles, we snapped out orders, we pulled wires, we coerced assistants. Most memorable in my mind was the half hour session we had with Tim Gerraghty.

Before we went to the chief's office, I was all for explaining to him in detail the precise nature of the leads which were drawing us to Havana. But Pete would have none of it.

"If we're going to get anywhere in this mess, we've got to keep our mouths shut with everyone. *Everyone!* Do you get me?"

I got him but still I didn't quite see how we could manage so abrupt a walk-out with any kind of countenance. It seemed cock-eyed! Crazy! Mad!

"Oh, to hell with all that. Now that I'm started, I'm going through with this Wyndham case, no matter where it lands me! However, you do what you want to!"

But Alcott's enthusiasm whipped me into line. Before my eyes swam visions of the story we would ultimately land.

"Aw, I'm with you, of course."

"Then quit kicking. I've got enough saved to carry us through."

I let him do the talking with Gerraghty. He did it pretty well. He explained that he had been working at top speed and felt he simply had to get away from the grind for a bit. There was nothing of importance on the immediate calender that his well-trained assistant could not handle. That he realized perfectly well this was not an allotted vacation and that his pay check would necessarily stop. Matter of fact, for the time he was away, he preferred it that way. The point was, he simply had to go.

I remember Gerraghty spilling a little of his mind and then suddenly asking him, "How long do you think you'll be away?"

"I can't say just now, but I'll get some definite word to you in a week's time. That I promise."

Gerraghty turned to me.

"And you, Ellis?"

My heart sank. "Well, I think I'll stick by Alcott just now . . . if it's O.K. with you."

Gerraghty knit his forehead and looked at me closely. "Same terms? No pay check? No expense account?"

"Yes, sir. Everything's in good shape. . . ."

We went over matters in detail.

At the door, Gerraghty put his hand on my shoulder, looked dubiously at us both and slowly shook his head.

"Look here, boys! I don't know what you're up to. But I've a tough notion it hasn't a thing to do with rest."

"Maybe you didn't get to be boss of this goddam paper without good reason," I laughed.

There was one other leavetaking before we left

the old *Globe*. Short and snappy. It was with Billy Farrel.

"Just a minute, Billy," Alcott said, cheerily yanking the boy after us as we slid into a down-going elevator. "We're signing off with the *Globe* for a little while, but *not* with *you*, young man. The point is, I've a hunch you're damned right to keep hot on the scent of that George Meenan lead. I'd do it myself if I weren't after something still hotter. If you turn up anything worthwhile, shoot it along to us post haste. We'll make it worth your while no matter what the paper does. A good starting point would be to have a talk with the old boy's private physician! Or, failing that, with the physician's secretary. But I'll leave it to you. The big thing is, dig up everything you can about George Meenan's death. Yes, even if you have to dig up the old gaffer himself. Well, here we are. . . . I'll be sending you our address soon as we have one. So long!"

Outside, I smiled. "The old bloodhound's still drawn by the Meenan scent, I see!"

"Sure. Either there's something to that rumor, or else it's a damned interesting coincidence."

* * * * *

We caught the Florida Special just as it was lurching out of Pennsylvania Station. Two dishevelled newspaper men with the world's all-time championship record for speed-packed valises. Worn out, we dropped into the green plush solitude of our last minute reservations and grinned at each other like fools.

"It may be an insane thing to do! But A Ignatius God, we're off!"

"Johnny Ellis, we'll be sane and sensible the rest of our lives. I'll even toss in eternity, if only the hunch leads somewhere."

Saying which, Alcott settled his gaunt length as best he could, mopped his face and just as we entered the Hudson Tunnel, flatly refused to say another word about Stephen P. Wyndham, his friends or connections.

He was still obdurate in his refusal to discuss the case when some forty-eight hours later, we stood at the rail of the boat, to which we'd changed at Miami, and watched Morro Castle looming large and gray through the dim golden mist of the tropical evening.

Partly from reaction, partly for deeper and more inexplicable reasons, a vague sense of discouragement had settled upon me, obliterating all the more hopeful angles of our mission. Each of us knows that mood. Twilight, a thousand miles between us and every accustomed sight and sound. I began to see myself as a complete fool starting off on this wildest of wild goose chases. Grimly I inventoried our entire stock of provisions, munitions and sinews of war. Fire hundred and sixty dollars, which Alcott had hastily drawn from his account, the rumpled remnants of our two round trip tickets from New York, a letter of introduction to the editor of the *Havana Post,* and a dismal and growing conviction we'd acted like a pair of sapheads in the supremely important matter of our jobs back home.

"Of course," I admitted to myself, "it would have all been a cinch, if only we could have explained the entire situation to the chief." But paramount, I realized was the need for absolute secrecy and quick

action. And a real bang-up scoop on this Wyndham
case would square accounts with Gerraghty. Anyhow,
it was a trifle too late for regrets. The die was cast
—whatever the upshot. And wasn't there old Miss
Wyndham's curse which was to bring us luck?

"Well, all aboard for Havana and maybe a solution
of this damned Wyndham mess!"

"All aboard for a holiday. And come what may!"
Alcott answered cheerily. "By the way, have you ever
tasted a real daiquiri?"

Gang planks lowering. The first babble of a foreign tongue. The nearby crescendo of city life. The
languorous heat of the tropical dusk. Bus boys, hotel
boys, baggage boys, fruit boys, droves of them, dark-
skinned, dark-eyed, darting in and about us with the
persistence of so many well meaning, good-natured
mosquitoes. The incongruous jangle of street cars
and taxis. Palm shadowed squares. Twisting, narrow
streets. Heavy white facades. Perfume, sweet and
heavy in the sensuous breeze. People! More people!
Still more people!

At the cheap commercial hotel where we engaged
a room we sent all our clothes out to be pressed at
once. We had to! Meanwhile, stripped to our B.V.D.'s
we drank daiquiris, and suddenly felt like lords.

"Johnny, I've been thinking. The best thing might
be to go over the ground at the Sevilla Biltmore first.
Take a good look at young Wyndham's suite! Get a
clear mental picture and all that. What do you say?"

"You damn fool! I suggested that the first night
on the train!"

Alcott laughed. "That's right. When I was trying
out that new solitaire of mine."

"Yeah. On the same memorable occasion when I tried to get your slant on what Charles Stone really had wanted with us on the telephone."

"But you knew!"

"That stuff about Miss Wyndham wanting to see us once more? That was only a lot of bull."

"No, I think that was straight enough."

"You don't trust Miss Wyndham?"

"None too much."

A half hour later, on the strength of our first four diaquiris, we floated over to the Sevilla Biltmore. From my spiritual elevation on a pink, ethereal cloud, I found myself enormously impressed by the stalwart modernity of the hotel and the air of brisk independence with which it reared its ten or twelve stories above the clatter of century old streets.

We found the lobby brilliantly lighted, palm-decked, overflowing with what appeared to my roseate vision the most thoroughly cosmopolitan throng in the universe.

With brilliant astuteness, I caught myself spotting the mid-western families, the handful of fashionably dressed, very sure New Yorkers, the high spirited crowd of "oh-such-nice-people" whom God had joined together in a cut-rate Havana excursion and nothing short of "home-sweet-home" would ever again rend asunder. With clairvoyant skill I picked out my own version of the soft little spinsters from Squeedunk and Lord-help-us-ville, who had been saving whole lifetimes for the fling. (To be sure, each of the women I selected may have boasted a dozen children or three husbands apiece, but I was in that peculiarly beatific state where facts make not the slightest difference to theories.) At sight I knew all the doughty millionaires whose doctors had recently advised a change of climate. With keen pleasure I pointed out for Alcott's benefit, the South American planters, who dark-eyed, heavy-set, and restless, kept weaving their way in and out of the crowd. With even more pleasure I pointed out to myslef the slim, eager, dark-eyed girls, bevies of them, sprinkled all over the place, attached, detached, unattachable, laughing, smiling, chattering. For discovering color, verve and life, I recommended four Havana daiquiris. To them I even attributed (though wrongly, as I subsequently found out) the gay, high warble of hundreds of canaries which I seemed to catch quite suddenly above the babble.

"Say, Pete, n'matter what happens, this place is jake with me!"

We found our way to the desk and asked to see the manager. In his own good time, Señor Fiordo emerged, keen-eyed and enquiring. We produced our press cards and explained, quite confidentially, as much of our mission as we thought good for him.

"Ah, yes. I remember well this young Wyndham. He was a very charming American gentleman. Si, si. It was with the emotion of profound shock that we learned a few weeks ago of his most terrible tragedy. So unexpected, the whole affair. Last year when he honored us, everything was . . . how do you say it? All so regular, yes? By the way, it would be a great courtesy if you will see that our establishment comes in for no unpleasant—er—er—notoriety in this matter, yes?"

Reassured on that score, he pressed a few buttons, interviewed an assistant and turned back to us.

"Ah, I am so regretful, gentlemen, but your request to see the suite occupied by Mr. Wyndham, it is impossible tonight. Could you call next week . . . ?"

"Next week?" we exploded in unison.

Señor Fiordo's smile was ingratiating. "Please understand. From the records I observe Mr. Wyndham and his friend occupied Rooms 208, 209 and 210. You would like to see all three rooms, would you not?"

"Of course!"

"But just now two American ladies are occupying Room 210. We cannot well disturb them, can we?"

In desperation we compromised our original demand and a few minutes later, found ourselves in a vast grill enclosed elevator ascending to the second floor, and briskly following one of Mr. Fiordo's young assistants down a long, cool marble lined corridor.

As the young man threw open the door of Room 208, I followed Alcott in, suddenly sobered, subdued, aware I was no longer spinning abstract theories but walking with living purpose over the footprints of another man's doom.

At the touch of the electric light, I knew at once Room 208 represented one of the choicest locations of the Sevilla Biltmore, an assumption in which the young night clerk promptly confirmed me. It was a large, almost baronial chamber, some twenty odd feet by about eighteen, coolly tiled in chaste white marble, with two windows long and wide, to catch

any chance breeze and dark Venetian blinds to keep
off the too impertinent glare of a tropical sun. A
large four poster bed, covered in damask, stood
against the right wall. At the side of the bed, was a
night table and lamp.

The other furniture of the room consisted of a
marble topped writing desk, a low, wide bureau
over which hung a massive carved mirror, a com-
modious chest of drawers, two large, comfortable
chairs and one straight one. A clothes cupboard
opened into the left hand corner of the room which
proved quite ordinary in all respects. Also, off to the
left, a short passageway some eight feet by six, led
past a bright, airy bath into the much heralded sitting room.

"I should really have brought you into this room
first," the young clerk said in flawless English, "instead of shoving the cart before the horse. But you
gentlemen seemed—ah—so impatient."

"Not just impatient! Positively panting, young
man! So much so, we'd part with a good deal just
now for a look into this next room, er—210. . . ."
Alcott's hand strayed carelessly toward his pocket.
"Those American ladies couldn't possibly stay in
their room on so lovely an evening. And regardless
of how *we look,* we're perfectly respectable. Honestly."

Alcott in this mood was hard to gainsay. The young
clerk beamed sympathetically upon us and drifted
out to see what could be done.

While he was gone, I crossed over to the single
window of the sitting room and peered over the

shallow railed balcony, down some forty feet or so to the quiet street that lay beneath us.

"Don't worry, Ellis, that window was never used."

"Why do you say that?"

"Both our witnesses have maintained that the room was in absolute darkness. If any one had tried to window, there, what do you think were his chances of remaining unseen?"

In a jiffy Alcott let down the Venetian blind full length and fastened it. Then closing both doors, he hastily snapped off the light. Instantly, the darkness pressed in about us like a black wool. Only a thin line of light shone from under and above the closed doors.

"And remember there was no light in any part of the corridor on the big night of February thirteenth."

I heard Alcott groping toward the Venetian blind. In another instant he had loosened it enough to allow him to mount upon the window sill.

"You win," I said laughingly, as in the faint glow reflected from the street lights outside, I caught the distinct outline of his figure.

"No one could possibly have come in or gone out that window with the old poker gang looking on."

"No."

Just then there was a sound behind me. I turned to see the hall door had opened quietly and there, silhouetted against the light of the corridor loomed the bulk of a short heavy set man.

"What do you want?" I said in annoyance. But

with a murmer of quick apology the door once more
closed and we were left to ourselves.

"That's a funny one!" I burst out to Alcott, but
he only shrugged.

"I've a hunch that may have been the *floor man* a
trifle over-curious about our movements."

We turned back to our task of examining the
premises.

"H'm. What of those windows in the bedroom?"
I asked.

Alcott laughed. "No! As a visiting Englishman
once remarked about our electric signs on Broadway—'they're *all* so deucedly conspicuous, don't
y'know?' "

I glanced down at the street with its idly saunter-
ing crowd. "Mebbe you're right."

Once more we turned on the lights and looked
carefully around, knowing beyond doubt, that somehow, someway that quite innocent little sitting room
with its adjacent quarters had played a strange and
vital part in the puzzling mystery of Wyndham's
end.

The room we surveyed was not quite so large as
the bedroom we had just left, but like the former,
it was attractively furnished. Wicker chairs, table,
settee, everything that could make for complete
tropical comfort! I had an idea it was one of those
prestidigitating rooms which could be outfitted by
the management as a bedroom or a sitting room as
the occasion demanded. But since during Wyndham's
occupancy, it had flourished as a sitting room, as such
we mentally registered it.

Just here at the risk of being repetitious I again

append the diagram of this suite; this time, no free hand drawing of an excited young missionary, but an exact reproduction of the hotel floor plan. To be sure the two plans correspond in most respects, and yet I feel convinced had I fixed their seemingly conventional arrangement more carefully in mind an endless waste of time might have been avoided, and what was more, a rendezvous with terror that was to last for ten seemingly eternal seconds in time.

The sitting room opened onto the public corridor and likewise by short passageways it connected with both room 208 and 210. To my cursory survey, the outer corridor presented an almost uniform pattern of doorways and lights. Only the cage-like shaft of the main elevator, some fifty feet away and the occasional stairways, Guest, Emergency or Service, broke its ordered regularity. One of these service stairways was located just opposite Room 210. Likewise, a large storeroom which we found upon investigation was used for linens.

I found Alcott emerging from an inspection of the shallow closet in the corner of the sitting room.

"X marks the spot where his sporting young Highness used to lock the sacred rods and racquets."

"H'm."

"Not room for much more in there, that's sure."

"Nope!"

At that moment the night clerk bustled back, rubbing his hands and announcing with satisfaction, "After looking over the whole floor for Miguel I find him in the store room just opposite. He bring the pass key for Room 210 right away." Then quite low, "Oh, that is unnecessary Señor. . . . Ah, muchas

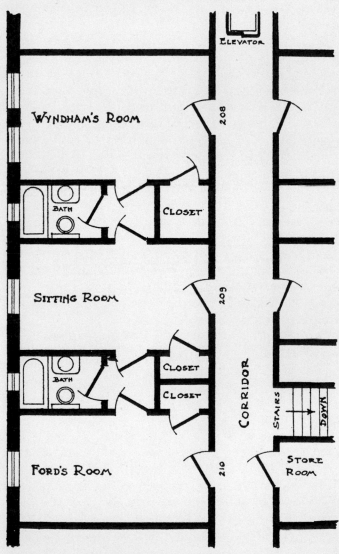

PLAN OF HOTEL SUITE

gracias! You understand, Miguel is our regular night man on this section."

Miguel was not long in putting in his appearance. True to Alcott's prediction, he was a short, rotund fellow who, decked out in his white duck uniform, resembled nothing so much as the proverbial snowball in July. He regarded us with large, solemn eyes and convinced that there were matters of grave moment, hanging upon our shoulders, he gave a loud, precautionary knock on door 210 and then opened it.

The room we surveyed was much like number 208. Only not quite as large. Also, just now it fairly reeked with the atmosphere of usage. A pair of sport sandals and some soft pink silk things were lying peacefully under the big armchair. A trail of talcum powder led cheerily off to the bath. Two half-finished lemonades were on the table. But with mental effort, I cleared the room of all vestiges of its late occupants and gave my full attention to its more fixed, less transient aspects.

"Ford didn't do so badly by himself when he stayed here."

"No."

Miguel glanced furtively at us, then two seconds later he seemed entirely preoccupied in straightening up the bed.

One window in this room instead of two! The same arrangement of passageway, bath and clothes cupboard! Door opening to outer hall! All the while Alcott coolly pacing up and down, craning his neck, examining the walls, the ceilings, the floor space.

Feeling ridiculously like the hero of a ten cent thriller, I fell to work on the short passageway that

led to the sitting room, tapping the walls to eliminate all idea of secret panels and that sort of thing.
But the solid substantial structure, above, beneath
and about us, gave back no suggestive lead. I hadn't
really thought it would.

Miguel smiled at me. "You, friend Señor Ford?"

"Yes, why do you ask?"

"Nothing. I remember him and Meestair Wyndham when they stay with us last year. Meestair Wyndham, very fine, Señor!"

I would have translated this simply to mean that
Wyndham had tipped very lavishly, but suddenly I
remembered Miguel's unsolicited appearance at the
other door, and wondered.

"Miguel, you didn't happen to be anywhere
around on the night last February when Mr. Wyndham was supposed to have disappeared?"

Blankness, complete and impenetrable! Miguel
concentrated his gaze on Alcott's movements. The
night clerk came to my rescue, repeating my words
slowly and clearly for him. Still Miguel's reaction was
difficult to gauge, solely because there was no reaction.

My patience began to ebb like the value of stocks
on an off-day. Then Alcott entered the picture.

"Miguel, my boy. One night last year your electric
lights all went out in the corridor. Everything dark.
See! We want to know, were you here that night?"

And still Miguel only regarded us suspiciously.

"H'm. Guess they had to burn down the school
house to get him out of the third grade! What's this
over here?"

In two long strides Alcott had crossed the floor

and stood pointing at the electric light switch on the side wall. There, spreading out from the plate, for an uneven inch or so, was a dull, scorched looking patch.

"What do you think that might be?"

I contemplated the mark a moment or so in silence.

"Damned if I know. It looks like an ordinary enough scorch."

"That all?"

"What do you make of it?"

"Very little and then again a devilish lot!" Alcott shook his head and absently rumpled his naturally recalcitrant mustache. "The trouble is it might date back three days, or three years."

Suddenly, inexplicably Miguel was at our side, glowering. From his pocket he took a rag and made a few brisk but ineffective passes at the discolored section.

"Some people make me seeck," he mumbled for our benefit. "All they see is one bad little spot. They no notice all the nice clean walls, floors and hallways. They no hear how everyone say there's no place in all Havana more nice, more clean than here. No! All they see is one ugly little spot. Well, soon we paint this room pretty like all the others. Very soon now."

"You can't do it soon enough," Alcott said in a tone of mock severity. "I'm surprised that the management of a first class hotel like this would permit its walls to remain so defaced for years."

Miguel choked in his indignation. "That mark not here for years. Not here one year." He looked at us darkly. "That mark I see first on evening after

night you spoke of when all lights go bad. Yes, then
I see that little place for first time!"

"Miguel. Are you sure of what you're saying."

"Si! Si! Course Miguel sure of everything what
happen like that! What you think I here for?"

"Can you tell us anything more about that night
when your lights went bad?"

But Miguel was now completely absorbed in brush-
ing up the talcum from the floor, so absorbed indeed
that he failed to hear Alcott's low chuckle and until
I called his attention, he even failed to see the green-
back we extended toward him. When he did see it,
his eyes lit up with pleasure.

"That, my boy, that's for keeping your heart so
loyally in your vacuum cleaner and scrub brush!"

But personally I wasn't too sure.

Nonetheless, in the corridor outside, softly, unaccountably I began whistling my favorite old tune.

> "I've taken my fun where I've found it;
> I've rogued an' I've ranged in my time."

But Alcott cut in. "You're whistling in the dark,
Johnny. This puzzle grows worse and worse!"

Chapter XII

MIGUEL DOES SOME TALKING

WHILE we were waiting for the elevator, Miguel
approached us hesitantly.

"Pardon, Señores. I no understand at first what you
mean about those lights. Si. Si. Miguel here that
night. But lights not my fault. No!"

I tried to keep the corners of my mouth from
twitching. "That's a great weight off our minds,
Miguel. Thanks for your help."

Miguel nodded and moved slowly down the wide,
cool hall, retarded not so much by his bulk as by
the burden of a very visible indecision.

As the elevator was descending Alcott turned
quietly to the night clerk.

"Would you have any objections if we talked a bit
further with that paragon of the scrub brush? I've a
kind of hunch the fellow's got something on his
mind."

The night clerk veiled his mild surprise. "Just as
you say." In a low tone he called down the corridor
after Miguel, then turned hesitantly back to us.

"I wonder if you would be so good as to pardon
me. Señor Fiordo will be thinking I am lost. I will
come back to you almost immediately. It is all right.
Yes?"

His manner was all civility.

"We'll manage all right. You've been no end of a help."

" 'Magnifico,' as they say in Barcelona, only don't bother to come back. We'll stop by the desk when we're leaving."

Two seconds later Miguel was at our side, regarding us shyly from out his large molasses like eyes. Alcott did the talking. I was glad of it, for I still felt uncertain about the fellow.

"Miguel, I'd like you to get one thing in your head. This gentleman and I aren't going to hurt you. No. Really." Alcott shook his head and smiled benignly. "We can see you are very happy in your work here. Fact is, except for a few of our fellow newspapermen, we've never yet seen anyone, anywhere, more positively joyous in getting after the dirt. I intend to tell Señor Fiordo when I leave here tonight that you're the most conscientious night attendant I've ever seen!"

Miguel did not quite understand all that was said but he grasped the main point. His eyes glowed in pleasure. His smile gleamed all red and gold, like the trappings of the most expensive night club. He grew positively garrulous.

"I glad. I—wife and four small ones. I want stay here. Before, when you ask me about lights I think you mean bad. Last year when that happen everyone start at me. 'Miguel what you do to the lights to make go out?' Truth, Miguel busy that night as usual with his work. Miguel do nothing."

"We believe that, Miguel. But that's not the point. Something did happen that night while the lights were out. Something very bad. . . ."

Miguel looked at us a little uncertainly. I made a guzzling noise and pointed to my throat. I closed my eyes and threw back my head to imitate the stark rigidity of death. Something of the pantomime registered for Miguel began bobbing his round hand in acquiescence.

"Si. Si. The nice Señor Wyndham!" He glanced furtively up and down the corridor as though vaguely apprehensive, and moving impulsively off he beckoned us to follow him.

Safely within one of the hall storage closets with the door discreetly shut, Miguel faced us resolutely.

"Something about that night, Miguel know. But Miguel want no trouble, see?" There was a very evident sincerity about the fellow.

"You'll have no trouble if you help us. We only mean to make it hot for those who don't." This last with a grand flourish of omnipotence.

Miguel nodded. "Si, si. Miguel want to help!" Yet somehow under the strain of trying, the fellow broke out into great beads of perspiration. The heat in the small closet was oppressive, but I didn't believe it was only due to that.

"That night, when lights go bad, I very busy, like always, on corridor. Bells ring, here, there! Miguel go everyplace. Sometime later that night when I pass room number 209 I see woman standing there close listening. I notice this woman because she crush out cigarette on my nice floor, then light another one, quick, take a puff, then crush it out. When I pass back next time, she still stand with her head close to Señor Wyndham's door, listening, while she drop the cigarettes and ashes all over my clean place. I think to myself. 'That a fine lady? No! Throw those cigarettes and ashes all over the floor!' I don't care what nice jewelry she have on her or what fine silk shawl, she twist so grand about her! I think to myself, 'She funny lady anyhow stand listening at the door like that.' I very angry. I look hard at her. Then quick Miguel recognize her! Yes!"

For an instant nothing moved in that stifling little store room but the lightning of thought. Then Miguel glanced around again to be sure the door was closed, and in his own good time he whispered:

"Upstairs on roof we have a big dance floor here. Very pretty place. Palms and nice music. The person who listen at door that night, she is girl that hotel pay to dance up on roof garden for guests. Very pretty dancer. I have seen her many times last year."

"Oh, yes!" Alcott said, his tone matter-of-fact. "Lolita Caros?"

Miguel nodded with excitement. "That right. How you know it was la Señorita Caros?"

Alcott remained matter-of-fact. "After all it's our business to know as much of this as possible. Just how does it happen you didn't mention all this before?"

Miguel looked at us like a big, helpless collie dog. "If Miguel was smart, he keep his mouth tight, now. What Miguel see, no one else knows."

We could not honestly argue that point. So Miguel proceeded.

"Not long ago, boy here tell me that something very funny have happen to nice Señor Wyndham on the night all my lights go bad. Then suddenly I think 'Yes! Yes! That surely it.' "

"And what made you so sure?"

A deep flush overspread Miguel's face for a moment. "A little thing I no like to talk of. But you see, Señor Wyndham have promised to give me whole dollar that night because I call downstairs so much for ice for his drinks. Well, Señor Wyndham never give me that dollar. And he not like these people who say, 'Miguel I give you this and that tomorrow' and then forget all about it! If Señor Wyndham had been live that night, he would have given Miguel the dollar."

"Oh, is that all?" I put in thoroughly disappointed. "Something might have turned up . . . so urgent, so important that the dollar was necessarily forgotten."

But Miguel was unswerving in his loyalty. "Señor Wyndham not that way. Something bad happened here that night. Miguel sure."

Alcott bore down on Miguel again, watching him closely with his hawk-like blue eyes. "Was there anything else unusual you noticed in the corridor to make you so sure of that?"

Miguel screwed up his forehead in thought. He was like a child in his earnest desire to help.

"Nothing, I think of now. People come and go same as always. Work keep me busy. I no chance to stand and watch." He said the last with disdain.

"Then we'll skip to the next morning. In cleaning up was anything unusual you noticed about Mr. Wyndham's suite? Disorder, bloodstains, anything suspicious?"

Miguel shook his head. "I no do morning cleaning and that day boy! Bah! He never see nothing."

"So that's that!"

With an air of finality I moved toward the store-room door, feeling as though I couldn't stand the stifling heat another moment. But apparently Alcott hadn't yet had enough.

"Er—one question more! When the lights came later that night, did you see la Señorita Caros again?"

Miguel shook his head solemnly. "No! When lights come on la Señorita was no where about. Later that night boy from roof tell us La Caros is seeck. She send word up she can dance no more that night. At that time I say to myself, 'No wonder that girl seeck. She smoke too many cigarettes.' Now I no say that no more."

"Is Lolita Caros dancing at the Sevilla Biltmore this year?"

Miguel shook his head.

"Do you know where she is?"

Miguel's voice was barely audible when he answered. "I hear she dance at the Chateau Madrid."

Alcott looked hard at Miguel for a moment. "By the way, Miguel, you didn't happen to be a little bit in love with the beautiful dancer yourself?"

Miguel flushed scarlet. "Oh, no! No! I good family man." He turned toward the door.

Suddenly, Alcott reached over and clenched Miguel's wrist in a vice-like grip.

"Then what are you afraid of, man?"

For a moment, Miguel looked at Alcott in stark terror. Then somehow, his childlike faith reasserted itself. He reached into his pocket and took there-from a soiled envelope that was post-marked from the States. With trembling hands, he removed a slip that contained a single typewritten sentence in Spanish. Haltingly, in a dull voice Miguel translated it for us. "It mean only this—'If you had eyes on the night of February 13th last, you better have not the tongue now. Look out.' "

Chapter XIII

"STRANGE INTERLUDE"

IN a gay lantern lit garden known as the Chateau
Madrid the head waiter seated us at a small table
near the dance floor. There, between a French menu
and an English speaking attendant we conveyed our
urgent need for a couple of daiquiris and a late
supper. We knew the evening was going to make a
bad dent in the exchequer. We knew, too, it was
unavoidable.

The *Havana Weekly Bulletin* had stated, with
superlatives of enthusiasm that Señorita Lolita Caros
was dancing once nightly at the Chateau Madrid.
With that much in our favor, it only remained for
us to cultivate the art of patience. And somehow,
lounging there beneath the tall shadowy palms and
the deep green glow of the tropical sky, waiting
seemed no great ordeal.

Around us soft waves of Spanish chatter rose and
fell. On a diminutive stage almost hidden by boganvillia, a group of Hawaiians plaintively strummed
their far away love songs. Alternate lights of rose,
violet and green lent the swaying couples on the
dance floor a strange remote quality, like the phan-
tasmagoria of a dream. The warm magic of the
tropical night was all about us. I lit a cigarette,

reflecting idly on the incongruity between so pleasant a scene and the dark reason for our presence.

Then just behind me I heard a girl laugh gayly.

"If it isn't Johnny Ellis in the flesh!" I looked around into the sunburnt face and smiling eyes of a sturdy young woman and in an instant I was on my feet.

"Why, Lynn!"

I beamed as though never in all my life had I been quite so glad to see anyone. Actually I don't believe I ever was. Yet to be entirely candid, there was about Lynn Dawson little that should have kept an old acquaintance still viewing her as exactly the ideal God-send for a moon-drenched Cuban garden. For all the warmth of her manner and her lovely blow away hair, I knew as no one else that Lynn had a disconcerting way of running off at odd moments toward Careers and Life Purposes and all that. Just the same, back somewhere in my post college days I'd been acutely in love with her and of such strong affection there's generally a long afterglow.

To our everlasting credit, no mention was made of how small the world was nor how little we'd changed. But all through the business of introducing Alcott I couldn't help wondering what stroke of good fortune had brought Lynn * down here. Then Lynn settled the question for me once for all.

* Dear Lynn. Whenever, . . Wherever, . . If ever you read this, forgive my dragging you into this tale at all. For your sake I might have abstained and I know it. Yet so definite though unconscious was the influence you exerted on my sojourn in Havana, I doubt if the story of that adventure could be honestly set down without you. But then, you feel as I do about this, I know.

J. E.

"No, Johnny, I haven't repented and I haven't settled down." She gave a gay laugh. "And, sh! If you won't tell anyone, I haven't set the world on fire either."

"That makes us about even," I grinned, ridiculously pleased that no new and unexpected barriers had reared themselves between us in the past seven years.

"But it really doesn't," she said, ruefully. "You aren't taking your first vacation in years with a couple of relatives on your neck." She made a wry face off toward a nearby table where her party were just being seated. "For the Lord's sake, and incidentally mine, come over and rescue me sometime soon! Anyhow, I'm desperately out of date about you, Johnny." She held out her hand and smiled.

"I dare you to join us now."

Lynn shook her head. "Can't tonight. But just try me another time. I'll be gratefully yours forever!"

She scribbled her phone number down. "Don't forget!" she smiled.

"Small chance."

I watched her move off to a table not far behind Alcott where a plump grey-haired lady beamed maternally and two men, in dinner jackets, promptly rose at her approach. Lynn doubtless said something in explanation of her stop, for one of the party, a man of about forty-five (and quite unnecessarily good-looking, too) turned his scrutiny in our direction. I thought his face looked vaguely familiar but for the life of me I couldn't place him.

Not that I wasted much time on the matter just then. Alcott was looking at me quizzically.

"Love's young dream, eh?"

I nodded casually, not even remarking how closely he'd hit to the truth. After all, I was growing used to Alcott and I knew for all his grey hairs and sober mien, he wasn't so much up on me in years.

"Seven long years ago," I confessed with would-be cynicism. "If I could have had my say, I'd been married to that girl and by now, perhaps had—er— a nice little electrolux and cocktail shaker. Today I wouldn't be tied down to any dame living. Not if she looked like Greta Garbo, had the brains of Frances Perkins and the income of our dear almost forgotten Hetty Green. Good God, no!"

Nevertheless, with that sticky sweet Hawaiian music in my ears, I found myself looking off through the tops of the palm trees, acutely reminiscent of the time when I hadn't been so serenely headed for a bachelor's path.

From the limbo of those days up rose the ghost of a certain infernal game that was Lynn's pet invention. We both knew its rules backward and forward. On that particular point Lynn had been insistent. She was such a straight shooting little devil, she wasn't taking the slightest chance of misunderstanding. The game consisted in pretending for whole evenings at a stretch that she wasn't at all bent on the career which we both knew perfectly well she intended to have at all costs; in pretending that my weekly pay, then, the munificent sum of twenty-three dollars per was entirely adequate to keep us forever in comfort and ease; in pretending that, instead of being cynically disillusioned about marriage (as the poor kid actually was, because of the smash-up

of her own parent's venture) there was a chance that
some day, some time, somehow . . . It was a thoroughly demoralizing game, I can tell you. I remembered how, after whole evenings of it, I used to see
her off for college on the midnight train and then
for weeks ensuing I'd be sunk six fathoms deep in
gloom. At those times I'd cuss myself for ever having
turned my back on the decent solid chance in my
uncle's business. I'd rail at high editors and the
phoney lure of the printers' ink. I'd gnash my teeth
at the grubby soul corroding limitations of my job.
But now looking back ruefully, I had to admit my
really great tactical blunder had been in helping
Lynn to her first job.

Alcott cut in. "People talk a lot of damned rot
about 'youth, dear old youth,' don't they?"

"At that, it's better than hardening of the arteries
and gout," I laughed. "Anyhow, no man should
marry his first girl. We've got to keep some illusions
in life."

Alcott narrowed his eyes down till only the crows-
feet in the corners suggested they were twinkling.

"That's why Lolita Caros has been on the floor
three minutes and you haven't turned to look at her
yet."

Incredulous, I spun around. There was no gain-
saying the facts. The Hawaiian music had ceased.
In its place the regular orchestra had struck up a
sharply accented tango. Spotlights flooded the center
of the floor, where with castanets clicking and the
inevitable shawl draped closely about her, a Cuban
girl still in her early twenties was threading her way

with sinuous grace through the intricate pattern of a Spanish dance.

Nonplussed I shook my head. "Say, I'd better pack my grip and report back to old Gerraghty. Fat lot of help I'm turning out to be!" I lapsed a moment. "Great guns . . . but she's a knockout!"

The exclamation was wrung from me unexpectedly as La Caros, arms akimbo, heels tapping, hips swaying ever so slightly, glided a few feet from our table. About the girl there hovered an indefinable quality of charm and freshness which somehow took me by complete surprise. Nothing tangible! Neither the utterly rakish angle at which she wore her Spanish sailor, nor the dazzling regularity of her white teeth set off by her olive skin, nor the flash of her dark shadowed eyes. And yet there wasn't a person in the garden who didn't seem to catch it as I did and strain a bit forward, eyes intent upon her. As for La Caros, it was obvious that she warmed herself in the glow of the admiration she kindled, basking in it, smiling now into this face, now into that, taking her public's enthusiasm as her natural due.

She was youth exuberant, vitality abundant, *joi de vivre!* Through all the intricacy of the dance, my eyes and thoughts followed her, while I speculated —oh, all the usual speculation of any man upon a lovely woman! And all the while there rose with mocking persistence, the spectre of a pink packet of letters locked in a lawyer's strong box, a thousand miles away. "Dearest Steve. . . . I count the days these two, three weeks. Then maybe I am in your arms again, and again I know what real kisses once more can mean."

Suddenly the music reached a sharp finale and was still. Lolita Caros bowed her acknowledgment to the enthusiastic applause of her audience, drew her brilliant shawl more tightly about her waist and was gone.

"Well, what do you think?" Pete was watching me narrowly.

"Simply that Dunlap was cockeyed when he tried to laugh that girl off as a possible cause for jealousy. It strikes me La Caros would be cause enough for a tidal wave, an earthquake or a good old-fashioned revolution. Whew!"

"Women are all a matter of viewpoint!" Alcott took a few philosophic drags on his cigarette in silence and looked off. "Anyhow, I don't think it was Lolita that Dunlap was trying to disparage, as much as the Green Eyed Boy himself."

"Maybe."

We didn't pursue the subject. The orchestra had struck up a familiar favorite, "Mon Homme." Once more the spotlights shone and La Caros was on the floor, this time accompanied by a dark-eyed youth, done up in a sweater and red neckerchief. I noticed that Lolita too had changed her costume for the scant skirt and tattered check blouse of an Apache girl. Her smooth brown legs were bare, only her high red heeled slippers and her eyes looked impudent and unafraid.

"There never was a man just like my man. . . ." The dark youth caught her roughly by the neck and swung her into his arms. Clasped tightly, almost annealed into one body, they went through all the usual forms of that much overworked dance of the Parisian gutter.

It was old stuff, of course. But in a new way. Never had I seen the Apache danced more superbly than there in that Cuban garden, with the very moon slipping up over the tops of the palm trees as though to look on. Once, when with especially vicious force her young partner hurled her from him, Lolita swayed, gasped and with a litheness that seemed the very apotheosis of grace, she came back again for more. Some few of the audience, enthusiastic, broke out into applause. Lolita's face was flushed with excitement. Languorously she looked at her supposed lover, even more languorously at those enthusiasts who shouted "Bravos" in the midst of the performance. Swifter and louder grew the music, madder and wilder grew the dance.

Once the suspicion crossed my mind that her Spanish partner was resenting a trifle too realistically the gracious glances she scattered so profusely about her audience. He said something close to her ear; then with a sudden excess of brutality he flung the girl from him. Four feet away, just by our table, she crumbled to the floor. The spotlight leaped our way. It was a purple moment to be sure.

There at our feet lay La Caros, so still that for a fatuous instant I wondered if she were stunned. Then suddenly she opened her large dark eyes, smiled straight at me, then at Alcott, and having done so, a flicker of a frown passed over her face. I was certain she was hurt, but as though divining my thought she shook her head, looked intently at us both again and a moment later glided back into her partner's arms and out on the floor to their grand finish.

During La Caros' third and last dance, some sort of colorful Mexican solo, I was conscious of her looking over toward our table once or twice. Lynn must have noticed it, too, for she scribbled a message on the back of her menu and sent it across our way.

Johnny, I'm making my bookings promptly, lest you slip away forever. Day after tomorrow at eleven we go swimming. La Playa Beach. By the big clock. Lynn.

Lynn darling, we swim at once if you say the word.

Unfortunately my signature was obscured by a long list of Cuban delicacies but it made no difference. I watched my waiter hand the message to her and laughed at her warning nod off toward Lolita Caros.

Thinking it was some more of Lynn's nonsense, I glanced her way when a short while later the head waiter touched Alcott lightly on the shoulder. But this time, I missed my guess.

"Pardon, señor. I was asked to deliver this to you by Señorita Caros."

Alcott's face was unexpressive as he took the envelope that was handed him, but he tore it open without delay. As the headwaiter lingered, Alcott addressed him quietly. "There will be no answer. I noticed La Señorita leave the garden a few minutes ago."

Then suddenly, as though from the clear air, Lolita's dancing partner was at our side.

"Señores," he began, looking from Alcott to me uncertainly. "I know not what La Caros has written you, but I give you warning. Pay no heed to that most lovely lady. She is—how you say—mos' impulsive in her fancies and her husband, he no like it. What is more he find strange means of showing his displeasure. He have me here nightly in the garden to watch her. The Señores had best be warned."

Saying which, the young fellow turned on his heel and disappeared.

Alcott raised his eyebrows in mild amusement and without a word, he handed me the note sprawled in the round, unformed writing that we knew so well.

Tomorrow night I am having a Charity Fete at my hacienda. If the two American gentlemen would care to come, I enclose tickets. I trust to see you. La Caros.

"Pete, you big stiff! To think I never once suspected your fatal fascination!"

Alcott brushed his hand across his weathered, scarred face and his jaw set grimly. "Don't be a saphead. Instead, you'd better chase up the motive. And there is one. You can bet your shirt on that!"

"Maybe. But here's where the case stops being a tough assignment and begins to look like a Charity hand-out to me."

"Going to the party?"

"Sure thing!"

"Well, count *me* out."

"And why the devil—?"

"Because it happens I've got a few lines out on this mess and a crazy hunch I'll work best if I give all the principals a wide berth till I'm sure of my ground."

"Have it your own way, but one thing sure, this little old bloodhound's hitting it off to the Charity Fete."

I was in high spirits. A couple of hours later, worn out, though still exuberant, I fell asleep in our stuffy down-town room and dreamed that the Cuban God was a very fine fellow indeed, with a Hawaiian banjo and a trayful of choice Havana daiquiris. Furthermore, he confided to me that his real name was Luck.

And so I snapped my fingers recklessly at warnings and the old Wyndham curse.

Chapter XIV

LOLITA CAROS

BUT I crowed too soon. The next day, hour by hour, proved it. Wearisomely, tediously, exhaustingly. And that, despite the almost miraculous brightness of the morning, and an enticing Gulf breeze that might have consoled any two more normal human beings, in our position, which is another way of saying any two with purposes less adamant than ours. At Police Headquarters on Empedrado and Monserate Streets, whither we'd repaired early in hope of a confidential chat with the Commissioner, we found, after cooling our heels a little matter of two hours or so, that Señor Jouffret was deeply involved in a red hot crisis which had broken loose in domestic politics. To the tune of doors swinging, phones buzzing and a battalion of excitable assistants hurrying back and forth, the chief assured us with profuse apologies of his "so great interest in the Wyndham case," and promised us in two days he would be free to go over every phase of the tragic affair with us. Meanwhile . . . "Ah Señor, there is a little matter of a bombing out in the Marianao district. . . . But you've heard, of course."

We hadn't heard then, but we were to get our fill of that bomb before the day was over. At the offices of the *Havana Post,* we ran straight into it once more.

There it had stirred up such a reportorial pandemonium that out of sheer fellow feeling we limited
ourselves to sending in to the editor our letter of
introduction from *New York Globe* with a short sup-
plementary note stating that we'd be around in a
day or so.

Outside, in the dazzling white glare of the tropical
day, we looked at each other glumly and mopped
the beads of honest sweat from our brows.

"Well," I began, doing my best to comport myself
on the approved lines of the young fellow who once
carried the message to Garcia, but grumbling withal,
"I'll bet next you'll want to trot all over Havana
inspecting every goddam registry in the town."

"That's one way of locating Wyndham's slippery
friends."

I surveyed Alcott as he stood there, nearly six
feet of gaunt lean resolution, unwilted by the sun.

"Aw, Pete, have a heart!"

"What d'you mean?"

"I'm hot as Hell! So are you!" I paused, then added
persuasively, "Well?"

"Well?" he echoed severely.

"What's the use? Ten minutes tomorrow at the
right source. . . . Give a guy time for a bite of lunch
and a drink!"

We had lunch and we had the drink. In fact, we
had two or three. At Sloppy Joe's, that old oasis for
parching Americans, we ran straight into a couple of
men whom I happened to know from the press back
home. Precisely how long they held us there swap-
ping stories, ladling out advice about this, that and
the other (but mainly the other) I haven't a notion.

I had the hazy idea it was growing late. I had the hazier idea that all problems were growing remote and metaphysical. Then abruptly, I passed my hand over my eyes and clutched hold of Alcott's sleeve.

"Pete," I said, in a hoarse low tone. "Either I'm seeing pink elephants . . . or else . . ." I broke off unable to proceed.

Alcott grinned reassuringly. "Your friend over there with the tall planter's punch?"

I swallowed hard, blinked my eyes and looked again. Of course! I should have known immediately. There was really no mistaking the broad smile and the strange myopic eyes that peered from behind their thick lens glasses across in our general direction.

"But how in hell . . . ?"

"H'm. I thought I recognized him when he came in."

"Queer!"

"Damned queer!"

The unexpected appearance of Charles Elihu Stone had a sudden subduing effect like the touch of that strange little wooden stick with which epicures some time take the bubbles off champagne. It pulled us up sharply, reminding us as nothing else could, of the sinister importance of our presence in Havana. In the space of three minutes we'd forgotten to smile at the point of Nick Grier's latest, we'd made the plump little proprietor fairly trip himself up in his haste to procure our check, we shuffled to our feet, mixed our hats, bade the bunch an abrupt farewell, and not until we were two blocks away did either of us venture a word on what was uppermost in our thoughts.

Then, like the ill-fated bomb of the early morning, Alcott exploded.

"Jesus Christ. I might be an adult about ideas, but I'm in the go-cart about action." He shook his head. "What an idiot I was to have mentioned our destination to that bird!" He said a good deal more at the moment, all duly deleted by the Censor.

Suddenly, for no good reason, I recalled to mind the chance remark that had been overheard on the night of Meenan's death. Then I grabbed Alcott's arm. "What makes you sure Stone's following us and not down here on some business of his own?"

"Just a hunch! But we'll have to watch our step, Johnny."

"What's his game?"

"Put that question down in your little black book! We'll know before we're through, that's one thing certain!"

For some reason, Alcott's bleak pessimism about this encounter didn't vanish with a cold shower and a shave; nor even with our magnificent tactical success in locating within our first four or five phone calls, the exact whereabouts of Calvin Watts, Judge Lamar, and Barton Dunlap. As we left our hotel room, some time later, Alcott stepped up to the desk.

"There was a young man here this afternoon enquiring for us, wasn't there?"

"Ah, yes. He took a room here, I think. One moment, Señores, I'll get the number."

"No need. We'll see him soon enough. I merely stopped to tell you that we may have to return home earlier than we expected. I'll let you hear in the morning."

As we left the desk, Alcott decided upon impulse that he'd drive out to the hacienda with me.

"It may just happen I'll be lucky enough to pick up some information outside the grounds while you do the honors within. Anyhow, it's not a bad plan to keep that fellow Stone guessing for a bit."

We found a taxi near the hotel entrance and showed the card with the address of the Charity Fete to an energetic little driver who stood nearby. With much bobbing of the head and a volley of Spanish he conveyed the idea that no one in all Havana could convey us there better than he. But when for a seemingly endless time he twisted this way and that through tortuous streets, shot at breakneck speed down wide boulevards and wound his way deeper and deeper into the Havana suburbs, I began to have my doubts. Nonetheless, despite all misgivings he pulled up at last at a spacious gateway . . . "El Verano."

Yes, there it was, exactly as on the card. At the hacienda just ahead were lights and music. As though taking cue from this Alcott stopped the driver and got out of the cab. I proceeded into the grounds, leaving Alcott standing solitary in the roadway, gazing off toward the building with an expression of puzzled interest.

The house I now approached was low, rambling and half hidden by flowers and palm trees. Whatever its dignity on ordinary occasions, this night it was gay with color and movement. Crowds in carnival array thronged the patio. Dozens of small booths vied with each other for novelty and beauty.

While I was still busy taking in the multi-colored scene La Caros appeared at my side.

"Ah, good evening! . . . So you did come at last?" She turned to a girl who was with her and said something in Spanish, the net upshot of which was that the girl relieved her of a large flower tray which she was carrying and moved off. Lolita smiled sweetly up at me.

"I wanted to wait for my dances until you got here . . . only you were so very late! Ah, but . . . where is your frien'?"

I proffered my best apologies for Alcott, gallantly inventing a business appointment that had kept him.

It was obvious, La Caros was disappointed.

"You like my hacienda?" she said by way of changing the subject.

"It's wonderful! An old one, isn't it?"

"Yes." She glanced around. "It's been in my husband's family many years." She broke off abruptly. "Tell me. Do you and your frien' stay long in Havana?"

"Oh, that's somewhat uncertain. We're here on business."

"I suppose one should not ask . . . what the beezness is?"

I smiled. "This time it doesn't matter. Our business is everybody's. We're newspaper men."

Lolita examined me with searching interest. "You would not make the leetle joke with me, would you?"

"No, why should I?"

La Caros shrugged. "Only because your frien'—

he do not seem just like the ordinaire newspaper gentleman to me."

"No?" I was amused. And yet basically, Lolita Caros' observation was correct. Pete Alcott wasn't the run of the mill newspaper man in any sense. As long as we'd known him around the *Globe* he never quite talked the vernacular, acted the vernacular nor behaved in any respect according to Hoyle. However, the important thing for the *Globe* was that he wrote Sports copy, like a house afire. And the important thing for Alcott seemed to be that here, a thousand miles from home, he had made a knockout impression on a very lovely lady.

This last fact irked me more than a little. La Caros had found chairs in a quiet corner of the patio and I was all set for drawing out from my very charming hostess a few facts about her own somewhat enigmatic self. But though I strove valiantly, it was obvious her interest was much more intrigued by the absent Alcott and without too much waste of subtlety she always managed to bring the conversation back to him. What was his name? Where had I met him? What was he like? After a half hour of wasted time I realized the young man at the Chateau Madrid was correct. Lolita's was certainly a most impulsive nature.

How long we might have gone on at our verbal fencing, I hardly know. But suddenly I was disturbed by a very singular observation.

"Señorita Caros . . . I'm afraid I am detaining you. There is a man on the other side of the patio who keep looking over here in no uncertain manner!"

Lolita shrugged indifferently. "It's most likely my husband." She paused uncertainly. "If you want, I will show you about the grounds."

Abruptly, she rose to her feet and moved off. I followed at her side.

"My husband behave like a spoilt child every now and then. You must not mind. We are not married long, you know!"

"How long?" I asked with a glint of sudden interest. *This* after all was the sort of thing I had come to get.

"Oh, four months or so!" It was obvious she wanted to put an end to the subject.

"Er . . . May I ask your married name?" I put in on a bright hunch.

She looked at me in surprise. "I thought everyone knew that. I am Señora de Sanchez."

"Not Señora José Sanchez?"

She smiled. "If you know so well . . . why then, do you ask?"

"Oh! There is a great deal about you I've been wanting to ask, Señorita Lola!" I said as disarmingly as possible.

"About me? Why so?"

"You once knew an American by the name of Stephen Wyndham, I believe!"

It was no mere fancy that La Caros grew pale in the moonlight. Stopping still in the path she looked intently at me. Then with an effort at control she said in a matter of fact tone, "Yes. I once like Stephen Wyndham very much. But he grew, how you say it . . . ? he grew cold with me!"

Precisely what any man should answer to a statement like that I never learned, modern education being so very inadequate to modern needs. Embarrassed, I changed the subject with some glittering platitudes about how tropical these tropical nights always were, and how charitable were Charity Bazaars. I also averred that it was growing late and perhaps I should be leaving. But at the mere mention of departure, Lolita seemed disappointed.

"Oh, it is early yet. And your frien', he might still come." She looked at me ingenuously. "By the by, are you and he relatives perhaps, that you interest yourselves so much in this Meester Wyndham?"

"You read the papers I presume?"

"Now and den!" She laughed. "When I have de time!"

"Then perhaps you know that Stephen Wyndham disappeared on the 13th of February of last year."

Las Caros' eyes grew large with amazement. "What you mean," she asked, looking directly at me. "Stephen Wyndham have disappear?"

"Precisely!"

"I don't understand!" But I got no chance to elucidate. At that moment, a man came around the bend and down the pathway toward us. In the green bright light of the moon I could see he was dressed in a dinner jacket and was smoking fast and furiously. I also noted that he'd arrived at the age where his waist looked a trifle too thick and his hair a trifle too thin. As he approached, he nodded sullenly to me, and then in an abrupt tirade of heated Spanish, he addressed himself to La Caros. Under the verbal onslaught, Lolita's color mounted, but her manner remained calm throughout. Once, in dulcet tones she tried to explain something but the man talked on, low and fast—fairly biting the words out with his even white teeth. Then swiftly as the storm had arisen it was ended.

La Caros turned to me, a faint sarcastic smile hovering on her lips. "This is my husband, Señor Sanchez! That boy I dance with last night have told him that I invite two American gentlemen to my party." She paused.

There was an awkward silence, during which Sanchez tried his best to look agreeable. "This is not our usual way of receiving guests. I am very sorry. My wife is young—and sometimes she forget she is away too long from her other friends. You will pardon us, I know!"

"But suppose it happen I do not want to leave yet?"

Señor Sanchez looked at La Caros coldly.

"Do not anger me again, Señora."

Nonetheless, Lolita stood her ground, until in ill-disguised rage, Sanchez moved off and left us once more to ourselves.

But somehow I felt my real opportunity had fled. As soon as I could with politeness, I proffered my excuses and said good night.

La Caros held out her hand to me as I was leaving. "Perhaps we will meet again before long. Adios."

"Good night, Señora!"

I found my taxi waiting where I had left it; and the little driver dosing not so very far away. Slowly, we started off down the roadway. Outside the gates, half hidden in the shadow of the tall shrubbery we had the good fortune to be hailed by Alcott.

"Any luck?" he asked as he sprang into the cab beside me. I was about to answer when suddenly our car made a sharp turn.

"Good God, look out!" But Alcott's warning came too late. The car was careening wildly. A wheel had spun off. How we ever extricated ourselves from that mess I'll never quite know. The one thing that saved our lives was that we had only just started and the car had not yet gained much speed.

Our little Havana driver, badly scratched and shaken up, dissolved into volleys of barely intelligible protest. Between gestures and indignation, I gathered nothing of the kind had ever happened to one of his cars before. Those wheels he indicated in fine pantomime, were on tight . . . tight! He was sure!

It was all queer business. Inexplicably, my hand wandered to Miss Wyndham's letter that I carried in my pocket. "Bad fortune pursues those who meddle needlessly in Wyndham matters. It is a kind of family curse." A ridiculous cold shiver went down my spine. Then I pulled myself together for hastening down the moonlit road toward us, I recognized the young man who had danced with La Caros the night before.

"Ah!" he exclaimed in seeming distress as he surveyed our broken down taxi. "You have met with no harm, I trust."

"Oh, no," Alcott said coldly. "And our driver's even optimistic enough to think he'll be able to get us back to town."

"That is well," the young man said with oily smoothness. "I come from Señor Sanchez. He had thought to offer you one of his cars."

But with a chilly air, Alcott turned aside. "Thank you. We'll make out all right, I think."

Later that night when we were about to turn in, Pete said cheerily through the darkness.

"Well, old boy, our sleuthing seems to be looking up a bit!"

"How do you make that?" I parried glumly.

"Tonight while you were holding forth with the fair Lolita I had a little talk with one of the gardeners."

"Yeah?" I yawned in boredom.

"Yeah. And it might interest you to know, Señor Sanchez has only just returned from a week's trip to New York."

"Still connecting that Meenan's death with young Wyndham's I see."

"Maybe something like that."

"And whom do you connect with our broken down car tonight?"

"Ask me that in another week's time!"

Chapter XV

AN UNEXPECTED VISIT

EARLY the next morning, when I was fuming about the room trying to cram an armful of crumpled clothes into Alcott's stubborn suitcase, the telephone rang. Needless to say, it rang inconveniently. I was rushed with impromptu packing and this was the morning when, despite murder, mystery and a generally cockeyed world, I intended taking a couple of hours off to go swimming with my old girl. Reluctantly, I picked up the telephone receiver, anticipating trouble.

"A lady downstairs to see Mr. Alcott."

"Mr. Alcott's out," I snapped. That was no lie. Having spent the better part of the night convincing me of the necessity of our getting away as soon as possible from the surveillance of Parson Stone, Alcott had hustled off at an early hour to find more secluded quarters.

"The lady asks if Mr. Ellis is in?"

"What?" I let out before I could put a brake to my surprise. Then I enquired the name.

Instead of an immediate answer I heard a ripple of Spanish, followed by a woman's voice, very low, at the other end of the wire.

"This is your frien' of last evening. It is important that I see you."

With no little curiosity I gave Lolita Caros our room number. Within a very few minutes she arrived, looking singularly pale and distraught. As she crossed the threshold of our room, I noticed she threw an anxious glance behind her as though in some way fearful of being followed. I noticed too, that although she was quietly and unobtrusively dressed, she wore a dark scarf drawn up high over her chin and her hat pulled low over her eyes. Because of the heat of the morning I closed only the half door to our apartment, a fact that seemed to cause a moment's apprehension, but without any comment she sat down.

"Your frien'—Meestair Alcott—where is he?"

I explained that a matter of importance had taken him out, but that he was expected back shortly.

"Oh!" For a moment La Caros looked uncertain as to whether she ought to proceed. Then she made a helpless gesture.

"It makes no real difference, I suppose. Either one of you gentlemen will tell me what I want . . . what I must know!"

It seemed a big order, so I kept my own counsel. She noticed my reserve and looked up at me, her eyes dark depths of entreaty.

"Please. Do not treat me so. It is more unkind than you know!"

The girl's sincerity seemed obvious. Her face was pallid with grey shadows, her hands opened and closed nervously.

"I am sorry anything has occurred to cause you distress. You must be more explicit!"

"That is why I come here. What did you mean

when you say last night that Stephen Wyndham have disappear?"

In the face of the fact that the press had been shrieking with the story for weeks, La Caros' question was absurd. I told her so.

But she shook her head with curious insistence. "You do not understand. I am kept very busy between the hacienda and my dancing. Since I marry," she hesitated then proceeded uneasily, "I depend on my husband for the news."

"And he omitted mention of this?"

She nodded.

"I see."

Then I outlined the newspaper facts as succinctly as possible, while she sat forward regarding me with a curious, puzzled look on her face. At the conclusion, she rose to her feet and stretched out her hand.

"Thank you. That explains much. I will say 'adios.'"

I moved between her and the door.

"Not quite yet, Señorita. Frankness is sometimes repaid in kind, you know." She glanced at me in sharp surprise. "Before you go, I'm sure you want to explain just how it happened you were listening at the door of Mr. Wyndham's room on the night of February 13th, last?"

The color rose in Lolita's face.

"Who have told you this?"

"That's unimportant. Er—I hate to bring the matter up, but it happens—er, you see—" I was getting embarrassed. "Oh, deuce take it! Señorita, you're involved in this Wyndham tangle a good bit more than you know!"

Lolita Caros looked at me a moment, then she shrugged. "Santa Maria, I don't understand any of this. But surely—I'll do whatever I can." Her voice fell low. "For him."

I tried to believe that she spoke sincerely but mine is a skeptical nature.

"You might begin by answering my question."

Lolita looked at me with candor. Then suddenly she smiled.

"Since you know so much, most likely you know what I have once been to Meestair Wyndham. Anyhow I make no lies about that."

I marveled inwardly at her frankness. She was proceeding without ado. "For a whole week before that night that you speak of—yes, for two whole weeks, I had tried to see Meestair Wyndham. For all those two weeks, he say to me he's busy here and there." Lolita sighed, her eyes far away. "You see, he think me a very stupid little girl—how you say it—light of love? Yes? Perhaps *that* was a little true. We are what we are! Isn't it so?"

She looked up at me appealingly, her eyes unaccountably welling with tears.

"Anyhow I get tired of always his excuses. That night I want very much to see him. There was a special reason, very urgent. When I called his room he tell me he have his frien's there. When I suggest I see him later he say he have an appointment. All the time I know I must see him. Between my dance numbers at the Sevilla Biltmore there was always forty minutes intermission. I think to myself I will go down to his room and see for myself if he tell me the truth about all these appointments. I slip my shawl around me and go to his room. Inside there I hear many voices. I listen close. It sound strange in there, like a beeg fight. I think I should leave but somehow I can't. Then after a while everything grow more quiet. I begin to think soon now he will come out. But just as I say this, everything in the hallway grows black like night. I say, 'Hurry up, Lolita, go away quick!' 'No,' I make answer to myself. 'I must stay and see Stephen when he come out.'

"So I waited there, crouched by his door in the darkness. Once some man come to the door, look out, say something, then turn back. The minutes pass. I don't know how many. I wait and wait. And all the time, no Stephen!

"At last I see a hallboy bringing a lamp toward the room, and I walk off quick so as not to be observed. But not very far, you know. Then as soon as that boy goes, back again I move to wait for Stephen. After a long while the lights come on; I know I must go. I am very disappointed for you see, my American frien', he never come out that door." She paused a moment, absently watching a large fly that had come in the window.

"You could swear to that?" I asked in suppressed excitement.

Her eyes met mine without wavering. "I could swear that by the Holy Madonna and all my hopes of Heaven!"

Swiftly I produced a hotel floor plan which I had obtained the night before.

"Señorita, think well! It's terribly important. This was Wyndham's room." I pointed to Room 208. "This was the room where the men were playing cards." I indicated 209. "And this, Number 210, was the friend's room. Now, precisely where were you standing?"

Without a moment's hesitation she indicated the sitting-room door.

"Facing which way?"

"Oh, when the light was on I could see the door to the sitting room and also the next door at number 208."

"What of Room 210?"

"My back was toward it. But if Meestair Wyndham had come out that door he would have had to pass me to take the elevator."

Then suddenly, at a moment's notice, La Caros pursed up her mouth as though in high amusement. She looked adorable. She knew it. She was tempting fate. She knew that too. What she didn't know was the simple fact that I had an appointment to go swimming.

"You Americans are—how you say it—very funny young men."

"Er—I suppose so. But let's not go into that. You said there was a special reason you wanted to see Stephen Wyndham that night."

All humour suddenly died out of the situation for Lolita Caros. Her expression grew tense.

"Yes."

"Will you be kind enough to tell me what could have been so urgent?"

Lolita's face grew hard.

"That I will tell you—nevair!"

"Tst! Tst! Never's such a long time, Señorita.

You'll get bored with me long before then, I'm afraid."

I moved a step nearer the door. Swiftly La Caros divined my purpose and changed her tactics. She pulled her scarf around her and looked at me smilingly.

"Santa Maria! I must go now, really. You will let me pass, please?"

She came very close to me.

Obdurately I shook my head. "First I must know why you thought it so imperative to see Mr. Wyndham on the night of February 13th!"

"I no tell you!" This with a sharp stamp of her foot.

Suddenly, without either of us being prepared for it the half door swung open and Señor José Sanchez, white and disheveled, stood at the threshold. His sudden entrance, like the devastating onsweep of some cyclone, left us both voiceless and aghast.

"*Cielo!*" he said with an effort of terrible calm. "If she don't tell you, I will." He was regarding Lolita with a fixed, glassy stare.

Lolita let out a little shriek and rushed to his side. There was a torrent of Spanish, low and anxious, but with one hand Sanchez grabbed her wrists and with the other he sealed her mouth.

"So," he said, looking at her calmly. "You went to warn him that night against me, and what I had confided. Bah, '*quien hace su cama con perros se levanta con pulgas.*' " He flung her from him and turned bitterly to me. "In other words, my young fellow, 'he gets fleas who sleeps with dogs!' "

Lolita's eyes blazed in anger and her hands

clenched. "You devil! No miracle I went to warn him against you. To talk to me like that! Santa Maria! First you tell me he have other girl! Next, you tell me he go away and forget all about me. Never once you tell me Meestair Wyndham is supposed to have mysteriously disappear. Why! *Why!* I wonder!" She looked at him suspiciously. Her slim body shook with the violence of her emotion. "And while we talk of this, something else come to me now. Yes, I wonder was it really only finance matters that take you so sudden to New York last week?"

I looked swiftly toward Sanchez to see what his reaction would be. But unruffled and supercilious, he stood gazing at his wife.

When the force of her passion had spent itself, he nodded to me. "Clever little actress, hein?" Then he made a mock bow, very low and sweeping. He looked contemptuously at the girl.

"Ah, Señora, you ask why I never mentioned this disappearance. Helas! Helas! I have such a great delicacy of sentiment and, remember well, a profound feeling for you!"

There was a peculiar significance to his tone that did not escape me. Swiftly I looked at Lolita to see what her reaction would be. Her face was deathly pale. Her lips parted. Then suddenly, before either of us could prevent it, La Caros had crumbled to the floor in a dead **faint.**

Chapter XVI

THE MAN IN THE ROOM
NEXT DOOR

IT was in the midst of brandy, drawn blinds and Sanchez's curious hovering anxiety and insane penitence that Alcott put his head into the room. In a glance he took in the situation. But the worst was over then. The superb Lolita was gradually returning to consciousness and even Sanchez was regaining some sense.

"You'd better get her home at once where she can recover in comfort," Alcott suggested to me at the doorway. Then lowering his voice. "Say, Johnny, we haven't much time to lose ourselves. I'll be back in a few minutes and by then," he glanced meaningly across the grey hush of the room, "I'd deucedly like to talk to you alone!"

"But good God, man! . . . You haven't an idea what we've stumbled on!"

"Yes, I have. Just the same get 'em out of here! Quick. Damned quick, if you can! By the way, be sure to tell them sweetly but firmly at parting that if either of them makes a move to leave Havana before you communicate with them, you'll put them both under arrest before they quite know what's struck them."

I wanted to argue. I wanted to cuss, but Alcott was

already halfway down the hallway. This once I felt myself in violent opposition to him. From the morning's developments I felt the Sanchez pair were more deeply enmeshed in Wyndham's strange end than either of us at first had supposed.

"Damn Pete and his fool ideas!" I mumbled to myself. It was with no little misgivings that I saw Lolita and José Sanchez to the doorway, and made it clear that one false move from them would land them in the hands of the Cuban police. However, at that moment they were impregnable alike to logic or threat. La Caros looked too dazed to even comprehend what I was saying, and though Sanchez nodded absently, by some strange monomaniacal absorption nothing seemed to actually register at the moment except that pale-faced girl who leaned unsteadily against his arm.

As the door closed I shook my head gravely and pulled out the inevitable little memo book. There, with a single dark question mark, I entered the names of my late callers.

As I finished, Alcott was quietly reentering the doorway. Just inside he put his finger to his lips and tossed a hastily written memo my way.

"No questions while in the room. Careful!" I read. Then, in a loud, good-natured tone he called out. "Well! Are you all packed, Ellis?"

"Pretty nearly," I grumbled. "If you'd plant your lean carcass on the end of this grip maybe I could get it fastened. That is, if you'd keep those flat boats of yours out of the way."

"Heave ho!"

"Don't heave ho on that bottle of Bacardi. You'll smash it."

"By the by, I got the reservations O.K. but they cost a pretty penny."

"Yep?"

"Sure. Gerraghty's a damn fool calling us home at the last minute. A few days more and we might have been finished with this job." Alcott banged the grips around with a great show of commotion.

"I agree!" But there was a wild inaccuracy in my statement. I didn't agree. I didn't understand. Fact is, if it hadn't been for the reassuring level look in Alcott's eyes, I should have been certain he was a little out of his head.

He guessed my mental fuddle and drawing me close against the side wall whispered in my ear. "Quick . . . take this. Inside there's a chair. . . ."

Into my hand he pressed a room key and nodded off toward the hallway. Once outside I observed with no little surprise that the key belonged to a room just two doors to our left. Without a moment's hesitation I softly moved in that direction and unfastened the lock.

The chamber I entered was an empty hotel room, quite typical, quite orderly and wholly barren of interest. I stood staring at it more doubtful than ever of Alcott's good sense. Then I remembered his crazy injunction about a chair. A straight backed one stood by a side doorway, which apparently led to an adjoining room.

"H'm, that room would be just next to our own," I thought to myself.

A moment later, I mounted the chair. On the level

with my eyes was a transom with a dark silk curtain over it. I pulled the curtain aside. What I saw at first was simply the dim interior of a room exactly like the one in which I now stood, and for that matter exactly like our own. Then over by the doorway (roughly corresponding to the one at which I myself was standing) I became aware of the figure of a man crouching on the floor, his whole attention strained and riveted on the keyhole in a mad effort to catch what was happening in our apartment. I experienced a peculiar chill of apprehension. There was a certain familiar set to the head. Then the man bent his ear a bit closer to the door crack and I caught a glimpse, of thick, double lens glasses. At that I got down and rejoined Alcott.

As I reentered the door I heard him cheerfully soliloquizing.

"So I said to the guy, if you can't get us two lowers, get us uppers, put us in the freight car, put us in the trailer, but for Christ's sake get us something on the train from Miami tomorrow."

With a wink I chimed in. "That was talking turkey! Say! I wouldn't like to see Gerraghty's face if we didn't show up."

For answer, Alcott swung a grip up in each hand. Then from the doorway he motioned me to sit tight until he telephoned me from downstairs.

The minutes dragged by heavily. Out of eye range of that odious keyhole, I busied myself moving the chair around with a semblance of great commotion, all the while keeping up a running conversation with a non-existent companion. At first, the by-play was amusing, then somehow it got on my nerves. At one point I got the distinct notion that Stone was softly and stealthily trying to force the door lock. Just then, very luckily Alcott phoned up for me.

As I left the room, I called back with one last grandstand flourish. "Well, Pete, I'll trot along and explain to Lynn!"

Lynn! Good old Lynn! I thought of her with a twinge of conscience, waiting cool and imperturbably good-humored out at the La Playa Beach— wondering (that is, if I was lucky!) what had happened to me. Well, it served me good and proper. There was no mixing women nor friendship, nor apparently any of the decencies of life into an ugly mess like this.

When I got into the cab which Alcott had waiting, I was still raggy and a little out of humor.

"Whatever your next halt old man, I'm going to La Playa to try to find Lynn Dawson."

"You'll find her all right. I sent her word a while ago you'd be a little late."

I looked at him in amused surprise. "Strangely enough, there are times when you seem moved by something very like genuine intelligence," I said, with no uncertain meaning.

After a bit, I relented a little. "By the way, it might interest you to know that information you picked up last night was okay. . . . Your friend Sanchez really *was* in New York just about the time of Meenan's death."

"Oh, I hadn't any doubt of it!" Pete said with a twinkle.

"Well, I had. . . . !"

* * * * *

An hour later, cutting through the clear green Gulf water at La Playa, stroke by stroke, my bad humor melted away. And still later, stretched out indolently on a deserted float I began to feel as though I could have drawn up a very presentable case for this business called living. The reason wasn't far to seek. Not two feet away Lynn sat, twisting up her funny, freckled nose and looking at me with her straight, clear eyes.

"You've changed a lot, Johnny."

"What did you want? Arrested development?"

"H'm, not exactly. But you're so much more serious."

I laughed. "I'll do a song and dance number as soon as I'm dry. I feel like it anyhow, just seeing you again."

"Don't be silly!" Pause. . . . A long one. . . . "What's worrying you on a grand day like this?"

And then, lying there on the raft, like a weed in the sun, I began to pour out to Lynn, the tale of our difficulties. I'd only just gotten well under way when she sat bolt upright, ripped off her red bathing cap and looked at me quizzically.

"Are you trying to tell me about that Wyndham case, too?" she asked with an unbelieving smile.

"And if I am?"

"Oh, nothing except I've been having Stephen Wyndham and fresh pineapple every night with my dinner since I'm in Havana!" She broke off in kind of wonder.

"Johnny, this is the funniest coincidence in the world, and now that it's happened, I honestly don't quite know what to do about it." She paused. "By the way, where are you staying?"

Cautioning her to secrecy, I gave her the address of the new hotel at which I was to meet Alcott.

"There's a good reason for my asking." But I needed no reassurance from Lynn. "Remember—oh ages ago—my speaking of Uncle Fred?"

I wrinkled up my forehead, thinking hard. "Vaguely. He was the great big howling success down in New York!"

Lynn nodded. "Exactly. The one I simply adored back in my salad days!"

"So what?" I said indifferently. I never went in for genealogies. Lynn knew it.

"Don't you remember his last name?"

I shook my head, thinking of all the water, fresh and brackish, that had spilled over the dam since those days. Lynn was looking at me humorously.

"It's Lamar. Sanfred Lamar!" It was my turn to sit bolt upright.

"Good Lord! Not *Judge* Sanfred Lamar? The one who knew Wyndham?"

She nodded triumphantly. *"Now,* what do you say?"

Say? Just then I said nothing. Instead I broke out whistling. Yes sir! To the Havana Gulf waters, to the blue sky, but best of all to my old girl Lynn, I sat there whistling my little pet tune.

> "I've taken my fun where I've found it;
> I've rogued an' I've ranged in my time."

Somewhere out of the furtive wind, I could hear Alcott's dry comment. "Think we're getting along, don't you old man?"

Well, doggone it! Maybe at last we were!

Chapter XVII

AN IMPORTANT BIT OF
EVIDENCE

I LOCATED our new hotel with a maximum of
effort and a minimum of speed. It turned out to
be a quiet little place in the heart of a secluded resi-
dential district, certainly the last place in the world
anyone would expect to stumble upon a couple of
newspapermen. A sleepy doorman, surprised at his
late afternoon nap, led me past a rusty iron fountain,
across a trim Spanish garden and thus directly to
the door of my room, which pleasantly fronted
thereon.

To my surprise, I found Alcott inside, propped
on the bed, a welter of books around him.

"What's the big idea?"

Instead of greeting he raised his eyebrow a fraction of an inch and continued reading in silence. At
the end of his chapter he abruptly slammed the
book to.

"Ever hear of Gross or Lacassagne or Locardi?" he
asked with a quizzical smile.

"Not some more guys in on Wyndham's poker
party, were they?"

Alcott shook his head and laughed. "Nope! Not
they!" Then, with an inclusive gesture toward the
heap of books around him, "Make your bow to a

bunch of pioneers, Johnny. Yep! Pioneers, my lad, of the vast unchartered realm of criminology." Then he finished in disgust. "But they'll get us all of no-wheres!"

I looked at Alcott closely.

"Say! How many daiquiris did you have this after-noon?"

Alcott laughed. "Not one. It so happens I spent an hour and a half at Police Headquarters, thirty min-utes at the *Havana Post*, and the rest of my time at a second hand book store at the end of Obispo Street."

"Hence this?" I indicated the mass of books scat-tered pell mell about the place.

"Exactly!"

"But why?"

Alcott looked away, a frown on his face. "We're in deep water. Terribly deep, old man. Frankly, this was sort of a call for help." He lit a cigarette ab-sently.

"H'm! You seem to have gotten the damned stuff by the carload," I remarked sarcastically, picking up first a worn French edition of "Manuel de Police Scientifique" by Reiss, and then two ponderous vol-umes entitled "Handbuch fur Untersuchungs Rich-ter," by Gross.

Alcott shook his head glumly. "You're right. Those guys are swell. They can tell you exactly how to look at a footprint and know whether the man that made it was carrying a bundle or not, how fast he was walking. All that stuff! Even our old friend Bertillon here. . . ." He stopped to reach for a book that had somehow (and I had my own suspicions *how*) landed five feet across the floor. "He tells about an 'effraction dynamometer' that can measure the exact amount of strength required to break down a door. He can settle once for all whether a forcible entry was effected by one or two men." Alcott gave a dry laugh. "Our big trouble seems to be that we haven't any footprints, we haven't any broken down doors, and our crime is nearly a year old!"

There was a tinge of weariness to Alcott's tone, a note of profound discouragement altogether unusual in him. I thought the news about Judge Lamar would buck him up, so I sprang it. But even that failed. Instead, he sat on the side of the bed flicking ashes over the floor, staring moodily at the welter of books around him. "It's as though we sat here trying to make bricks without straw!"

Out of the heap of books I picked up an English treatise, and commenced glancing through it. Its theme was that the detection of crime rests more with the chemist, the physicist and bacteriologist than ever with the police or other agents. It hammered so steadily away at this point, that I was just beginning to understand Alcott's discouragement, when suddenly he sprang up and reached for his hat.

"Good God! I've got a hunch, Johnny. A good one! We'll get our 'footprints,' we'll get our 'straw!' Wait here. I'll be back in an hour."

In three strides he was out the door. Nothing else to do, I sat down and resigned myself to a cheery little study of subtle poisons that kill in an hour, of the strange powers of psychological suggestion, of delusions that can obsess the criminally defective and such like, until a rap on the door called me back to actuality. Outside, against the sunny silence of the garden, I found my old friend the doorman standing irresolutely, a note outstretched in his hand. Hardly pausing to reflect on the singularity of any letter finding its way to us so soon after our change in quarters, I took it from him and tore it open.

My dear Mr. Ellis—

Lynn Dawson has just informed us of your presence in Havana, together with a hint as to the reason. It is imperative that we get together as soon as possible so you'll find me close on the heels of this note. Judge Lamar is with me.

Calvin Watts.

"Where's the man who gave you this?" I burst out to the doorman with such excitement that, though the fellow spoke no English, he gathered my meaning and nodded back to the entrance.

"Send him and his companion here."

Two minutes later, crossing the garden toward me, I saw a fine looking, squarely knit man of middle age whom, now in the bright afternoon sunlight, I easily recognized from the newspaper pictures as Judge Sanfred Lamar. I wondered how I had ever missed his identity the first night when I saw him with Lynn at the Chateau Madrid. Hair greying at the temples, strong, clear features, deep-set blue eyes, there was about Lamar the unmistakable air of distinction and stamp of leadership that generally makes men of his type stand out from the crowd. But just now it was the young man at the judge's side who managed to engage my interest. Why, I could hardly have said. He was a tall, rangy fellow in his early thirties, with unruly dark hair, a broad generous mouth, crooked nose and haggard eyes.

As Lamar came up he gripped my hand in greeting. "Forgive our intruding this way. My niece Lynn assured us you wouldn't mind. And there was no controlling my young friend here!" He nodded toward his companion. Then, on second thought he added pleasantly, "By the way, I'm Sanfred Lamar, and this is Mr. Calvin Watts, of Baltimore."

Watts looked at me directly. "You don't mind our busting in like this, do you?"

I smiled. "If you hadn't come along today, by tomorrow I would have busted in on you at the Almandares Hotel and the Judge at his villa in tha Vedado section. Yes, and Mr. Barton Dunlap at the Presidente."

Calvin Watts ignored the fact that I had run down all their addresses. He ignored the wild disorder of our book-strewn room. He ignored the chairs I proffered. All the while his tired eyes bored through me searching, questing for something he didn't seem to find. Then, without waiting for Judge Lamar to speak, he came directly to the point.

"Damn it all! What do you make of it?"

"That was what I was going to ask you," I said quietly.

The young man waved aside my question brusquely. "For God's sake, let's can the formality! I'll lay out my cards first because the Judge's niece has told us you're straight shooting and O.K. All right. Get this. I was Stephen Wyndham's best friend. We knew each other since we were youngsters. Yale together—all that!"

Watts broke off abruptly and turned aside. "Oh, what's the use!" Then, on second thought he decided there was some use, for he proceeded. "The whole point is I cared about Steve Wyndham as though he were a brother. And yet, good God! Well, you know the facts. Some one did Steve in. I was there, present on the very occasion. What did I do? I allowed myself to get stuffed with a lot of banana oil. I spent six months playing around with airplanes and polo ponies. Man! you won't believe it, even my friend Judge Lamar, I guess, can hardly do so, but until the papers broke with the story of Steve's disappearance, never once did I question but that Steve dashed off on one of his usual impulsive jaunts." Watts ran his hand through his hair distractedly and looked me straight in the eye. "Good God! Can you imagine the way I feel?"

I could. I could also imagine it was no very satisfactory dilemma for a friend. I felt oddly sorry for the chap. There was something so forthright about him, you couldn't help feeling that way.

Even the Judge warmly came to his rescue, putting his arm over Watts' shoulder with an impulsive generosity that dissipated, once and for all, any preconceived notion I might have had that here stood the usual sanctified executor of the law. "I've tried to make this boy realize that the responsibility falls alike on everyone of us who was present that night."

Watts ran his hand nervously through his hair. "Oh, let's get this all up to date and done with! The week this story broke I dashed back here to Havana. I saw Judge Lamar, who, as you seem to know, usually vacations down here. Together we've

hunted high and low for evidence. We've dredged for
Steve's body. We've searched the records of crema-
tories, hospitals and asylums. Not a trace has been
found. We're at our wits ends, honestly. There!
Those are all our facts to date. The whole meager
array of them. Now what have you to offer?"

I must have looked my indecision. Anyhow, Judge
Lamar shrewdly guessed it, for his eyes twinkled
exactly like Lynn's.

"Look here, young fellow. Don't you let us in-
veigle you into talking unless you so wish. That's
spoken as a counsel; and, er—as the relative of an
old friend!"

The laugh that followed cracked the ice. I told
them as much as I thought safe, which is another
way of saying that I told them nothing very important. Not that I entertained the slightest doubt of
either, but at the crucial moment I remembered my
pledge to Alcott, and that effectively tied my tongue.

When I had finished, Lamar and Watts shook
their heads. "It doesn't get us much further!"

"Not exactly a burst of light, I'll admit."

Just the same I got them to reconstruct for me,
bit by bit, their story of the fatal night. All tallied
neatly with what I had already heard. I questioned
them about the Wyndham will and Parson Stone. To
no avail. Judge Lamar knew less than I did, and
although Watts was vaguely aware of some mystery
about the will, just what it was he had never heard.
I got them to check my hotel plans and the diagram
of the men at the table. Lamar was helpful, in his precise, clear way, but Watts was impatient of all such
detail. One half hour of it he managed to stand; then,

with sudden impulsiveness, he turned away from us and commenced walking up and down the room.

"What's the use? Good Lord! To you newspapermen all this is just another murder feature! Nothing else!"

I realized a new line of approach was necessary. "Look here. Our very detachment and coolness are the best qualities that could be brought to bear just now. After all, where's your righteous wrath getting you?"

Watts stopped short in his pacing, wrapping himself around my idea like an amoeba about some particle of food. "I guess that's true," he said slowly. "Only to us who knew Steve it all seems such a rank outrage. He was the whitest guy that ever lived. Really!"

"I believe all that. Still . . . when you're close to a person you lose your perspective."

Watts was unconvinced. "You didn't know Steve as I did. He wasn't the sort of fellow to whom anything like this should have happened. He didn't go around acquiring enemies."

I jumped at the opening Watts offered. "Nonetheless, you admitted awhile ago that on that very night you had to stop a fight between him and Sanchez."

For a minute Watts looked taken back. Then I heard him echo precisely what Barton Dunlap had said back in New York. "Oh, that didn't mean much. Steve's affair with that Caros girl was over and done with. We all knew that. Why the very morning before his murder, Steve had warned me that I'd better quit making bets on the chances of his remaining single. I got the notion that he might be settling down any time within the year."

"How do you know he didn't have this Lolita person in mind?"

Watts looked at me intently. "Steve didn't say. Just the same I had a damned good idea it wasn't she."

I wanted to whistle or whoop. Something lay ahead. I could feel it. Very quietly I aimed my bolt. "Right here you have one of those simple little elementary facts which is getting *you* nowhere. Whereas," I smiled, with Metternichean cunning, "if laid out before a cooler, more unbiased eye . . ."

Calvin Watts looked genuinely uncomfortable. "What you ask is impossible," he said. "It brings in the name of a particularly nice person who's had trouble enough of her own lately without being bothered with this mess. Furthermore, she was miles away from Havana on the night of February 13th."

"Omit the name," I said persuasively. "All I want is a new slant."

Obstinately Watts shook his head and it was only after an infinite amount of digging and probing that I gathered the fact that the girl in the case was married, and very unhappily so, at the time that she and Wyndham had first met. Furthermore that the attraction between her and Stephen had been instantaneous, mutual, and the honest-to-God thing.

I let Watts finish, and then very quietly I faced him. "By the way, did you happen to know that on the morning of February 14th, Wyndham had an appointment with this very same woman in Pinar del Rio?"

My question must have exploded Watts' consciousness like a shot.

He wheeled around on me. "How did you know that?"

"Simply enough. I got it from your friend, Barton Dunlap."

Calvin Watts' open face turned scarlet and his jaw dropped. "The dog!" he said in a low tone. "The dirty low down bastard!"

"You're a little rough on the chap," I ventured, but Watts only stared at me.

It was Judge Lamar who quietly explained. "He should be. That girl at Pinar del Rio was Dunlap's wife."

Chapter XVIII

THEORY, PLUS A FEW
STRANGE FACTS

"NOW listen, Pete Alcott!" I burst out that evening. "I'm warning you. If we turn up one more suspect in this case, I'll go just plain bughouse from the strain. Anyhow, why did you ever come busting into this mess? Before you happened along, I seem to recall great stretches of peace and quiet and the marvelous blessedness of not one single clue."

By the light of the street lamp which we were passing, I saw Pete smile faintly at the extravagance of my jest; but he didn't trouble to answer. It happened just then he was indulging in a fit of temperament, the only genuine one I had ever observed in him. I remember the occasion with peculiar vividness. We were tramping along the Maleçon. He had suggested the walk shortly after I'd finished telling him my story of the afternoon. Along our path the sea waves with wild, impetuous force were hurling themselves against the grey embankment, shattering to silver spray, washing the pavement around us, sprinkling our faces, suggesting somehow by their unceasing boom and obstinacy a little of our own plight and the equally impenetrable wall of mystery against which we were matching our strength.

When Pete spoke it was as though he were echoing

my thoughts. "Well, if that sea doesn't shatter the wall it gets over it somehow, by God!"

I remember noticing his face when he said this. Thin, fine features set in determination and silhouetted clearly against the luminous sky. It did more for my morale than a shot of whiskey.

"Think hard. You're sure they didn't give you a clue as to where Dunlap's ex-wife could be located?"

"Nope. We could wire Billy Farrel, though. That little ferret would dig it up."

"I wouldn't bother him just yet."

Again we tramped in silence. Absently I noticed the moon had a ring around it. I noticed the huddled masts of the fishing boats, dozens of them, tossing at their moorings near the foot of the Prada. There was an inexpressible magnificence to the night.

Abruptly Alcott spoke up. "I guess it would be too much to hope that you remembered to ask Lamar and Watts whether they were smoking in Wyndham's rooms on the fatal night?"

"Oh, nothing's too much to hope," I said lightly. "Take my own case. I'm hoping old Gerraghty won't part with our invaluable assistance just because of this little spree. I'm hoping to see Lynn Dawson once more before this confounded case drives me completely nuts. I'm even hoping you'll quit acting so almighty patronizing before I knock your damned block off."

Alcott laughed. "And what of that little matter of smoking?"

"As to that: Judge Lamar and Watts were smoking early in the evening. The Judge recalled that Watts had smoked him out of his last Havana cigar. But by the time the lights went out both had stopped. The way Watts remembered was that he'd looked for his lighter and had not been able to find it at the time."

"I see."

"Hell, I *don't*. I always feel like a damn fool putting that question. I could see that Watts thought it was blamed queer, too."

"Forget it then. Or call it just another of my crazy hunches. At this precise moment I've a peculiar longing to hear your theory of the case, Johnny."

I chuckled. "My theory? Theory? Singular did you say. Good Lord! I'm inundated with theories, man. Over production. Drugging the market. I can let you have almost any kind of theory you want. Romantic ones! Sinister ones! Mercenary ones! Insane ones! Theories to fit the Tall and Slender, the Stylish Plump, the Short and Stout. You ask for *a* theory? God, man! I'm fairly wimbling with them."

"Quit stalling and let's have them."

"All right, I'll try to be sober. First, there's that charming little damosel, Miss Isabella Wyndham. You know, every time I feel the least discouraged about the ultimate possibility of our unravelling this mess, I want to call for a cop and a pair of steel handcuffs and once more ring the doorbell of the stately old Wyndham mansion. Remember the fish-like coldness of her face at the window, that day? Brr! Man, if that sister didn't actuate Wyndham's killing, she simply had a lucky break. She would have one day. Anyhow, I don't trust her. She's Suspect One. That woman has the eyes of a fanatic and the cunning of a cat. And something is preying on her mind. We saw that the first day. As further evidence there was that note she sent to Parson Stone the morning after our visit and that peculiar letter of warning she sent to you to keep your nose out of her affairs. And what of her pledging the bulk of the Wyndham fortune to a Chinese mission? It sounds like buying your way into Heaven to me. 'Who bids highest? I'm a poor crawling sinner. I hated my brother and all that, but I gave my money to convert the heathens!' No sirree! I don't like her."

"I don't either. But these days we don't indict a person on sheer prejudice, Johnny." He nodded off across the water toward El Morro Castle, and I, having picked up a little of the history of that gloomy old fortress, knew precisely what he meant.

"But I'm not relying on prejudice," I countered hotly. "There's her side-kick, Parson Stone. What exists between those two? What brought a seemingly poor student to Havana at the height of last season? Even more to the point, what brings him back here now? I've a notion he's all against our little investigation. I've a further notion he's against us. Anyhow, the day I ring the Wyndham bell, I'm bringing an extra pair of handcuffs for that young prize package. He's part and parcel of Theory One! And he stood to profit by Wyndham's death you can rest assured."

Alcott bent his head forward as though absorbed by what I was saying. It was a generous but unconvincing gesture. No matter how impregnable I might deem my logic, I knew he would take the same facts and integrate his own theories. Nevertheless, I was encouraged and plunged on.

"In short, I believe Miss Wyndham had no love for her brother and a good deal to fear from him. I think she felt his fortune in her hands would serve much better ends. She may even have heard of the possibility of Stephen's marriage and the chance of losing his portion for good and all. Between herself and Stone was a tie of long association and perhaps something stronger. She sent Stone to Havana where she knew Wyndham was staying. As for the rest. . ."

But Alcott cut in meditatively. "The rest? That hinges largely on these questions. Could Stone have known of Wyndham's plan to leave the poker crowd that night? Could he have conceived and executed this particular design to murder and dispose of his body? What of the lights and the burnt mark on Ford's wall? You're 100 per cent right as far as you go, old punk, but to build a complete case in this instance, I've a hunch we'll have to concentrate on *method* as well as *motives*."

I accepted his challenge. It was easy. "All right. Young Stone could have had someone aiding and abetting him, couldn't he? After all, there was a locked closet which it seems Wyndham's nice thoughtful friends didn't even bother to look into. And that timely darkness could have been part of his method or it could have been merely coincidental."

Alcott nodded his head. "Don't bet too much on coincidence."

I brushed past his objection. "Well, my main point is I'd arrest Parson Stone and Sister Wyndham at the drop of a hat if it weren't for a few other curious facts."

"Four to be exact," Alcott put in with a knowing smile. "Four other hale, hearty and perfectly adequate suspects."

"No, three."

"Are you starting with Barton Dunlap?"

"Yep! though I hardly know why. His wife had fallen in love with Wyndham we know, but after all, behind that fellow Dunlap seems to have been a long record of the Roving Eye, and a great capacity for consolation. I think he's on my Black List solely because he's a Grade A stuffed shirt and I don't like him."

Alcott spoke up quickly. "I'd add to that. I believe Mr. Barton Dunlap was insanely jealous of his wife. The phenomenon isn't exactly infrequent, you know. Furthermore, he denies the emotion a little too vigorously for my taste. And after nearly a year, his loss is still burning him up. Anyhow, I'm afraid I agree with young Watts. The fellow's a dog, and a low down one at that."

I looked at Alcott sharply. "You speak of him with more suspicion than Parson Stone."

Alcott nodded. "Perhaps," he shrugged, "I didn't mean to, however!"

"Of course," I admitted, thinking out loud. "He did have an equal opportunity of committing the crime."

"A better opportunity," Alcott cut in dryly. "If you remember your diagram he was sitting just next to Wyndham."

"Good God!" I let out sharply. "And his talk about being drunk that night might have been a lot of stale boloney."

"It's possible. Only let's not set our minds on anything just yet. By the by, shall we turn off here?"

We had reached the end of the Malecon and had to

turn some place; that much was sure. But so absorbed was I at this particular moment I hardly noticed when we set our backs against the harbor, with its tangled outline of fishing craft, fortresses, and steamers, and began proceeding up the broad Prada toward the Hotel Sevilla Biltmore. I was much too busy talking.

"And, of course, that Sanchez pair isn't exactly easy to laugh off, you know. You should have seen those little love birds when I did this morning. Something's amiss there; take it from me. Our friend Stone may have invented the long knife he saw in Sanchez' hand, but it's entirely within character. That's the worst of it. And from those pink sachéd letters back in New York, we know the lovely Lolita still had a weakness for young Wyndham. She made that very clear regardless of what he may have felt. I'm a little leary of these volatile Southern temperaments. It's possible our pretty dancer went to warn Stephen Wyndham against José, as was suggested. It's possible she went for some more cussed purpose of her own. It's even possible, though at this point I suggest that you take my temperature and call an ambulance, it's even possible that she and José are in cahoots, and are acting up a little for our benefit. I honestly don't know; I'm dizzy; I'm going cuckoo. But, anyhow, that is the end of my trail of suspicion."

Alcott looked at me incredulously. "Not really? You lucky bum! You haven't even begun to be bothered as yet. Wait till you reflect upon Hugh D. Ford and that neat little sum he withdrew from Wyndham's account just before his marriage."

But I cut Alcott off there. "You sound like the tabloids. By the way, have you noticed how that particular item has leaked out and been pounced upon?"

"Well, there are those that smell a rat there, even if you don't."

"Rot," I said curtly. "If you'll use your brains you'll remember he wasn't even in the room at the time."

Alcott laughed. "Good Lord! Like all experts, Johnny, you show a positive genius for avoiding the minor errors as you rush forward to the major fallacy. How do you know Ford was not present? What makes you so damned sure? Stone spoke of meeting him in the corridor when he went outside. He could have been in the next room all the time. Dunlap told us of that adjoining door opening and closing, didn't he? And somehow that little scorched patch by the electric plate suggests gently but insistently to my mind that someone was there. Oh, no! Johnny, my boy, you don't know what worry really is as yet; you haven't even faintly tapped the possibilities of this case for genuine headaches."

"How do you get that way?"

"Well, not once in any of your theories, have you mentioned George Meenan's peculiarly opportune attack of heart failure. I can't forget that particular episode so quickly even if you can. To be sure, the unknown gentleman who accompanied Meenan to his apartment on his last night could conceivably have been any one of the men you mention, for curiously enough *every one of your suspects were in New York at the time*. But who was the most likely visitor? That's what I keep asking myself. And why was it necessary that George Meenan, political backstage boss, should be put out of the way?"

"Oh, you make too much of the matter," I put in by way of protest. "Farrel told us that was just a lot of wildcat talk."

"Then he seems to be changing his mind. Take a look at this!"

He handed over a cablegram sent a few hours earlier to us in care of the *Havana Post*.

AS PER SUGGESTION HAVE BEEN STEPPING OUT WITH SECRETARY OF M'S FORMER PHYSICIAN STOP TWO MOVIES AND THREE DINNERS HAVE NETTED FACT THAT M NEVER HAD SIGN OF HEART TROUBLE IN HIS LIFE STOP THIS PRETTY CERTAIN AS WEEK PRIOR TO DEATH HE HAD BEEN AT OFFICE FOR ANNUAL PHYSICAL EXAMINATION AND EVERYTHING OKAY STOP ALSO LEARNED DOCTOR IN CASE IS CONNECTED WITH CITY HOSPITAL STOP WHERE DO WE GO FROM HERE BOYS

BILLY FARREL

"All of which may be the case," I grumbled. "But personally I think we have enough on our hands with this Wyndham mess, without dragging George Meenan into the broth!"

"Have it your own way, Johnny." Pete lapsed into silence, but I was all for third degreeing him a bit.

"Well, where's your next hot trail of suspicion?"

Alcott looked at me without a smile. "Oh, what's the use? I could mention a half dozen clues that would make anyone else take notice, but you don't pay any attention to those I do hand out."

"That's rotten unfair."

"Not altogether," Alcott smiled. "I told you some

time ago not to overlook the disappearance of that little gold medallion."

"Oh, that," I said, with magnificent ease. "Lawyer Stone was only trying to keep his nephew out of the case."

Pete's eyes twinkled. "There you go. *Motives* again. Forget them. Most of the crowd there that night seems to have had a motive, and small help that is. No. Whoever planned this crime—or crimes, if you will permit me—was a shrewd, calculating individual with the cunning of a devil and a good bit of luck. *Method,* Johnny, that's our only real lead on the Wyndham end. *When we ascertain the method, we'll nail the guilty one.*"

"Well, how about getting started?"

For answer, Alcott studied the rear approach of the Hotel Sevilla Biltmore, which almost miraculously appeared just opposite.

"We could start right here."

The hotel passage that we pushed our way into was fairly deserted. From a partition somewhere down the hallway came the sound of boys' voices, bell boys I presumed, talking away in a soft jargon of Spanish. Much further off we caught the faint rattle of dishes and the far-off odors of a kitchen. A few feet from the doorway a portly old fellow in a rocking-chair struggled to read his evening paper in the dim illumination of the exit light.

Glancing up, he spotted us as Americans. "What do you want?"

His directness took us by surprise. On the spur of the moment Alcott pushed me forward, a convenient goat for the sacrifice. "I've a friend here who's looking for a job as night watchman at a hotel like this. Any chance here?"

The fellow scratched his head and looked me over critically. It was easy to see that I didn't quite come up to his high ideal. Nonetheless he gave a toothsome smile and broke the news gently as possible. "No use. Night man myself. Six years now."

Alcott seemed vastly impressed. He let out a low whistle. "That's a record. Great Scott! We happen to be writers and we've knocked around a bit. But I guess a fellow gets to see a whale of a lot more of life in a job like yours."

The night man agreed. In fact he launched into detailed proofs of the fact that threatened to become endless. I was just beginning to get a little surfeited with the minutiae of our new acquaintance's autobiography, when Alcott broke in. "You've got a wonderful memory, all right. But at that I'll bet there's plenty you forget."

The fellow shrugged. "Not much."

"All right. Let's see about that. Do you remember, oh, about a year ago two men who happened along this way on a very rainy night?" Pause. "My guess is that they had no business down here and perhaps asked you how to get upstairs without going out in the rain again."

The night watchman looked at Alcott sharply and his smile suddenly vanished. "So many people come and go here. I no can say things like that." But any one with half an eye could see he was lying.

"Oh, you'd remember these fellows all right. There were only two who went up and three who came down; and one at least was very thoroughly drunk."

But apparently the night man's wonderful memory had failed him completely. He shook his head and looked oddly uncomfortable. "No. I no remember anything like that at all."

Undismayed, Alcott dug out a dollar bill from his pocket and tossed it to him smilingly. "I can see it sometimes pays better to forget than to remember. Just the same, you've been a lot of help. Good night."

Outside among the clamoring realities of the gay Southern night, Alcott turned jubilant. "That's one fool hunch that worked all right. Johnny, my boy, I think we're in for a break."

He should have said "breaks." A car whizzed by, barely missing us. Mercifully, I was yanked back from near death by Alcott's vise-like grip on my arm.

Safe on the pavement, Alcott opened up. "Damned queer that car shooting by like that!"

"It was on the wrong side of the street!" I managed to gasp.

"H'm. And it turned the corner before I could see who was in it!"

"Well, that time I beat you! There was a dark, heavyset fellow driving, who looked suspiciously like José Sanchez!"

"God, no! He wouldn't dare an attempt like that! No matter how hot he thought we were on the Wyndham trail."

But I couldn't argue the matter with Alcott just then. I felt cold sweat gathering on my forehead, and in desperation reached into my pocket for my handkerchief. In pulling it out, Miss Wyndham's letter of warning fluttered, phantom-like, to the pavement. *"Bad fortune follows those who meddle needlessly in*

Wyndham matters." A long shiver passed over me. Suddenly I felt icy cold despite the warmth of the night.

Alcott picked up the note. As he handed it back he looked at me narrowly.

"Not getting superstitious, are you Johnny?"

I scratched my head and grinned. "Well, I own up there have been times in my life when I've enjoyed myself more. Just the same, the old Wyndham curse isn't turning me back just yet awhile."

"That's the stuff. Anyhow, before you decide too definitely that that crazy driver was Sanchez, it might not be a bad idea to call his estate and see where the charming gentleman is to be found."

We found a telephone exchange and a pretty little dark-eyed operator put through our call. The report came back that Señor Sanchez had been absent all evening. Further, he had left no message as to where he could be located.

I turned to Alcott in triumph. "I guess that will hold you for a while."

But Pete was non-committal.

It got me sore.

"For Christ's sake, sometimes it's more than a duty to spill one's mind, it's a positive pleasure. Of all the pigheaded punks I've ever seen. . . ." I broke off, overcome for words. "Yes, and while we're on this subject. You can kindly illuminate me as to the purpose of that wild dash of yours this afternoon."

For answer, Pete treated me to a dose of silence. Very soothing silence, to be sure; during which time we tramped through the humid night, past monuments and people, past spectrally white buildings and palm-lined public squares, in fact the greater part of our way back home. Only when we had nearly reached the gate, Pete bestirred himself to talk. "Gosh! I hate acting this way, old timer. The trouble is I'm groping in the dark myself, and it's all so devilish difficult to explain. When I rushed out this afternoon, I wanted to catch the late Havana papers for an ad."

"An ad?" I echoed, more mystified than ever.

"Here. Take a look."

He tossed a slip of paper over to me and I read the English part.

$500 Reward for information of any strange or untoward event occurring on or about the night of February 13th last, which might tend to throw light on the end of a young American millionaire who disappeared at the time from the Sevilla Biltmore Hotel. Communicate with Chief of Police, Havana.

When I finished I shook my head glumly. "Good Lord! You're a bigger fool than I suspected. A little experience of this sort of thing and you'd know you'd be swamped by communications from every blamed nut in the United States and West Indies."

"I rather hope so."

"Well, you'll manage this yourself. That's sure." I spoke glumly. Suddenly I felt inexpressibly weary. Luckily for me, we had reached our gate. I pushed into the garden, knowing without looking that the hour was very late. Somewhere in the darkness I heard the fountain dripping softly. Despite my mood, the night seemed charged with a warm, magical peace. Then suddenly, when we were more than half way across the garden and nearing our door, a shadow slipped past us. It was a broad, heavy-set shadow, strangely clumsy with speed. Then I gripped the rail of our balcony, for in the light of the street lamp, I caught the gleam of thick lens glasses. When the outer gate clicked, I swallowed in a kind of relief.

"Do you know who that was?"

Alcott nodded briefly. I noticed he had already switched on our light and was examining the window by which Stone had apparently gained entrance to our room. Once he stooped and picked up a letter that Stone had evidently dropped in his flight. He frowned for a moment over the strange, oriental symbols, and then, unable to decipher them, laid the letter aside.

"That bird works fast," he said tensely as he peered out into the night. "We'll have to hustle if we want to beat him."

Chapter XIX

THE FIRST ARREST

I THINK it was on the same memorable night as Stone's strange visit that in the midst of a sweet and dreamless sleep, I was rudely awakened by the crash of part of our ceiling as it fell to the floor. It had barely missed Alcott and me.

"Good Lord! That was a close call!"

I remember standing in the midst of the debris and plaster, nervously tearing Miss Wyndham's note of warning into a hundred bits. "Right here and now!" I said with fervor. "I swear off all connection with that old hag's letter. A fine trail of luck, it's brought us, anyhow."

At that moment, Alcott was absorbed in a painstaking examination of the wreckage, but he paused to smile.

"You're a superstitious mug, Johnny. This old dive is so moldy and ancient, it's a wonder the whole place doesn't come to pieces."

"Yeah. That may answer for this. But what about Sanchez and that loony taxi tonight?"

"Oh, I've a hunch that was pure chance, too. After all there must be a thousand Cubans who resemble Sanchez."

"Sez you! Well, keep right on! And the wheel that came off our taxi?"

"Perhaps accident, again. Though that I'm not willing to say with finality."

"Well, I'll say '*boloney.*' There's something about this whole mess I don't like, Pete. I'm telling you straight. It's making my hair stand on ends. It's giving me the jitters. It's. . . ."

But Alcott was grinning at me cheerfully. "Johnny! Johnny! Pull yourself together. You'd think we were stalking through some absurd melodrama where everything that happened to the hero is the cool and calculated work of a hidden fiend. No, old punk!" The smile died suddenly on Alcott's lips. "I've been thinking about it all night and it's 'no go.' The brains we're matched against are far too shrewd for that."

"Maybe. Just the same, I'm getting out."

"Because of a few curses from an old lady in Manhattan?"

I scratched my head and dismally surveyed the wholesale havoc about us. "I don't say it's old Miss Wyndham. I don't say *what* it is. I just say I want to get away from this mess and quick as ever I can."

Alcott looked at me askance. "Not quitting, are you?" The way he said it sobered me up.

"No! but one thing sure—I'm getting out of this goddamed hole!"

Alcott shrugged. "Something tells me you're foolish to bother. Stone's watching us. We know that. And my hunch is, we won't shake him with our next move. No, unfortunately. Nor with our next hundred!"

On sober reflection, I realized Alcott was right. To move did seem futile with that hawk-like Parson on our heels. Consequently, we settled the issue by having our belongings switched to another room down the same section. We engaged the quarters to the right and left of our own to insure some modicum of privacy. We destroyed every tell-tale paper that we did not want to trundle about on our persons, and we made very sure to lock windows and doors whenever we went out. Nonetheless, it was uncanny how the feeling persisted that we were being spied upon by stealth or followed.

I remember with peculiar vividness, one early episode that lent weight to this presentiment. Alcott and I had decided, as a routine precaution, to wire Jimmy Farrel to do a little checking up on Calvin Watts and Judge Lamar. We were accepting no one too whole-heartedly just yet. Accordingly, we dropped by the Post Office to dispatch the necessary message. As we were leaving the Telegraph Bureau, for some inexplicable reason both Alcott and I looked back. There, already at the desk, talking in soft, sibilant tones to the clerk, we recognized the now familiar bulk of Charles Elihu Stone. He must have sensed our glances upon him, for suddenly he turned about and spread his broad accordion-like smile full in our direction. Cold and fishy, that smile now seemed, with a depth of malevolence in it.

Once outside in the Havana sunshine, I opened up.

"Look here, Pete. We've stood just about enough from that bird. Let's have a showdown here and now."

Alcott shrugged. "What's the point?"

"Well, I'm for telling him to mind his own damned business and quit pussy-footing around after us, this way."

Alcott smiled. "And you really think he'll listen?"

"Maybe not. But it would be a satisfaction anyway."

"Well, count me out! I'm not ready for Stone just yet, no matter what you think you are."

Saying which, he left me to call instead at Headquarters for whatever letters may have arrived in answer to that absurd ad of his in the *Havana Post*.

There was no accounting for the fellow!

But I was all steamed up. Even Pete's philosophical unconcern did not deter me. Fairly smarting with annoyance, I turned back into the Post Office and walked directly up to Stone.

"What's the big idea of all this?"

Stone glanced at me with that singular smile of his. "The big idea of what, Mr. Ellis?"

"Oh, come off. The big notion of your following us, spying on us, prying into our affairs, as you have done."

That audacious smile broadened.

"But what could possibly make you think I'm following you?"

"Oh, I'm not here for small talk," I said in irritation. "But I'll give you fair warning. You better leave off. Do you get me? If you don't, we'll make things hotter for you than even this Cuban climate."

"Try it!" Stone looked at me coolly and his smile grew a trifle less broad. "Perhaps I know what *I'm* doing even if *you* don't."

And having delivered himself of that cryptic utterance, he turned on his heel and was gone.

The next occasion on which I saw young Stone was some two nights later when, temporarily forget-

ful of the whole Wyndham muddle, I had taken
Lynn Dawson to the Fronton for our first look-in on
the great Cuban game of Jai-alai. The amazing agility
of the players, the mercurial enthusiasm of the spec-
tators and, moreover, Lynn's own humorous side
remarks were absorbing my entire attention when
suddenly I caught a fleeting glimpse of Stone moving
among the throng on our right. However, at that
moment, it seemed unimportant. Luxuriating in
Lynn's companionship for this first stretch in years,
I could manage to rise magnificently above such
minor annoyances as the prying Parson.

Things were going better, I told myself. But the
real truth was, I was seeing Lynn with a vengeance
these days. Every hour that clues slackened or work
reached a temporary standstill, I'd find myself sneak-
ing off with her for a set of tennis, a swim, a round
of talk and cocktails . . . all, of course, just for—er
—old times sake. Judge Lamar was off on a three-
day fishing trip, her mother had gone back home,
and Lynn needed looking after, I argued. Alcott
shook his head over me or roundly cussed, "For
God's sake, quit whistling that damned old tune."
(I think I was whistling "The Ladies" from morning
to night these days.)

But it made no difference. Somehow it was too
exhilarating to discover old lines of sympathy un-
broken, new interests akin, in a girl who had the
gayest, straightest, tenderest eyes in all Havana and
the most infectious laugh I'd ever heard. After that
first date at La Playa, I had admitted ruefully to
myself that Lynn was as grand as ever. At the end
of my second I perceived she was even better than

that, and by the end of the third I realized in dismay, that I was breaking out again with every symptom of the old flame. Worst of all, I didn't seem to mind.

As for Alcott, no matter how much he scoffed at my lack of sense during these days, the score seemed about equal between us. If in his eyes I was a fool; in mine, he seemed in training to be a moron. During this time, he made divers and sundry references to mysterious trips and missions he was making about the island, but no matter what hour of the day or night I'd come home, I'd find him, shirt sleeves rolled up, perspiration rolling down, poring over the stacks of letters that slowly but surely had trickled into Police Headquarters in answer to that inexplicable ad of his in the Havana papers.

And a conglomerate lot those letters were! Typed, scrawled, printed, signed and unsigned. Some posted, some handed in without even that formality; soiled and torn, meticulous and tidy; Cuban, Mexican, American. A steadily mounting pile of testimony to the innate vagary of the human species. But not one iota of those countless letters would Alcott miss. It was a preposterous waste of time. Half a dozen times a day I told him so.

However, my remonstrances did little good. Invariably, I was met by the same obdurate shake of his head and exasperating smile.

"Run along, Johnny, and play if you want. I'm not forcing you to help me, am I?"

One afternoon, coming in late from an excursion with Lynn, I was particularly amused at him. The harvest of queer happenings on or about February thirteenth was growing more abundant judging from the mass of letters on the table. In detail, one man wrote in to report about a sugar mill which had mysteriously burned down near his place on the night of the thirteenth, fourteenth or fifteenth, which date he wasn't just sure, but he was certain, quite certain it was last year or the year before. A woman from Mexico City described the terrible fright her child had been occasioned by a so-called supernatural visitation that had occurred on precisely the date mentioned in the press notice. One, Señor Aguero, reported that his year's savings had disappeared from an old butter crock where they were always kept. And to cap it all, at Tampico a cat was reported to have given birth to thirteen kittens!

"All of which certainly throws great bursts of illumination on our Wyndham case," I broke out, sarcastically.

Alcott quietly pushed a soiled sheet of paper toward me. "At any rate, here's something that might be important."

I turned the sheet over gingerly. It was written in pencil and was barely legible:

I seen your notice in the paper & dunt know as this'll interest you but thought I'ud writ it. Anyways on the night you menshun, I an my brother found a man stretched out on the starboard side of our fishing boat which had been tied up at Havana more'n eleven days waitin' fur the bad wind and wether to let up enuf for us to get clear of the harbur. When we furst seen the guy all messed up there and bluddy among the ropes and fish hooks and riggin we wuz already 20 miles out at sea. Mebbe you'd say we should have turned back and told the Police about this guy but it wuz our furst good break in weeks and the Red Snappers were sed to be runnin pretty good just then & we couldn't afford to take a chanct on getting stuck in Havana harbur again. Anyhow the guy wusn't dead but he wus awful banged up around the hed. We done what we cud fur him takin turns cooking and settin up with him. When we got him to feelin a little better he'd lay by the hour out on the deck in the sun, keepin his own company. He wus a funny one. Never a word cud we get out of him as to where he'd come from or who he wus or nuthin. Sometimes he'd help us haulin or washin up but most of the time he seemed kind of absent-minded. When we put in at N'Orleans to sell our catch, he wus lookin thin as a rail and white too. We told him we'd be going back ter Cuba and wud tak him back with us but he shuk his hed and sed he'd ruther stay in the States. Then he thanked us for our care and blew off, the Lord knows where. It wus the last we ever seen of him. But the date in yer notice put us in mind of him. Specially becuz he wus so unnatural quiet, it made us think him a bad customer. If you want more perticulars write

> Porkie Smith
> Sailors Cove
> Key West
> Florida.

"And thus commences an elevating and literary correspondence between you and 'Porkie,' I suppose." I contemptuously tossed the letter across to Alcott.

"A mutually remunerative one," Pete smiled. "I intend to see that Porkie Smith gets the $500.00 reward. That is, when, as and if, I can lay hold of the $500.00."

I looked at Pete in curiosity. "Jesus. You really think that seaman's yarn important?"

Alcott smiled lazily. "H'm, very! And I've a kind of hunch you'll one day agree."

"Damn fool!"

But that sort of bickering got us nowhere. Much more to the point seemed the results of little Billy Farrel's research back at the Home Office. Forty-eight hours after our communication to him, two characteristic cables arrived at the *Havana Post*.

CALVIN WATTS ONLY SON OF ONE OF FIRST FAMILIES OF MARYLAND STOP FATHER SENIOR MEMBER OF WATTS AND BRUTON BANKERS STOP CAL ALSO CONNECTED WITH FIRM BUT NOT ENOUGH TO BOTHER HIM STOP FROM ALL REPORTS SEEMS TO BE GREAT WHITE HOPE OF ENTIRE JUNIOR LEAGUE STOP REPUTATION DECENT BUT THE GUYS STILL YOUNG STOP HEARD SWELL STORY LAST NIGHT ABOUT HAILE SELASSIE STOP GUESS YOURE DOING YOURSELF PROUD IN HAVANA WHILE THE OLD FOLKS SLAVE BACK HOME STOP NO DONT STOP

BILL FARREL

The other dispatch was equally to the point.

DESPITE HARD WORK CANT RAKE UP MUCH DIRT ON LAMAR STOP BORN UPSTATE MUCH IN ORDINARY WAY STOP RESIDES WHEN IN CITY AT RESIDENCE GRAMERCY PARK STOP AGE FORTY THREE AND STILL UNMARRIED STOP SAID TO BE AMBITIOUS GENIAL AND INDEFATIGABLE ABOUT WORK STOP VACATIONS REGULARLY IN HAVANA IN WINTER STOP HIGH SPOT OF CAREER TO DATE SEEMS TO HAVE BEEN SCHMIDT MESS LAST YEAR WHEN DUE TO BRILLIANT JUDICIAL CHARGE EIGHT PHONEY INDICTMENTS WENT FLOOEY AT TRIAL STOP BY THE WAY GERRAGHTY LOOKS MADDERN HELL EVERY TIME YOUR NAMES ARE MENTIONED STOP

BILL

Over cream cheese, jelly and black coffee in the sunny dining room of our little hotel, we smiled over Bill's cables.

"Right off the bat, Johnny, what's your impression of Lamar?"

"Straight shooter and okay! Billy's report only rounds out the picture."

"And Watts?"

"The same of course."

"So much for that!"

Our talk drifted from personalities to events. We speculated idly how long, on the shifting sands of our present social and economic world, the phenomena of rich young playboys like Watts and his crowd could persist. We drifted to current events, where both of us thoroughly disillusioned and cynical shook our heads over a rough and tumble world where reformers, crime waves, fads and presidents come and go. I remember we even touched on the growing menace of the racketeer. That was no trifling matter. Despite all the outcry from platform, pulpit and press, the virulent evil seemed spreading far and wide like a hideous cancer in the nation's life instead of being effectively rooted out once and for all. The very make-up of our morning paper proved the point. "St. Louis Bank Teller Killed in Machine Gun Raid." "Sausage King Takes One Way Ride." "Police Sergeant Succumbs to Racketeer's Bullet."

"Jesus! It's a damned poor commentary on our agencies of law enforcement."

"H'm. Maybe the corruption doesn't stop short with the racketeers!"

"Of course not. Still, poor Johnny Public pays and pays!"

"Yeah. That's the rub." (Pause) "By the way, were you surprised at the outcome of those Schmidt charges last spring?"

"Maybe at first. But it seems there wasn't a scrap of real evidence to hang on the guys."

"I know. We got the rumblings of the matter even down in Florida."

We finished our lunch in silence. On my side I was speculating at what moment I could make a decent get-away. Outside the day was blazing and clear, a grand afternoon to take Lynn exploring through the older quarters of Havana. After all, I reasoned, Alcott and I could talk forever, but so far as progress on the Wyndham case was concerned, whether due to the old Wyndham curse or what, it was obvious, perfectly obvious, I argued, that for the time being we were completely becalmed.

Becalmed did I say? At precisely that moment, there was a slight commotion near the door of the dining room. I turned to see a police officer striding our way, his every step protested by our woe-begone head-waiter. The oddly sorted pair arrived at our table simultaneously.

In broken English the head waiter proffered a thousand apologies that our luncheon should be so rudely disturbed.

"These policement—ah, they are so insistent."

This one certainly was. Straight into my Guava jelly, he extended a large official looking envelope from headquarters. It was addressed to Alcott, but at a nod from him, I tore it open.

The typewritten communication therein was surprising, to say the least.

As per your honored instructions, I am writing to inform you that Señor José Sanchez and wife were arrested this morning when trying to leave Havana for Rio de Janeiro on the S.S. Orestes. They had the passage engaged under the name 'Esteban' but due to the vigilant watch you had instructed me to keep, I was fortunately able to frustrate these plans and notify headquarters.

Señor Sanchez was in a very nervous state when the arrest was made and offers the most heavy bail. The lady thus far stubbornly refuses to answer all questions, repeating hysterically that the arrest is an outrage. She even audaciously demands to face you and your friend, assuring headquarters that you will see she is promptly released.

"Wha-at!" Alcott broke out, evincing the first real interest he had shown in the entire communication thus far. "Here, let me see that!"

I handed the letter over to him with an unpardonable smirk of satisfaction.

"Well! What have I been telling you all along about that Sanchez guy? He never looked good to me from the beginning. But you'd have none of it. Oh, no! it couldn't have been him in that crazy car! And that loosened taxi wheel was just chance. . . ."

But I was wasting my breath. Alcott, hearing not a word, was absorbed in re-reading that missive from Police Headquarters. Beneath his quiet exterior I could see that something in the situation interested him.

"You can tell them at headquarters that we'll be

over right away." Then to the head waiter, "Better hurry our check along if you want us to sign."

I caught the fever of his suppressed excitement. And then precisely at that moment my heart gave an extra beat, for hurrying across the dining room toward us, I recognized—of all people!—Lynn Dawson. Very tailored and tan she was looking, and very obviously bothered by something. However, with her usual debonaire smile, she brushed aside the police officer who was still lingering at our table.

"If you're nice, you'll wait to arrest these young men until another time. I simply must talk to them right away."

The officer laughed and moved away.

Lynn took the chair which I drew up for her, her perturbation more evident than ever.

"Whatever shall I do?" she began after the immemorial fashion of all sturdy young women whose minds are already made up. "This radio arrived for Uncle Fred the very first day he went off fishing. I think it will interest you."

She drew a message from her small white handbag.

"Of course, I should have opened it there and then, but alas! mine is such a strong character."

She laid the message on the table before us and we took it in with one swift absorbing glance. It was dated four days prior.

SANFRED LAMAR
CALLE PASEO 32
VEDADO, HAVANA.

JUST LEARNED FROM PANAMA PAPERS THAT MY NAME HAS BECOME INVOLVED IN WYNDHAM MIXUP STOP MY WIFE

AND I ARRIVE HAVANA WEDNESDAY MORNING STOP HAVE
WIRED ATTORNEY TO MEET US STOP WILL COMMUNICATE
WITH YOU AT ONCE

                                        H. D. FORD

My jaw dropped in amazement.

"But today's Wednesday! He must be here," I said stupidly.

"Oh, he is, Johnny, no mistake about that. At this moment he's pacing up and down the patio out at Uncle Fred's, in a temper so hot it almost matches his carroty head. Whew!"

"Good Lord!" I ejaculated slowly.

It was Alcott who interrupted with the air of Richard III calling for his horse.

"Listen! Don't let the grass blossom under your feet, old timer. You beat it back to the house with Miss Dawson and get a crack at that redhead without delay. I'll trot along to headquarters to see what's happening to that Sanchez pair. And believe me, we both had better hurry! S'long!"

Chapter XX

A VERY IRATE YOUNG MAN

BY the time that Lynn and I arrived out in the Vedado district and at Judge Lamar's quiet, palm-shaded residence, Hugh Ford had abandoned his posturing. Instead of an angry lion pacing up and down the patio, I found a lamb in immaculate flannels and a blue yachting jacket, stretched out in an easy chair, a planters' punch by his side, his attention absorbed in a copy of Machiavelli's "Prince" which he seemed to have picked up at random from the library shelf. He glanced up in surprise at our entrance. A sunburned, keen-looking, young fellow, smooth-faced, well-knit, direct-eyed. For some reason even his mop of flaming red hair seemed on him not unattractive. When I added to his obvious physical assets what I already knew of his unquestioned ability in the field of political writing, I no longer wondered at his personal popularity. I don't think he did either. He looked to me as though he revelled in his success, in all the flavor and fatness of it.

Lynn introduced us without delay, explaining my own interest in the Wyndham case and assuring him I could be of quite as much help to him as her uncle. However, on that point, Ford was good-natured but skeptical.

"I've only waited around because the butler tells

me Mr. Calvin Watts phoned he would be out about this time."

And much to my dismay, instead of opening up on his own connection with Wyndham, Ford draped himself artistically in the grilled iron doorway and proceeded to turn the conversation to the Galapagos Islands and the lure of the tropics.

"God! Those nights there!" he said at one point. "Imagine, Miss Dawson! Shimmering green moonlight and the stars so close you feel as though you could reach up and gather handfuls of them."

Lynn was enchanted. Not I! I would have much preferred learning how he had reached out and gathered fifty thousand dollars from Wyndham's private brokerage account. Oddly, persistently he began to recall to my mind a certain chap with whom I'd once roomed after college, one of these dreamy young aesthetes with a soul far above such craven things as money. He had gone over immensely with all my girls, sending them orchids, taking them to the swankiest places for tea, always on my savings of course. Sometimes he even magnanimously invited me to come along and, while he dwelt loftily on the magnificence of life in the Renaissance, or the magic of pre-Raphaelite poetry, I was permitted the supreme privilege of settling the check. Of course, we split up after a time, for there are limits to human patience, but deep within me, I still nursed a grudge against that fellow and his whole species.

But at the moment, something more than the old grudge was working. "Mr. Ford," I said, cutting straight into the middle of a rapturous description of the sun-flecked coral beaches and deep booming

surf on his South Sea islands, "I'm kinda curious
about something. Why of all the books around this
place does any guy on a nice, pleasant day choose this
particular one?" I had picked up the open copy of
Machiavelli's "Prince" from the table where I had
seen him lay it.

Ford's grey eyes looked sharply at mine, accepting
the challenge.

"If you've read it," he said with a shrug, "there's
no need to ask that question. If you haven't, I might
suggest there are great chunks of political wisdom
in it."

"As for instance this one peculiar little passage?"

I pointed to the page at which he had left it and
with a growing sense of distrust, I now read aloud
from a recently underscored passage:

" (It is) offtimes necessitated for the preservation
of his state that he (the prince) do things inhuman,
uncharitable and irreligious, and therefore, it is
convenient his mind be always at his command, and
flexible to all the puffs and variations of fortune;
not forbearing to be good whilst it is in his
choice, *but knowing how to be evil when there is a
necessity.*"

I looked up at Ford significantly. "Shall I go on?"

"Suit yourself" he said coldly. I read on, a con-
temptuous note in my voice.

"A prince then is to have particular care that nothing falls from his mouth but what is full of the fine
quality aforesaid, and that to see and hear him he
appears all goodness, integrity, humanity and religion, which last he ought to pretend to more than
ordinary, because . . ."

I left off abruptly for the simple reason that Ford, pale in the face, had snatched the book from my hand.

"I get the drift of your damned insinuation now." He planted himself squarely before me. "Listen here, if you, like half the rest of your confounded newspaper tribe, think I've had anything to do with Steve Wyndham's end, you better get to hell out of here. I've had five drinks and I've a gun in my pocket. Do you understand?"

Lynn gave a startled cry and rushed to my side, but I wasn't shot just yet.

"Steady Lynn. Clear out for a few minutes like a dear." I looked meaningly at Ford. "I don't think your irate guest wants any more bloodshed. He's just got a load on his mind. It's making him peevish."

Lynn looked beseechingly at Ford. "I wish you'd give me that gun." Without once relaxing his expression, Ford took an automatic out of the pocket of his white flannels and threw it carelessly on a tiled topped table which stood nearby.

"Now! If there is any shooting around here we'll start off even."

Lynn heaved a sigh of relief and went out into the garden. Left alone, Ford's stony expression underwent a swift change.

"Look here. I hadn't intended to open my mouth without due advice of counsel, but you goad a fellow to it." He smiled affably. "Shall we sit down?"

Inwardly I thought the transition from the thunder of his outburst to this tone of easy going confidence was too sudden, too suspiciously sudden, in fact. Whatever assets Ford had, one that he certainly lacked was poise. He started uncertainly.

"I'm going to tell you briefly what I know of this mess about Wyndham, but I advise you not to interrupt me. I'm doing a fool thing to talk to you at all, and if you give me time to think I may change my mind.

"First and foremost, get one thing clear. I have absolutely no knowledge as to how Steve met his end. He and I were about as thick as two men could be. We've been friends since the time we were at Yale. I knew all the snarls in his family life and sympathized. I knew, or thought I knew, all the ins and outs of his affairs in the sporting world, the social world, the financial world. The only thing I never knew, and no one else did either, was what Steve was going to do next. However, that's aside from the point.

"When I saw him last, we had been down here on a holiday. I was in for some hard work in the Spring, expecting to do a big write-up on the racketeer situation and I was glad for the chance to play. Furthermore, and this is something I'd like to keep out of this story but I guess it's what is called a contributory factor, I had just met the young lady who has since become my wife, and in the varnacular, I was hard hit. I think that in part accounts for my crazy, insane, mad oblivion to everything that was actually up those days. The only comforting reflection is that Steve was in pretty much the same shape himself at the time.

"I remember on the very day, that has since become so momentous in connection with Steve's end, Miss Devereux had arrived in Havana. Until that happened, I had actually planned to be in on the now momentous poker game that was scheduled for that night. It's too bad I wasn't there. But those things are fate, I guess.

"When Steve came in from golfing that afternoon, he'd been out with Meenan and Lamar and Brady, I think. I still have a mental picture of myself doing a nose dive into my best white flannels, and Steve walking up and down the floor as though very much perturbed and undecided about something. He was looking unusually grave.

"I remember at one point he stopped pacing the floor and said abruptly: 'Red'—that was what he always called me—'I've got something important to spill to you.' I think I answered offhand. 'Can it, old man. Ten minutes ago, Kay phoned that she's in town.' Steve turned without a word, and went on into his room to take a shower.

"I finished dressing and was on the point of a hasty exit when Lamar dropped by for a few minutes chat. I never was less hospitable to anyone, but at that, despite the difference in age and everything, he's a regular fellow you know, and he gathered something was up and let me run along.

"I was with Miss Devereux from that hour until shortly after midnight. When I came back to my rooms . . ."

"I beg your pardon," I said coolly, breaking into the middle of Ford's story, "would you mind telling me where you spent the time?"

Ford looked at me searchingly. "We had cocktails and went dancing at the Almendares Grill. Later we debated dressing for dinner and, since it looked as though it was going to rain, we compromised instead on a quiet informal supper for two at the Casino."

"Is there anyone besides your wife and yourself who could testify to that?"

"I'm afraid not. There are times when two's company you know!"

"Well, go ahead!"

"As I was saying, when I got back to my rooms it looked like pandemonium had broken loose. Steve was gone and everyone was speculating how and why and everything else under the sun. At first, I was as puzzled as the rest for there were certain elements I didn't like. One thing was the matter of my inner door being locked and my outer unlocked in a way altogether contrary to our custom. Some of the bunch tried kidding me about this, saying after all I didn't really know what I was doing these days. But I did know about those doors, that's sure, and I would have stuck it out on that point until it was cleared, had I not found this note from Steve under a whiskey bottle on my bureau."

Ford took a folded paper from his jacket and handed it over to me. It was written on Sevilla Biltmore stationery. I read what was evidently Wyndham's last note.

Something has arisen with regard to Carol. In consequence am leaving at around twelve to-night. If for any reason you don't hear from me within the next week or so, settle up my bill here, have my things packed and checked over at the Biltmore Yacht Club. Also, if any emergency turns up in business, attend to it as per always. Thanks and s'long!

Steve.

I gave the note back to Ford, saying simply, "Well?"

"Well! There's not much more to relate, sad to say. I killed two weeks around Havana without once getting any word from Steve. Then very carefully I followed his instructions, sent his bags over to the Yacht Club and hied myself back to New York, and straight into one of the toughest magazine assignments I ever tackled."

"No sign of life from Wyndham all this while?"

"Absolutely none, nor as I saw it was there any reason for any. I was conversant with all his affairs and he knew he could trust me to muddle through somehow in the emergencies. Also, he had plenty of cash with him when we were in Cuba, and a very sizable letter of credit to fall back on.

"Furthermore, and try to keep this in mind, I was working like mad on my own account just then and conducting a pretty dizzy courtship in my off-hours."

"Yes," I said good-naturedly. "You made all the newspapers sore as hell marrying so quietly in November."

"That's neither here nor there!" Ford answered unsociably. "The point is I was some three thousand miles away on what was supposed to have been a honeymoon when this damned news breaks that Steve's disappeared or been murdered or something."

"Jesus, hadn't you begun to think so, yourself?"

"No."

"Not even a suspicion all this while?"

"No." Then Ford quieted down a bit. "In all that while only one thing did strike me queer. Along about July, on a steaming hot day when I was dashing over to the Plaza for an appointment with Miss Devereaux, I ran straight into—er—er—the very girl whom Steve had been so stewed up about all year."

"Cut out the riddles!" I broke into Ford's story. "We know the girl in the case was Barton Dunlap's wife."

Ford shrugged. "All right then. I was shocked at the change in Mrs. Dunlap. She'd always been lovely in a sort of magazine cover way. Wonderful light hair! Violet blue eyes! Everything in fact that should entitle a girl to a life of gardenias and ease. But on this occasion there was an air of indefinable worry in her face that I hated to see. Furthermore, I had an idea she was dressed a little shabbier than I'd ever known her to be. She was generally awfully stunning, you know.

"We exchanged the usual pleasantries in short order. She mentioned she'd just returned from getting her divorce in Paris. Then suddenly she sprang her neat little bombshell.

" 'How's Steve getting along?'

"My jaw dropped. 'I'd supposed you knew more about that than I did!'

"She shook her head and looked away.

" 'No. Steve and I are about quits, I think. Something or other happened; what's the difference what? I had to leave for Paris a good deal earlier than I had planned. . . .' She spoke hurriedly. 'You know, my sister and I sank nearly every cent we had in a bad sugar speculation. Of course, I had rather expected to see Steve in Pinar del Rio before I left.'

She smiled gamely. Then abruptly she turned her head away.

"I took her hand for I saw her eyes were wet. I remember saying rather awkwardly, 'You've got me guessing, Carol. I know you don't need me to tell you what Steve thinks of you. However, I can any day you want.'

" 'Let's forget all that,' she answered quietly.

" 'Will you come up to my office some time soon? I'd like to have a talk.'

" 'Maybe.'

"We said goodbye. For five minutes I speculated idly on what their smashup could have been about and what-the-devil had so suddenly changed Steve's plans when I knew for a fact, that at the time he left his note, he was expecting to see her. Then I met Miss Devereux and—well, that was that!"

Hugh D. Ford stretched himself out again in the big easy chair and seemed to rest content. I decided he was a callous egg. Just the same, I enjoyed watching him. There's a sort of magnetic something about these mortals who think they've pulled themselves up to the very heights of life.

After a moment or so, I said, "I'd give a damned lot to talk to your friend Mrs. Dunlap just now."

Ford's answer was a surprise.

"You might reach her at 'El Mirasol.' That's her sister's plantation down near Pinar del Rio. It happens I radioed both to her and to Phillip Brady to meet me down here in Cuba without delay."

"Good work!" Pause. "There's nothing further you could add that might help us?"

"Nothing."

"I don't suppose you ever thought to enquire as to whether Wyndham had drawn on his letter of credit or bank balance since the time he blew out."

"Not until this damned news broke. Since then, I've been keeping the radio apparatus hot."

"With what result?"

"One curious one. Not a penny of Steve's bank balance or his letter of credit has been touched since the beginning of last February. That has me worried. It suggests there may be something in this damned talk."

"H'm. Since you've arrived in Havana did you think to check up on his baggage?"

"Yes. That was the first thing I did. Every item of his stuff is exactly as I left it. The whole thing's got me guessing. It's blamed queer!"

Queer? That put it mildly. There was a silence in the room broken only by the lazy droning of the dragon flies and insects in the garden. Somewhere on the verandah outside I heard a footstep, I didn't know whose. Hugh D. Ford picked up his Planters Punch and drained off the liquid from the melting ice in the bottom.

"Er—I hate to bring a personal matter up," I broke out at length, "but what of that fifty thousand dollars you drew from Wyndham's account at Manning and Wilson's?"

Ford sat forward and ran his fingers through his mop of red hair. He looked ridiculously embarrassed. "I thought we'd come to that. Well, get this! And it's not for publication, you understand. I drew that money as a loan to save the last of Carol Dunlap's holdings. I did it without her realizing the source of the money, knowing perfectly well that Steve would have wanted me to act so and that had he been there, he would have offered fifty times that much. Now do you see?"

I was about to answer when suddenly I heard a cynical laugh in the doorway. Looking in that direction, to my utter amazement, I met the now familiar gaze of Parson Charles Stone. He watched my surprise with cool indifference.

"If you believe that!" Stone nodded meaningly toward Ford, his eternal smirk spreading over his face. "Ask your red-headed friend, just what he was doing with a hotel room down the same corridor as his own, on the night of February 13th? It's an interesting little point I'd forgotten to mention in our talk back in New York!"

At this seemingly simple remark, Ford's face went purple with rage and his hand clenched.

"You crumby hoboe, you . . ." he began and lurched forward to strike.

But Stone dodged swiftly. Once more safe behind the grilled door, he called back sarcastically. "So sorry to have bothered you. I just dropped out here in hope of finding Mr. Alcott."

Then we heard his footsteps hurrying down the gravel path.

Chapter XXI

THE LADY IN THE CASE

SOME explanation was due from Ford there and then, but before I knew it he was out of the door and down the gravel path after Stone. I remember pacing up and down Lamar's living room, trying with fierce energy to fit the various odds and ends of this insane puzzle into some plausible picture. But it seemed futile. Nothing made sense. Nothing seemed logical. Two and two added up to eight, to thirteen, to fifty! I poured myself a drink.

After a while, and I hardly knew how long, Lynn came in the door. She looked flushed and warm, and with the perversity that rules all such occasions, I noticed her shoe lacing was coming untied.

"Well, thank the Lord! *You're* still here!" she broke out.

"Sure thing."

"Mr. Ford just phoned to excuse himself for his abrupt departure. Said his wife was waiting or something. I should leave a message for him at the Yacht Club as soon as Uncle Fred returns."

"Well, if I'm not a son of a gun!"

"What's the matter?"

"Nothing. Only an orthodox devil on trial would know better than hand out that line of bunk."

"What's up?"

"Wish to God I knew. I'll be seeing you this evening, honey."

"Well, I should hope so."

She blew me a kiss.

But even so, I slung down the road, hot and out of temper. My first impulse was to corner Ford. Then I thought better of the idea.

The day was superb, blue skies, wisps of clouds, the gulf stretching itself jade colored and serene off toward the untroubled horizon. Ford could wait. By good luck, I found a taxi.

"The nearest airport and pronto!"

Blankness complete and impenetrable.

"Airplane. Zoom! Up! Sabes?"

I made signs. The man smiled.

At five that afternoon, on the outskirts of Pinar del Rio, I found myself driving into the grounds of "El Mirasol." Obviously, the place had known better days. Its coral stucco gates were fading. The dusty white road that wound up to the main house was in bad need of repairs. Large portions of the building seemed too old to hold themselves erect any longer under the intense tropical sun and looked almost on the point of sagging. Just the same, some inexplicable air of charm was running rampant. Was it the tangled profusion of boganvillia, and oleanders, of hibiscus and palms? I wasn't sure.

Inside a piano was playing:

"Alone . . . alone, with the sky of Romance above!
Alone . . . alone, on a night that was meant for Love!
Oh there must be someone waiting,
Who feels the way I do. . . ."

I rang the bell. Somewhere far off a dog barked. The door was opened promptly by a Cuban boy in white ducks.

"Has Mrs. Carol Sutherland Dunlap arrived?"

The piano playing ceased. I heard someone walking across the floor.

"I'm Mrs. Dunlap."

I found myself looking at a slender young woman who was so disconcertingly pretty, that had I been ten years younger I would have promptly forgotten what I'd intended to say. However, feeling just then like a contemporary of Methuselah's, I forgot only half of it.

"I've come a good way to talk to you," I said as disarmingly as I knew how. Then I proceeded to introduce myself and tell her of the mission that had brought Pete Alcott and me adventuring to Havana.

Mrs. Dunlap looked at me with unfeigned curiosity.

"Perhaps you had better come in," she said with quiet dignity. She led the way back into a sort of conservatory where the piano stood. I noticed she had on a pale blue tennis dress. It did nice things to her hair and eyes and the sunlight streaming through the latticed windows did the rest.

"I'm not going to beat about the bush, Mrs. Dunlap. I'm here because we're trying our darnedest to unravel this Wyndham tangle and we need your assistance badly on a few side points." I hesitated and looked at her closely. "That is, if the whole matter isn't too painful to you."

To my surprise, Mrs. Dunlap looked unmoved.

"It's not painful at all." Her head went up

proudly. "That is, not now." There was a pause. "What do you wish to know?"

"It's beastly awkward having to ask you. Do you mind if I'm intimate, personal and impertinent, for a few minutes?"

Mrs. Dunlap smiled. "I'll try to endure it." She selected a cigarette from the box on the piano and offered me one likewise.

"You have my word the matter will be entirely confidential." I stopped short. It's always difficult to talk to a pretty woman about an affair which you know was unhappy. In addition to which her Irish terrier had just come in and was bounding all over the place. "Were you and Stephen Wyndham ever engaged?"

Mrs. Dunlap smiled at me. "I was still a married woman at the time Mr. Wyndham—disappeared."

"I know that. What I mean is . . . ?"

But Mrs. Dunlap didn't give me a chance to finish. Her eyes looked amused, and faintly incredulous.

"Are you tactfully trying to decide whether any uncertainty about me could have led to the situation which so tragically arose?"

"Yes. I'd like to eliminate that as a possibility."

"You can," she said quietly. "Mr. Wyndham had no reason to doubt for a moment that I cared for him, nor that I would have married him the moment I was free."

I began to like Mrs. Dunlap's candor almost as much as her profile. "You're a straight shooter," I said with admiration. "Now for the next point. On February 13th, we understand that Wyndham received word that you were leaving for Paris sooner than you expected. Is that true?"

"Yes. I phoned him directly at his hotel. We had had some silly little misunderstanding prior to that. The usual nonsense. This once I threw ceremony overboard and explained that I would be leaving the following day. It happened at that time I was in very troubled waters, financially."

"What was his attitude?"

"Oh, I didn't mention finances."

"No, I meant about your leaving?"

"He wanted to come down to Pinar del Rio at once."

"Why didn't he?"

"I explained there was an endless amount of packing and a lot of people around the place, and it would be one or two at least before I could finish up. I told him my preference would be for him to come down early the following morning. I think I even implied it would mean a great deal to me to see him."

"What did he say?"

Abruptly Mrs. Dunlap got up from the piano bench on which she had been seated and crossed to the window. She ran her hand absently through her light gold bob. I couldn't decide if she was disturbed by her recollections or by my question. After a while she turned around and faced me frankly.

"I *thought* he said he would come. Afterwards, when I neither saw nor heard from him I was sure I had been mistaken. I was indignant with myself for having made the overture. I had no intention of playing 'Poor Butterfly' to his, or any man's whims. I made up my mind to put him out of my thoughts completely and irrevocably. For ten months I went around being bitter and cynical and disillusioned in the approved fashion. I think I even went in for heartlessness on the grand scale."

She smiled a little sadly, her violet blue eyes looking directly into mine. Mentally I computed that a few looks like that could do as much damage as a flask of cold poison, a machine gun or a dash of T.N.T. At the same time, I decided that I'd better be quitting these southern latitudes.

And suddenly and inexplicably the grim tragedy of Wyndham's end smote me anew. The very softness and sweetness of this woman standing opposite me; the warm, lush breeze that came in fitfully through the window, the rich vibrancy and promise of life all about, and the strange unlucky chance that cut a young man off in his thirty-fourth year . . . for causes still unknown!

Mrs. Dunlap's voice was low, tremulous as she proceeded. "You can image how I felt when some weeks ago the newspapers first began printing rumors that Mr. Wyndham had disappeared."

I nodded sympathetically, wondering withal if there wasn't a little more comfort in knowing, once and for all, that your lover was dead and faithful rather than alive and roving. However, Mrs. Dunlap's perturbation didn't seem to bear me out.

"May I ask what you did when you learned this?"

She looked at me helplessly.

"What could I do?"

Our acquaintance being so recent, I was unable to rush gallantly to the breach as I would have liked to have done. Besides which, Carol Dunlap was so unutterably lovely, I doubted seriously if she could have done anything, even had she so wanted. Somehow, it seemed to me, that would have been expecting just too much.

But no matter what my inward reflections, I had come to Pinar del Rio primarily on business.

"We have learned that your former husband was appraised of the fact that you expected to see Wyndham on the morning of the 14th. Was it through you?"

"Yes," she said in a low voice, "after the papers began hinting at some terrible mystery in connection with Mr. Wyndham's silence, I went to see Mr. Dunlap."

I looked at her narrowly. "Did you think it possible that Barton Dunlap was implicated in the crime?"

Suddenly Mrs. Dunlap sat up. Her cheeks were flushed, but I noticed she kept herself perfectly in hand. A faint shadowy smile hovered about her lips. Her tone was one of firm decision.

"You're a pleasant enough person but you do ask the most troublesome questions. Please understand me. I went to see Barton Dunlap for reasons of my own. And now if you'll excuse me, I really must dress for dinner. It's growing late."

She moved toward the door. Like a jack-in-the-box, I jumped out of my chair and stalked after her. "Would it delay dinner too long if I inquired first if you ever received a loan of $50,000 from Hugh Ford?"

Carol Dunlap paused a moment and her eyes opened wide in surprise.

"Did *he* tell you that?"

"You're not answering me, and I regret to say you may have to answer that publicly before we're finished."

Again she gave me that faint shadowy smile.

"That may be. But just now I really must be going upstairs."

Thoughtfully I looked after her as she crossed to the door. At the threshold she paused uncertainly.

"Forgive me, Mr. Ellis, if I seem unobliging. I see, we can't talk after all. There's too much that needs explanation. Goodbye and good luck to you, and your friend!"

Her voice suddenly broke. She turned quickly away and in another instant she was gone.

For a few moments, I stood irresolutely where she left me. From the first landing I thought I heard a stifled sob. Self-conscious, feeling like an interloper for the first time in all my years as a reporter, I quickly turned and left the house.

When I was racing back by plane to Havana that evening I took myself very thoroughly in hand. It was the only thing I could do. Twilight had fallen and the whir of the motors was too deafening to permit conversation with anyone but one's self.

"Now look here old man. You've seen enough in your day to know better than to confound the outward aspect of guilelessness with the genuine article. As for these pretty faces! Bah! Remember your old primer work. The light that lies in a woman's eyes can lie very ably upon occasion. Don't be taken in by this Carol Dunlap. She's probably phony."

To which some instinct within me made answer, "Aw, quit talking like a simp. That gal's been through hell, but she's on the level or I'll eat my hat!"

Chapter XXII

A VERY UNUSUAL
APPOINTMENT

B Y the time I reached Havana, it was long past
eight o'clock and the city was rousing itself
from the warm languor of the day for its plunge into
nocturnal gaiety. Even from far off I could discern
the colored lanterns on her many roof gardens, and
see the searchlights of the taller buildings threading
their way among the stars. But to all the siren call of
pleasure I was deaf at the time.

Through the friendly offices of a young Cuban of
the airport I succeeded in calling our hotel.

"Ask if Mr. Peter Alcott has come in," I begged
him.

After an interminable time the answer came back
in the negative.

"Has there been any message left for Mr. Ellis?"

"No."

In desperation, I had my new friend try Police
Headquarters. But there, though we explained in
minute detail my connection with the press, and
patiently waited a very long time, we had no better
luck. As the young man was about to ring off, I
thought to have him enquire whether Señor José
Sanchez and his wife had yet been released.

Five minutes, ten minutes elapsed while we held on. At last:

"Señor Sanchez and his wife are being held in custody in connection with the murder of the American, Stephen Wyndham."

"Wha—at!" I caught my breath and managed to stammer. "On whose warrant?"

Another lengthy silence.

My young friend at the airport shook his head and smiled. "You make things move queeker, up in the States, isn't it so?" He turned back to the phone.

"Eh. . . . *Que?*"

There was a rapid fire of Spanish conversation and the young man looked at me in bewilderment.

"It is a little difficult to understand. It seems under private cross-examination the stories of Señor and Señora de Sanchez do not quite tally."

"Well . . . I'll be . . . damned. . . ."

I thanked the young man and moved on into the night. My thoughts were reeling. Despite my own suspicions up to this time, now that the charge was actually filed, I couldn't quite believe it. Too many tangled skeins! I pulled out my little black memo book and looked again at the long list of questions that had accumulated there from the start of the case. The last few alone kept me guessing, especially in the light of this latest development.

What was the significance of Pete's questions to the doorman at the Sevilla Biltmore? Of that sailor's answer to his ad? What sinister purpose kept Stone shadowing us day and night? What of Ford's unexplained presence in that hotel room on the night of

Wyndham's disappearance? And his lack of a real alibi?

I would have given a hundred dollars flat for the chance to buttonhole Pete at that moment and to thrash out some of the major complexities of the situation with him. I was agog to hear what had occurred that afternoon at headquarters and perhaps, even more eager to spill my own adventures to him. But rack my brains though I did, I could think of no place to reach Pete.

So it was with an entirely clear conscience that at last I hailed a cab and drove out to Calle Paseo 32 to keep my appointment with Lynn.

By the time I arrived at Judge Lamar's residence, Lynn had almost given me up for lost. But though she treated me to a fine imitation of dejection I could see she had been playing, with clear-headed vigor, at a game of Russian bank laid out before her on the table. She caught my glance at the empty place opposite hers.

"Oh, Uncle Fred got back this afternoon!"

At that moment the Judge himself came into the room. He was looking a little tired but I noticed he had acquired a good coat of tan for his three days' outing. He greeted me with all his usual affability.

"I hear you fellows have been having a good bit of excitement around here since I've been away."

"Rather. Did Lynn tell you the latest?"

Lamar nodded, tolerant and amused. "Yes. I've been trying all evening to reach Ford at the Yacht Club. He's not there."

"And I've a kind of feeling he won't be!" I said glumly.

Judge Lamar looked at me with a quizzical smile that wrinkled the little crows feet in the corners of his eyes.

"Why do you say that?"

"Something came out this afternoon that Ford didn't count on!"

Lamar picked up the deck of cards from the table. For a few moments he shuffled them as though undecided. When he spoke it was with a kind of quiet, mellow wisdom.

"If you want an unsolicited opinion, young man, I think you're dead wrong. Hugh Ford may be a hot-headed temperamental son-of-a-gun but my guess is he's straight. You fellows are letting this business get on your nerves." His face brightened suddenly. "You ought to try landing a sailfish now and then."

I forced a smile. "That doesn't help solve this case."

"Well, does this?" Lamar looked at me directly. "When I came in this afternoon Calvin Watts was waiting here. The boy looked white and haggard. I don't believe he'd slept in days. He said he'd just seen Ford, Dunlap and also Phil Brady, who had apparently been dragged down here from the coast. Then he sat down and begged me to go over with him every detail of that night in Wyndham's rooms. He was groping, he was frantic—for the tiniest minutiae of detail. He wrote out lists of those who had been drinking, of those who had been smoking, where the money was stacked, where the cigarettes, cigars, matches and whiskey each stood. His eyes had a strained, peculiar look in them. Suddenly he got up. 'It's what I've been saying all day,' he said in a curious, tense voice. 'It's the question of those matches that solves this crime.' He looked startled. He looked ghastly. He said goodnight and rushed out. I'll frankly confess I was worried about him. If I were well enough acquainted here in Havana to have known a good doctor, I would not have allowed that boy to walk home alone."

"Jesus! He didn't expect to walk, did he?" I said, in surprise.

Judge Lamar nodded. "He said it would soothe him."

I turned to Lynn laughingly. "There's a moral to the Judge's story. What do you say to going dancing with me before I pull a brainstorm or start writing editorials or go generally haywire?"

*   *   *

For a long time afterward, that evening with Lynn remained impressed on my mind. It wasn't that it was the last halcyon spell that preceded the storm, a final hour of tranquillity before a series of events that were to shake us like some convulsive nightmare. No, the hold of that night in my memory was Lynn's alone. She was sweeter than I ever remembered her. Sweeter, softer and inexplicably nearer. I remember the orchestra kept playing "Siboney," and "Spanish Love," with plaintive persistence. I remember that the strongest bachelor's resolve was almost wilted.

When I reached our room that night it was long past two o'clock. The air was hot and sultry. I rather expected to have to tiptoe across the porch, and noise-lessly slip into bed, but to my surprise half-way across the garden I saw a yellow patch of electric light in our window.

Inside I found Pete pacing up and down the floor. I noticed he was fully dressed except for his coat, which in an excess of impatience, warmth or what you will, had been flung across the bed. For some inscrutable reason he looked worried and harassed. His face was pallid with shadows. His grey hair was rumpled. An absent-minded nod and "hello" were the only salutations I got out of him.

"What's up?"

For answer he crossed to the bureau and picked up a note.

"Read that!"

Something in his tone aroused my curiosity. I glanced at the hastily penned letter. The envelope was addressed jointly to Pete and to me. The note was short.

Must see you tonight without fail. Have discovered something of gravest importance in connection with Wyndham's end. Will return to your hotel at one o'clock sharp. If you are not in, will wait.

Calvin Watts.

I looked up at Pete as I finished.

"No sign of him yet?"

"No!" he answered in a strained, staccato way. "And I've been back here since twelve."

"That's funny." Then I proceeded to impart to Alcott what Judge Lamar had told me of Watt's condition earlier in the evening. Alcott listened to me with absorbed attention.

"The Judge told you Watts had already seen Ford,

Dunlap and Phillip Brady?" Alcott repeated the names with emphasis as though he was mentally checking the list.

"I just finished telling you that."

"And Stone?"

"Lamar didn't mention him. But Watts may have seen him for all that."

Alcott relaxed into a grin, his first that evening.

"He would have if he'd been around Police Headquarters, that's sure. The bird was waiting for me when I came out. Only luckily I saw him first."

"Good Lord! What *is* he up to?"

"God only knows. Get on with your story. You were saying Watts looked like hell and acted worse."

"Yes." I spared Pete no detail. By the time I reached the point in Judge Lamar's story where Watts was supposed to have jumped up with his crazy exclamation that it was the question of the matches that solved the crime, Alcott crossed over to me and grasped me roughly by the shoulder.

"Look here, Johnny. For God's sake! No clowning now! You're dead sure that's exactly what he said?"

"Sure thing." I looked at Alcott with genuine surprise. His chin was set tensely and I noticed the muscles in his face were working with suppressed excitement. "What's up?"

"Nothing. Still—I'm worried. Damnably so! Ring for the night man. It's just possible that Watts may be waiting somewhere in the lobby."

I rang. But the night man's advent seemed interminable. Meanwhile to kill time, I poured out to Pete the story of my afternoon's adventures. During most of my account Alcott stood in the doorway, peering out into the night, watching, waiting the arrival of the porter. I was beginning to think my whole account a mad waste of breath, when he turned around to me, the old flicker of interest alight in his eye.

"What was that Charles Stone said about Ford?"

I repeated Stone's curious statement. "He said, 'Ask your friend what he was doing with a room down the same corridor as his own on the night of February 13th?'"

Alcott ran his hand through his hair. "H'm," he said, as though thinking aloud. "I'd like to know the answer to that one myself."

"Aw! Suppose you talk to him directly. You may get further than I."

Alcott made no reply.

"And while we're on that, you lazy bum! Don't you think it about time you took a crack at a few of our leads directly. You haven't talked to a single damned one as yet—excepting old Miss Isabella."

Alcott turned around with a sudden smile.

"She was *enough!*" He paused abruptly, his smile died and a hard note crept in his voice. "I'll see them all, but in my own good time."

The porter's arrival at that moment cut us short. He was a scrawny, blinky-eyed old fellow, whose repose had obviously been interrupted by our ring. Briefly, peremptorily, Alcott directed him to search the main lounge for an American gentleman who might be waiting there for us, and to bring the man to us with all possible speed. The night man nodded and shuffled off into the darkness.

After that the minutes dragged by as though

weighted. From time to time Alcott turned on me with a barrage of seemingly irrelevent questions about Stone, Mrs. Dunlap and Ford. But for the most part he paced the floor, abstracted and moody, ten fathoms deep in his own reflections. Up and down! Up and down! Up and down! There was a feverish unrest in his manner.

Drugged by the monotony of his footsteps, and the humid warmth of the night I became gradually aware that I was very tired. With increasing wistfulness I began looking at my open bed. I felt a simple old-fashioned yearning to turn in.

"Aw, Jesus! Pete," I said, when I could struggle no longer. "There isn't a chance of that Watts guy turning up any more tonight. Maybe you're not wise to it, but at this moment it's precisely ten minutes past three." I aimed my remark as a plain little homespun statement of fact.

Its effect on Alcott was amazing to observe. He wheeled around as though he had been struck.

"Ten past three!" he said, in a flat, incredulous tone. "I'd no idea!" For a moment he stood looking at me like a man who was seeing ghosts or hearing voices. Then he strode across to the bed and picking up his coat, he shouldered into it like an automaton.

"What a fool I've been! What a complete damned fool!" he kept repeating under his breath. "I should have known."

At the door, the night porter suddenly appeared, his taciturn solitary presence looming out of the darkness and announcing to us more clearly than words that his search had failed. I gave him some change and waved him away.

Alcott stood rooted in his steps, running his hand through his hair nervously. "God! Sometimes brute logic is as dangerous as brute force. Don't sit there staring, Johnny!" He gave a humorless laugh. "There's something horrible afoot. Something devilish. Like 'when church yards yawn and hell itself breathes out contagion to this world.' Good God! Why didn't we foresee this?"

To see a person of habitual reserve shaken by intense emotion is an arresting phenomenon to say the least. Galvanized, I sat bolt upright unable to take my eyes from him.

He was moving with swift decision now. From under his bed he pulled his old grip. I watched him open it, and take from a small compartment in the side, a revolver whose presence I had never once suspected heretofore.

"What the devil's eating you?" I burst out, as I saw him slip the gun into his pocket.

Alcott turned to me, his face set and grim. He rubbed his hand across his eyes convulsively.

"Grab your hat and come along, Johnny," he said, almost fiercely. "Calvin Watts won't be coming here tonight. What's more I've an awful hunch he won't be going anywhere for a long, long time."

Chapter XXIII

A SHOT IN THE NIGHT

A FEW moments later Alcott and I were jumping into a taxicab.

"Almandares Hotel!" Pete commanded almost hoarsely. "And *veloz!* pronto!"

The night was black and intolerably warm, despite the fact that a fine drizzle had begun to fall and the wind was rising.

On our drive Alcott hardly spoke a word, but as the street lamps whizzed by, I could see that his face had lost none of its strained, tense look.

We turned in the driveway of the Almandares grounds, and immediately I became aware that something unusual was up. Just ahead, between the smooth trunked palm trees, there was the gleam of lanterns, and the flash of searchlights. Out of the rain loomed dark forms trampling the grass and examining the shrubbery and trellises.

Alcott sat forward. Under his breath I heard him mutter, "Too late! Good God! I was afraid so!" He ordered the driver to stop and in three strides he had joined a knot of men who were standing in shivering curiosity near the roadway.

"What became of the body?" he demanded so peremptorily that I found myself starting. For a moment the cluster of men stared blankly at each other and at him. Then, as happens in almost every Cuban group, some one of the party understood English and stepping aside, he bowed and answered us in a low voice.

"They moved him away in an ambulance over an hour ago."

Alcott swallowed. Neither I, nor anyone else could have been sure of what he said. I caught something that sounded oddly like "fiend" and then the next thing I knew he'd stalked off and left me.

When I caught up to him, he was in the thick of the wet, bedraggled group of policemen, camera men, newspaper reporters and hotel employees who had all spurred hither to this focus of excitement. I saw him buttonhole a hardened old reporter from the *Havana Post* whom we had both previously met. Jeffers was the man's name. He was an American by birth and a funny, shabby little fellow with bad teeth and worse hair.

"Over there! Mr. Alcott!" The man was saying with excitement. "Look! You can still see the blood in spite of all this infernal rain!"

I followed the direction of his outstretched hand, where the ground, despite the now sudden and torrential downpour, was still darkly stained with gore. A shiver of apprehension went down my spine. It comes back over me again as I think of that scene. The circle of grave sombre faces, lit by the occasional flashes of lightning and the dim glow from the lanterns, the wind moaning like a soul in distress through the tall palm trees, the flower-bordered hotel path, and there in the center, that crimson tell-tale pool of blood.

As in a dream I heard Jeffers talking: "It appears the poor guy was walking peacefully up to his hotel when his assailant shot at him from behind that bush!" He nodded off a half dozen paces.

"Were you there?" Alcott asked with a flare of interest.

"Nope. But there were footsteps behind there, that is before this rain started coming down. And then the body was lying in a way to suggest it."

"I see," Alcott said gravely. "At what time was all this?"

"Sometime past twelve. We fix the hour largely on the advice of the doctor who came along with the ambulance."

"No one heard the shot?"

"Oh, yes! Shortly after twelve the night clerk and some of the guests heard a report off on the grounds. However, they paid no attention to it. So many cars backfire these days. They just set it down to that!"

"Too bad!" I broke out. "A little promptness and they might have tracked the criminal."

"I doubt it," Alcott said with weary emphasis. Then he turned back to Jeffers. "Who discovered the body?"

"Two of the hotel guests. It seems, they were coming in from a party some time after one, and saw, or thought they saw some unusual bulk over here in the shadows. They stopped to investigate. Ten minutes later the night clerk was phoning for police, first aid and all the rest of the works! It was then I hopped out here!"

"Funny, no one noticed the body before then."

"Well, the grounds are rather deserted at night,

you know, and the poor guy seems to have picked out a pretty dark spot in which to keel over."

"It's ghastly."

"It's got me beat. The man's watch and wallet were left untouched so there's not even a good, old-fashioned theft to pin it to!" Jeffers turned up his coat collar and looked slantwise at the heavens. "Zowie! Did you ever see such a downpour?"

I never had. The rain was teeming. I felt rivulets descending my back, dripping from my hat, seeping into my shoes. "Good God! let's move under cover!"

Of a sudden, the wind had come up with tropical force, beating the vines and bushes this way and that, howling through the tops of the palm trees. Lightning licked the black sky, and the thunder seemed to crack all about us. Even before my words were out most of the crowd were scurrying this way and that for shelter.

Only Alcott seemed strangely loathe to leave the spot. His clothes were drenched. At each minute the storm was becoming more menacing, and yet it seemed as though that small rapidly disappearing pool of blood held him rooted and spellbound by its fatal secret.

When reason could put up with this situation no longer, I touched him on the arm. "Look here! you crazy sap! If you're all set for an early death, I'm not!"

With a profound sigh, Alcott shook himself out of his reverie. "Clear off, if you want. I just can't get over this confounded mess. God! I should have forseen it. That's the worst of it! Poor fellow!"

"I'm not budging from this spot till you do." I

was honestly bothered about Alcott. However, the words were hardly out when a wild gleam of lightning tore through the sky, illuminating for one blinding instant every object about us. In the crash of thunder that followed, I clutched hold of Pete's arm.

"Holy God! over there! Behind that tree trunk! Did you see what I did?"

"Stone!" he whispered between closed lips. "He's been there fifteen minutes."

"What's he up to?"

"God knows. He keeps watching us like a hawk."

I grabbed Pete by the arm in genuine earnest. I remember my voice was husky as I said, "Let's get going. There's been enough crime around here for one night!"

Pete shrugged. "Maybe this once you're right, old punk. Anyhow, that bird is beginning to give me the creeps."

We turned swiftly up the path to where the Almandares, white and still, seemed slumbering peacefully through all the wild cannonade of the storm.

A few minutes later we entered the lounge. Its polished marble floors, its cool banks of green, its dimmed lights brought a fleeting sense of serenity, but not for long. Reminders of the night's grim business were all about us, evidenced in the scattered knots of police and reporters, who, like ourselves, had taken shelter here from the storm.

Alcott made his way straight to the hotel desk, where a slender dark-eyed night clerk was regaling a group of late comers with all the gory details of the crime. In the group, I suddenly caught sight of the tall foppish figure of Barton Dunlap. He was dressed with all his usual sartorial elegance. Alcott saw him too and drawing me aside, he waited unobtrusively for the clerk to finish and the group to move away. Then without ado, Alcott produced his press card and introduced himself to the young man.

"We won't keep you a minute."

The young clerk smiled. "It's quite 'okay' as you Americans say. We do not have disturbances like this so often." His dark eyes kindled. Obviously, he was relishing the excitement.

"At what hour did you come on duty tonight?"

"At seven o'clock."

"Since your arrival has anyone called to see Mr. Calvin Watts?"

The young man hesitated. "I'm sorry. We're not at liberty to divulge. . . ."

At that moment, Alcott beckoned to a short, massive Police Inspector who had been looking over at us uncertainly.

"Didn't know I'd have need of you twice in the same day, Inspector Montara," he said laughingly. "For Christ's sake! Tell this young man he can speak freely and that we know how to hold our tongues. Oh, by the way, this is a friend of mine, Mr. Ellis."

The Police Officer's presence worked wonders. As though by miracle the night clerk's garrulity returned.

"Si! Si! There were two callers. A gentleman and a lady. Just a moment, please." He rummaged in the room box and took out a slip. "Ah! There is the message! Maybe it will help."

Alcott opened the envelope with indecent haste. Within was a short note and a strange one.

Remember my warning. The odds are all against you.
                                        Hugh Ford.

"At what time were these people here?"

"At perhaps nine o'clock! I would say."

"I see." Pause. "And this very tall fashionably dressed gentleman who was talking to you when I came up." Alcott was referring to Dunlap, of course, "Was he here earlier this evening?"

"I do not know. But he asked very many questions about the affair, so I assume he could not have been there!"

"H'm. Did Mr. Watts have any other callers during the evening?"

"I do not think so."

The police officer intervened with a broad smile. "I have checked this myself, Señor Alcott. There were neither callers nor messages."

Alcott shook his head thoughtfully and turned again to the clerk.

"Did Mr. Watts put in any phone messages during the day?"

The young man looked dubious.

Again the police officer spoke up. "I have also talked about that with the operator. There were no phone messages, Señor."

Alcott smiled and patted the officer's back. "We need you around home, Montaro. Cuba's really too cramped for your talents." He paused a moment.

"By the way, how did you leave our friend Señor Sanchez at Headquarters?"

Suddenly the inspector looked uncomfortable. He gave an embarrassed cough. "Er—er—Señor, I am very sorry to report, but in spite of everything I could say, that José Sanchez managed to get himself, how do you say it, freed on bail at ten o'clock this evening."

"Wha—at!" Alcott ejaculated in sudden interest; then, after a pause, "Did you think to have him shadowed when he left Headquarters?"

"Er—er, Señor, it so happened I was not there at the time."

Alcott let out a low whistle. "Montara," he said gravely. "You stick right here in Havana. I was mistaken in what I said a while ago. We have a thousand like you back home!" Pete lit a cigarette.

Montara looked over at me. Anyone could see he was as woebegone as a licked puppy. To ease his tension, he made a brave stab at conversation. "Very soon, you Americanos will be thinking Havana no very safe place for your little vacations, eh? First, that young Americano who get killed last year. How you call him—Wyndham? And now this young man tonight."

Alcott was blowing a series of smoke rings ceilingward. "Don't fret, Montara!" he snapped, mercilessly. "Americans in general will still be safe enough in spite of your carelessness. Anyhow, the Wyndham mess of last year and this dead man here tonight are both the work of the same cold diabolically cunning hand."

The idea took a seemingly endless time crawling

into Montara's brain. When at last it registered, he broke out in wonder.

"Señor Alcott, you really believe this?"

Alcott looked the little Inspector over coolly. "I know it."

Inspector Montara smiled and shrugged. "You right about so many things, maybe you right about this. Only one thing I know you're wrong about, Señor." Dramatically, he bided his time. "This young man who was shot tonight, you say he was killed, eh? But non, Señor. He's unconscious, si! . . . But he still have a small chance at life."

Alcott strode over and grasped Montara by the shoulder. His face was white.

"What makes you say that?"

"I got the word not ten minutes ago from the Mercedes Hospital."

When Pete turned back to me there was a strange look on his face. "Listen here, Johnny," he said with quiet decision. "We've stalled around long enough. No matter what it costs, rent Wyndham's old suite at the Sevilla Biltmore for tomorrow night. Set up a table with cards and chips. See that there are plenty of drinks on hand; and, oh yes, plenty of cigars, too. Round up every living person who was in on that damned poker party of last year. Lasso everyone else who was anywhere around. Drag them there, tie them, kidnap them, but get them there by ten o'clock sharp! We must have the old scene in every possible particular. And, oh yes! Be sure to have a couple of police on hand too! We'll need them, Johnny."

"What's the big idea!"

"A last play! Or maybe, a last tragedy."

He turned on his heel.

"Where are you off to?" I called in curiosity.

He looked back with a peculiar smile. "Sorry, but I've a kind of hankering to see that guy at the Mercedes Hospital."

PART THREE

Points Unknown

Chapter XXIV

THE ROUND-UP

WHEN I try to think back calmly and coherently on the events of the day that followed, my memory staggers, reels and despite a record of fairly dependable service this once it fails me completely. There is a confused blur of frantic phone calls, frenzied interviews, hotel authorities, Police Headquarters, infinite yards of administrative red tape, countless wearisome details and over and above all the necessity to see and to persuade into coming to Pete's absurd meeting place the six men who represented all that was left of that once strange and fateful party.

Six pretty queer men at that, I kept telling myself as I cornered each. Somehow that private verdict bolstered my nerve. And after all what else could I think of a group, who no matter what their excuses had sat by for nearly a year since that mysterious occasion when a so-called friend had vanished from their very midst into the unknown.

Needless to say I did not rely too implicitly upon their several assurances that they would meet me without fail in Room 209 of the Sevilla Biltmore Hotel at ten o'clock that night. As I left each I took care to station on watch a plainclothes man from the best Havana Agency with instructions to keep a sharp look-out and notify me promptly if by 9:30

P.M. his quarry looked as though he were heading anywhere else but to our net.

However, I could have spared myself both trouble and expense.

At ten o'clock precisely I looked around the suite that had once been Wyndham's and congratulated myself. The stage was set in every detail, from the marble topped table and wicker furniture of last year, down to the minutest particulars of ice, drinks, cigars, chips and cards. Yes, and at the last minute, by some white flash of inspiration I'd even remembered to draw the Venetian blinds.

As for the cast? Outside in the corridor, mystified but obedient, Miguel, the night attendant, took up his stand as he had almost a year ago. And inside the room, in varying attitudes of annoyance, boredom, interest or curiosity lounged the men who were once brought together by the simple bond that they all liked poker, and now by the more tenuous tie that they had all been present on the occasion of the last known appearance of Stephen P. Wyndham.

The situation was hardly conducive to ease or affability. The atmosphere seemed charged with an electrical tension. On the surface Barton Dunlap and Hugh Ford seemed chatting as nonchalantly as though their meeting were occurring on the golf links or in their club room or under any conceivable circumstances other than the present. However, out of the corner of my eye I noticed a few peculiar things. One was that Ford was smoking with nervous incessancy. The other was the phenomenon of Barton Dunlap's tie. A small thing to be sure, but puzzling withal. Because, despite all his usual sartorial correctness, his tie was on quite awry. And the color was in ghastly disharmony with the rest of his costume. Furthermore, I noticed he had already gotten away with half a bottle of brandy and was still going strong.

Judge Lamar who stood at my side noticed the latter. "Look here, Ellis!" he said with his usual air of tolerant omniscience, "better lock up your liquor, or your little party will be turning into a free-for-all souse!"

"Let it!" I said wearily. "And here we go with it!" I poured a stiff drink for the Judge and myself. As though in common impulse, we raised our glasses. "To Lynn," I said suddenly, with a change of mood.

The Judge drained his drink and reached for a chaser. "What's the big idea?" he said gravely. "I don't mind for myself, but young fellow, you'd better keep your wits about you."

"Aw, my friend Alcott will be breezing along any minute now to take charge of this show. Anyhow, I'm so damned tired, it would feel simply great to get pie-eyed drunk this once."

That was the God's truth. Furthermore, the atmosphere of that room was getting on my nerves. Across from me, Charles Stone was sitting aloof and detached, smiling at me with that everlasting sardonic smile of his. Smug and imperturbable he seemed behind the bulwark of his would-be admirable character, but never for a moment did he seem to take his eyes from me.

Nearby, glowering at us all in rage, and filling the room full of his cigar smoke, was Señor José Sanchez. Every now and then he walked sullenly down the passageway to what had been Wyndham's former room, and where, just now, Señorita Lola had been permitted to ensconce herself in a deep and moody solitude. There was something questionable about that pair. When I tried to view them, as I had the night before, as the sole key to the disappearance of Stephen Wyndham, Señor and Señora de Sanchez may have seemed a very inadequate answer to all our many complexities. But now that I actually faced them, temporarily free and at large, well—that couple bothered me more than a little. I can tell you that.

As I look back on that room, I think the only thoroughly unconcerned person present appeared to be Mr. Philip Brady of the West Coast and Fine Art Studio. I'd met him for the first time that day. Of medium height, blond in a baby-doll way, he ambled around, addressing now this person, now that, his deep blue eyes and high voice proclaiming more plainly than words ever could the fact that he was about every other inch a man. He was garrulous and amiable, telling everyone how he'd flown down from Hollywood upon the receipt of Mr. Ford's radio, how terribly upset he'd been at the first intimations that anything was amiss; how awfully impressed he'd always been with young Wyndham ever since he'd met him—oh, years ago, during a sojourn in India.

"I was just appalled about this affair! It's just too frightfully awful! We think we have occasional sensations out in Hollywood, but dear me! Dear me! When I think of this!"

By eleven o'clock, the strain of the occasion was beginning to tell on us all. Conversation petered out. An ominous silence filled the place. Pete Alcott had not turned up as yet, and minute by minute I was growing more anxious about him. Furthermore, even with a couple of police in the corridor outside, and the ordinary quota of human curiosity to back me, I began to doubt my ability to hold this ill-sorted crowd together much longer. At last, to relieve an unendurable situation I suggested we try a few hands of poker.

With varying degrees of affability the men there fell in line. The question of stakes was quickly settled. Dunlap and Ford suggested high limits. I, of necessity, had to hold them to low ones. I got the crowd to seat themselves in precisely the same positions they had occupied nearly a year ago.

At the head of the table, near the door that communicated with Ford's room, we left a vacant place, the place that had once been Wyndham's. Next to it, on the left, Barton Dunlap, moody and silent, sank his huge frame. I suggested to young Stone that he take the next chair, (the one which actually had been occupied by Watts on the ill-fated night), but Stone shook his head, and looked me over with his peculiar smile.

"I don't play cards as you well know. What's more, I'd rather look on, just as I did last year!" He paused, then added insolently, "Anyhow, don't bother about me. You better figure out what's keeping your friend, Mr. Alcott."

The fellow gave me the creeps. And then for no ascribable reason there arose in my mind's eye the image of Miss Wyndham's pale face as she had peered down at us that day from her second story window, cold and malevolent.

Stone drew up his chair behind Sanchez. Lamar and Brady took the next seats. And still there were three empty places. Grim toll of the passing year. Wyndham, Meenan and Watts! What strange dark skein of fate united those men in common destiny? I wondered. But wondering got me nowhere. Certainly, I knew that by now. Gloomily, I motioned Hugh Ford to Watts' vacant place, pulled out Meenan's chair for myself and commended to deal to a table that looked like this:

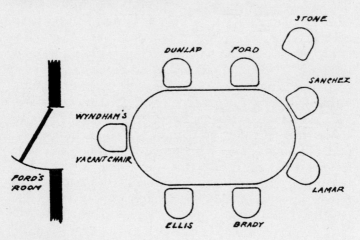

As I remember, we had played exactly three hands and were just commencing the fourth, when as I live, move, and have my being, the damn thing happened again, exactly as it was supposed to on that previous occasion, and before anyone realized what was up, the entire room went pitchy black. The lights in the corridor had failed, too, judging by the sounds outside. I couldn't figure how, or why it had all come about. It was the one grim touch that lay outside my plan and it gave me a vague sense of disquiet.

From out the Stygian darkness that engulfed me came an immediate burst of anger and exclamations of surprise. Then an instant later matches were struck, cigarette lighters flickered on and every man at that table peered about at the startled and annoyed faces of his companions around him.

"What's the big idea?" Ford broke out in a dour tone as though he held me personally responsible for the inky darkness.

But I didn't get a chance to answer. In the moment the followed, the hall door swung open and I heard Alcott's lazy drawl, "Gosh! I'm sorry to be so damned late."

As he crossed to the table within the pale range of our light I observed with surprise that he was looking especially well groomed. Fresh shirt, clothes pressed, hair slicked back, all that sort of thing. And in the same glance, I noticed, too, that he was very pale and for some unaccountable reason, deeply shaken.

Without any ado, he made his way to the vacant place at the head of the table. As he glanced around at our flickering matches and cigarette lighters he suddenly smiled as though at some entirely private joke of his own.

"Had a kind of a hunch those matches and lighters would be working more quickly this time than they were supposed to on the last memorable occasion. But it's a rather peculiar thing that this should be so." His voice was low and even. "Doesn't it strike you that way, gentlemen? Not individually, you understand. For any one person's lighter could fail him. But collectively, now! You'll admit it's really a little queer."

Every pair of eyes at the table was focussed with sudden interest on Alcott's tall, spare form as he stood there in the circle of wan, uncertain light. Over the entire scene hovered something spectral, supernatural.

The flickering of the matches threw vague shadows over Pete's face, elongating some features, throwing one scar into complete oblivion, bringing another out into high relief, making his mop of grey hair seem almost white by contrast with the gloom all about him. But it was the burning intensity of his eyes as he turned to Barton Dunlap that held my own.

"For instance with you, Mr. Dunlap!" he said in that same low, even tone. "How does it happen that you manipulate your lighter so well *now* and on that last occasion, from all accounts, it failed you so completely?"

Barton Dunlap, despite all the liquor he had consumed, looked up at him sharply. His come-back was instantaneous and heated. "If you're set on knowing, I'd loaned my lighter to one of the men."

"To whom?"

Embarrassment. "Er—I don't remember."

Alcott smiled. His eye swept the table, past Ford who was known not to have been part of the fatal poker game; past Stone, who had already avowed that he never smoked; on . . . straight to Señor Sanchez.

"And you, Mr. Sanchez? I notice you keep striking those matches against that little box in your hand.

Was it so inconvenient for you to have done that same thing when you last sat in this room?"

In an instant José Sanchez was on his feet, glowering in our direction. "I put up with enough these last two days. I no stand any more." He looked bellicose enough to give his words special force. Then suddenly, Lolita darted from out the darkness to his side and whispered something in his ear. His mood underwent a swift change. He looked with attentive interest at the man at the head of the table. Then his hands unclenched. Sullenly he said, "Why do you not make to enquire if I had the matches before you talk like this, eh?"

Alcott was nonchalant. "Because I observe that little box in your hand is a valuable one. It has your monogram and it looks as though it might be more than a year old."

"That much is true," Sanchez sourly admitted. "But on the occasion you mention I could not find this little box of matches which I keep always beside me. Only after the lights come on did I see it down on the floor."

Alcott turned to Judge Lamar. "And you, sir?"

"The same holds. I never carry a lighter, but I distinctly remember at the time of the disturbance groping about on the table for the matches that had been there, and finding *none*."

"And you, Mr. Brady?"

Meditatively, Mr. Brady's slender white hand pressed his forehead. "Well, now, let me see. Let me see! I always do carry a lighter. Not the lovely jade one I now have, to be sure. This was a recent gift from one of my stars. Charming thing, isn't it? Ah!

it's made me very happy. But let me see. I must have had another lighter with me that night. And why didn't I use it?"

"Why, indeed?"

"*You* borrowed it from me, didn't you, Judge Lamar? Ah, no! no! Now I remember it was the big gentleman on the other side of me. Yes, that Mr. Meenan."

Alcott looked Brady over with mild curiosity.

"A statement which, like most of the others here tonight we are unable to verify. But no matter. Did Mr. Meenan give your lighter back to you before you left that evening?"

"Oh, yes! As a matter of fact, I remember now. Mine was the only lighter that worked during all that dreadful darkness. I remember seeing it in Mr. Meenan's hand!"

I stirred uneasily in Meenan's chair. There was a grey hush of expectancy in the room. Tense faces! Taut nerves! Then Alcott's voice, still smooth and unruffled.

"Don't look so disturbed, gentlemen. No one can be indicted for murder, simply for failing to use his lighter at the psychological moment. It only happens that each of you willingly or unwillingly were duped that night into playing straight into the hands of the criminals within your midst."

A wave of indignant surprise swept over the group. Barton Dunlap forgot his superciliousness, Señor Sanchez his private grievance, young Stone sprang impulsively to his feet, then thinking better of his intention, subsided once more in his chair.

Only Alcott, undisturbed, went on in the same low, even tone:

"For you see, gentlemen, you all sat in on a very horrible crime that night. Under the cover of that cunningly planned darkness, within a very few feet of you, Stephen Wyndham was knocked over the head with some hard, jagged object. My theory is that he fell forward just where he sat, instantly unconscious. He may have uttered a groan at the time, for several of you in your accounts of that night have mentioned hearing some sound that could have been taken for a groan. But each of you attributed that sound to the prevalent tomfoolery. That was your error and Wyndham's very bad luck.

"While you joked and sang and laughed here in complete darkness, I've a kind of hunch, the door behind Wyndham was stealthily unlocked. Yes, this one here!" Alcott turned and threw wide open the door to the room behind him.

"There! Don't look so surprised, gentlemen. By now you surely must realize there were two men in that adjoining room all evening. Not your own set, of course. Pretty tough customers, those, I'd say. But how else do you suppose that electric light fuse was so opportunely blown? How else do you suppose Wyndham's body was so quickly and ingeniously disposed of?

"Oh! Don't look so horrified, Mr. Ford! And so taken back, Mr. Brady! There was a neatness and precision about this whole crime that surely must recommend it to any group of intelligent men. That intervening door was locked, of course, and if you heard no sounds from Mr. Ford's room that fatal evening, remember you were intended to hear none. It so happens, I myself performed the same little trick tonight. A short while ago, while you were playing cards, I entered Mr. Ford's room and blew the electric fuse and I believe, you gentlemen heard as little on this occasion as you did on the last."

I think we all gaped our surprise, much to Pete's embarrassment. For this one time, at any rate, I saw him disconcerted enough to mistake the low whistle Dunlap let out for mine. Under the shelter of the table he gave me a discreet kick and then said aloud:

"Instead of all that whistling Johnny, I wish you'd rustle us up a candle or a lamp. We could stand a little light around here, the Lord knows."

I nodded and moved off to obey orders. Still Pete didn't seem entirely at ease. As I left the room, I heard him saying:

"I wonder, Mr. Lamar, if you'd mind taking Ellis's place here. I'm never too sure of what that young explosive is going to do next."

That there was something behind the easy banter of Alcott's tone struck me at once. And when some few minutes later I returned to the room with the solitary candle Miguel had found for me, the conviction had grown upon me. I placed the candle in the center of the table (much to the general relief), settled into my new place and looked discreetly about me. To my right, Sanchez, with bloodshot eyes, was watching the scene with nervous expectancy. To my left, Brady smiled, affable, wide-eyed, insouciant.

Meanwhile, Alcott, his mouth set grimly, was proceeding in his low, even tone. "Yes, gentlemen, my theory is that Wyndham's unconscious body was passed through that door, into the hands that waited there to grasp him. Then quietly, noiselessly, that door was once more shut and locked. And all the while, in here, remember, chairs were being overturned, and you gentlemen were singing, laughing and cutting up, egged on, doubtless, by those who had most to gain.

"My hunch is that the two gangsters (and I say gangsters not without reason) who waited in the next room, hoisted Wyndham's limp body up between them, slapped one of their hats over his eyes, and with their arms firmly around his body, and with his arms limply and lifelessly about their necks, managed under the cover of that infernal darkness, to get him down the service stairway, and out the rear door. On the street outside, there no doubt stood a waiting car, ready to convey them to some stretch of the waterfront where they could dispose of their guilty burden without leaving a trace. Yes, gentlemen, that's my theory, though God alone can prove it. However, I've a few facts that do corroborate it, oddly enough!"

He looked around at each of the men at the table, studying their tense faces, biding his time, playing like an orchestra leader for his maximum effect.

"Some of my minor corroborative testimony is the sudden appearance on the morning of February 14th of a discolored mark on the wall of room 208, just by the electric switch. This was made no doubt when that fuse was blown. Also there is the fact that shortly after midnight on the night of February 13th, (to be exact at about 12:30 A.M. on the morning of the 14th), three men passed out the service door of this hotel, two of them lending what seemed to be the helping hand to a man who appeared dead drunk. Interesting, isn't it? Yes, but more interesting still is the fact that last night, young Calvin Watts was shot down in cold blood, because, poor cuss, the actual significance of your unused lighters suddenly occurred to him and with more clarity than seems to have been good for his health, he let his knowledge be too widely known. Regrettable! Of course! Tragic! Yes! A thoroughly contemptible crime quite worthy of the hand that plotted the end of Stephen Wyndham. Which brings me, gentlemen, to the strangest part of all. . . ."

The dead silence of the room was broken only by the chance sounds from the corridor outside. Young Stone leaned forward, his myopic eyes wide with expectancy. On Sanchez' forehead great beads of perspiration were breaking out, trickling slowly down his face and neck. Brady had abandoned his wide, clear look of blue-eyed innocence, Lamar his air of casual omniscience. Only Ford and Dunlap sat by motionless, tense, imperturbable.

"Yes, the strangest fact of all, gentlemen, is that each one of you assembled in this room tonight, excepting only Mr. Brady, I believe—each one of you, I say, had a very good reason to have struck that dastardly blow in the dark. For each of you, as I see it, stood to profit in his own way from Wyndham's untimely end."

There was a gasp of protest from that semi-darkness. Then Alcott's voice above the tempest.

"Oh, gentlemen, it won't do to get excited. There are police in the corridor just outside."

Chapter XXV

THE CHARGE

THE effect of Alcott's announcement was electric. As abruptly as the storm had arisen it subsided. Everyone still looked as though they would have liked to have given Alcott a sock in the jaw, but as usually happens when everyone wants to do something, no one actually does anything. In consequence, Alcott got a momentary chance to peer through the flickering candle light at the circle of set, angry people around him. Whatever was churning in the hidden recesses of his mind, at that moment, God alone knew. To me, his eyes looked a trifle mad, but his manner, as always, was calm and unruffled.

"Yes, I repeat it, gentlemen. With the exception of one person here, every one of you stood to profit very neatly from Wyndham's untimely end. Oh, yes, we may as well face the facts, unpleasant as they are. Even the charming Señorita Lola doesn't seem to have been above reproach." Alcott's eyes sought hers out through the shadow. "Hm, yes. By the way, Señorita, I learned today that when you took up your stand outside Wyndham's door on the fatal night, you carried this little trinket with you!"

Alcott took a narrow steel stiletto from his pocket and casually tossed it down on the table in front of him. "An ugly little thing, isn't it?" he said eyeing the blade in the wavering candle light. "Especially for a pretty woman."

Lolita's voice came tremulously through the shadows. "You know not what you say, you Americano. That stiletto was for my heart, not for *his*, if I found he no longer loved me."

Alcott shrugged impatiently. "Maybe. Just the same, my charge holds with regard to you all." He made an inclusive gesture around the table then turned slightly to his left, peering intently through the darkness at the well tailored bulk that loomed beside him. "As for you, Mr. Dunlap, I've a hunch you bore Stephen Wyndham a grudge because, no doubt, he knew you for the cad you really were."

The sheer audacity of Pete's attack took my breath and then I grew cold with apprehension for him. For Dunlap had pushed his chair back and risen unsteadily to his feet.

"Yes, Mr. Dunlap," Alcott went on coolly. "You knew that Wyndham was in love with your wife and that she, due to your abuse, neglect or what you will, had come to care for him. Well, sir, jealousy may *sometimes* be an overrated emotion, but I'd say *not* in your case."

But Dunlap's endurance had snapped somewhere back in the darkness. "By God," he muttered drunkenly through his set teeth, "if no one's going to shut this maniac up, I will." His arm shot out, but Alcott caught it in a sudden vise and pushed him unceremoniously back in his chair.

"Don't be incautious, Mr. Dunlap! It makes you look so guilty. After all, I'm going to have my say this once, though Hell itself breaks loose. Do you get me?"

There was a rising outburst from the table: "The fellow's mad. . . ." "What's the big idea? . . ." "Do we have to put up with this?" . . . "Aw, quiet, it's a good show. . . ." "Rats." "Why doesn't someone fix the lights?" An angry ripple.

But with a fixed, steady smile, Alcott went ploughing ahead. "And get this straight, gentlemen, I'm aware there's enough desperation in this room tonight to blow me to Kingdom Come. All right, but let me warn you, I'm not exactly a fool. Before coming here, I took definite precautions, so that no matter what happens to me, gentlemen, justice will somehow be done."

"Good boy!" I said inwardly, impressed anew by Pete's cool courage, his crazy-right hunches; in fact, every damned thing about the guy.

And all the while, Alcott forging recklessly ahead. With a slow smile he had turned to Ford.

"As for you, Mr. Ford, you were in bad need of ready cash, I believe. Standard of living out of scale with regular income. Hopelessly infatuated at the time, from all reports. You held a valuable power of attorney from Stephen Wyndham. On the whole, it would have profited you considerable to have been able to draw every now and then on Wyndham's estate without having to give an accounting to anyone. Or wouldn't it? There! Don't protest!" For Ford's jaw had dropped open abruptly, and he sat forward peering at Alcott through the semi-darkness as though he were not hearing or seeing aright. But Alcott, impervious and unheeding, took an envelope from his pocket and laid it before him. "There are the dates and the amounts of your withdrawals from Manning & Wilson, together with a few other items of information you may find of interest. You can look it over at your convenience."

Ford wasted no time in doing so. Idly I wondered what the other items might be. The withdrawal of funds from Wyndham's brokerage account, and that mysteriously unexplained room on the night of Wyndham's disappearance were the only facts that I knew against the man. And they seemed enough.

But Alcott was proceeding.

"Now for you, Mr. Stone." He looked quietly into the myopic eyes of the young missionary. "You were frantic to return to China. You didn't have a red cent to your name. Stephen Wyndham never liked you. But Miss Isabella . . . ah, now, if *she* were suddenly to come into the whole of the Wyndham fortune? It might mean a return trip to China. Why do you start, my lad? Miss Isabella has always told you her brother was no count. She's hated him since boyhood with a murderous hate. If he dies—well, there's just one sinner less in the world, you reason. Ah, yes," Alcott's voice grew low and tense, "and remember, a chance to go back to that young Chinese girl whom you loved."

"Look out what you say or I'll tell a few things!" The words hurdled at Alcott through the shadows. I strained to see Stone's face at the time he cried out. He was sitting forward in his chair, white and nervous. And this once his foolish smile seemed frozen on his lips.

And still Alcott's voice, like a steel whip cutting through the darkness.

"As for you, Señor Sanchez, we went into the facts against you rather thoroughly at Headquarters yesterday. You've already admitted to the police your insane jealousy of Lolita Caros. You've admitted to the Police that you had threatened Wyndham's life —oh, just in joke, I think you said."

Alcott's lips curved sarcastically. "But what you didn't confess to the police, I've a notion, was the lead weight you held in your fist when you were fighting with Wyndham and the long knife that you drew from your pocket that night in the dark."

There was a silence in the room so deep and prolonged that I thought it must be impenetrable. Then suddenly, I was aware of Lamar's good-natured drawl.

"Well, I say, don't I come in for my share of the general culpability?"

Suavely, Alcott turned toward him in the shadows. "Of course, Judge Lamar," he said in a particularly deferential tone. "Quite as much as the rest. There was your anxiety as to how much Wyndham knew of the part you played in the matter of those now almost forgotten Schmidt indictments. What was more, there was your black fear of what he might do with the unpleasant facts, with which he faced you on the afternoon of his last appearance."

Judge Lamar got up quietly and came around to my chair. "Is your friend quite all right?" he whispered to me, indignation and incredulity mingled in his tone.

I hardly knew what to answer. Inwardly, I was rather puzzled and worried myself. Alcott's calm seemed strained to the breaking point and his eyes burned with an intense gleam that I'd never seen before.

"Oh, yes, I'm quite all right, Judge Lamar," Alcott said wearily, as though divining what had been said. "And if you'll be so kind, I'll crave your indulgence a few moments more."

"As I was saying, gentlemen, we've motives in our midst a plenty. And yet, as we all know, a man does not go to the electric chair simply for motive. No," he said, and his voice sank to a tense whisper, "we have to nail this crime home a little closer than that."

"What in hell's the matter with you, Pete, old man?" I thought, half-aloud. An instant's pause. Then once more the old cool self-possession.

"Now, then, gentlemen, ask yourselves, who among you could have perpetrated this crime? You look blank. You shake your heads. And you're almost right. I've a hunch the person who struck the blow did not do it without an accomplice! I've a hunch that it was this accomplice who very cleverly manoeuvered your matches and lighters away from you! I've a hunch either the man or his accomplice was well acquainted in the underworld! Oh, yes, *particularly well acquainted!* I've a hunch that the decision to commit this crime was not long in formulating and that it followed very close upon the chance discovery that Wyndham was planning to leave Havana at midnight! I've a hunch that it necessitated access to Ford's room sometime during the fatal day, in order to obtain the key to that hall door! I've a hunch that the need for action loomed desperate, imperative, immediate! I've a hunch that the man who did

all of this was a master at that one supreme tribute
that vice must always pay to decency—I mean hy-
pocrisy. Yes, a sort of modern disciple of Macchiavelli's Prince. In other words, gentlemen, I've a hunch
we might ask the police in to arrest Judge Sanfred
Lamar!"

Chapter XXVI

GUILTY?

FOR a few seconds after the thunder clap of Alcott's statement, a pall of silence hung over the room. No one moved or uttered a sound. It was as though we were all stupefied, frozen to stone, by the very audacity of such a charge. I have an indistinct recollection of Alcott mopping his forehead and saying with faint sarcasm.

"In my indictment, I might also include the Honorable Mr. George Meenan. Only he had the good luck to have been quietly done away with some ten days ago in New York. Yes, gentlemen—when, my guess is, Judge Lamar grew a trifle uneasy about his fellow conspirator."

But no! The whole thing didn't hold water. It was too fantastic. I simply couldn't or wouldn't believe it. It was as though there was a void somewhere in my brain; as though the ground was opening beneath my feet; as though with the known dignity and honor of Judge Lamar, the very foundations of organized society were slipping.

I have a vague recollection of the sound of Lamar breathing shortly and heavily in the darkness. He still must have been standing behind me, for the sound came close to my ears. Then as though in a dream, I remember seeing him turn and stride back to his place at the table, a colossus of white indignation.

"I don't know whether you realize the seriousness of what you've just said, young fellow. That George Meenan myth I won't even stoop to discuss. I believe there is a death certificate that can prove the falsity of that. But with regard to the rest. . . ."

The Judge confronted Alcott squarely, his words weighted with deadly authority. Only the knuckles of his hands, showing strained and pale as he grasped the back of the chair in front of him gave a clue to his inward tension. "I warn you! Unless you retract your damnable charges here and now, I shall institute an immediate suit for slander against you, naming these gentlemen as my witnesses."

The Judge's poise was magnificent. He looked Alcott coldly up and down, a strong man facing his adversary, taking his measure cannily. The thought struck me of what incalculable force the man's reputation was. There wasn't a person at that table who wasn't solidly behind him.

In the balance, I felt Pete going down, down, irretrievably down! Until this point, I'd patiently swallowed all his reasoning. I'd talked myself into believing I saw most of his grounds, remote though they were. But now the water seemed closing over his head, engulfing him.

Nonetheless, even in the face of the tumult, Alcott's voice with the sting of ice:

"I retract nothing, Judge Lamar."

"Look out, you fool!" Anger glowed in Lamar's eyes, but he remained fixed in his terrible glacial calm. "You say, that Stephen Wyndham had learned of some alleged complicity of mine in the matter of those Schmidt acquittals?"

"Exactly."

"And what precisely was the nature of the complicity?"

Alcott, standing haggard but erect among the quivering shadows, flung his answer back defiantly. "Simply that you had accepted a bribe and the promise of political advancement for your white-wash of the Schmidt crowd when they came up for trial before you."

I was thankful to hear Judge Lamar's laugh in that semi-darkness. "Good God! If you weren't so altogether preposterous, I might be able to take you seriously."

He had voiced precisely what everyone present was feeling. You could see it in the lessening tension at the table. The whole thing was too monstrous and absurd. I began to feel a dim regret for my own haphazard association in the muddle. After all, just where did Pete get off to. . . . ?

But Alcott's jaw was set. "Perhaps you'd better take me seriously, Judge Lamar."

The Judge's face darkened with good old-fashioned wrath.

"And can you tell us why, if Mr. Wyndham was aware of all this, he should have neglected to bring these facts to light at once. There's young Ford over there who would have snapped at them. Wouldn't you Hughie?"

"Quite true," Alcott interrupted in a low voice, never even giving Ford a chance to answer, "but suppose Wyndham had no time to do so. Suppose he learned those facts only on the afternoon of his last appearance?"

Again the Judge laughed, the cool, easy laugh of one who feels himself as impregnable as Gibralter. I thought his bearing was superb; I was wishing I might borrow a little of it when I came to facing Gerraghty as I knew I would be doing in the not too distant future.

"I presume Mr. Meenan and I took a few drinks too many, and with the fumes of liquor still in our heads decided to take Stephen Wyndham into our confidence. Well, you can tell it to the Jury, young man. I'm through." Judge Lamar turned aside in obvious disgust.

"Not that story exactly!" Alcott persisted in his tense, low tone. "But I'll tell one that is equally strange." He took from his pocket a cablegram which he laid down coolly on the table. "This cable is the answer to your boast that I talk nonsense when I say that George Meenan was quietly murdered in his New York apartment. As for the rest. . . ." He paused and I noticed his eyes fixed Lamar with a cold, steady look. "Men are often overheard in the lockers of their Golf Clubs, Judge Lamar. And when they think themselves alone they are sometimes, perchance, a trifle indiscreet."

Judge Lamar eyed Alcott sharply.

Pete was standing tall and erect at the moment. A strange light gleamed in his eye. In the fitful shadows of that hotel-room he looked curiously impressive and awesome, like some self-appointed instrument of wrath.

"You'll have a hard time proving that to a court," Lamar said with sudden asperity.

Very quietly, I saw Alcott lean across the table toward him.

"Do you really think so?" he said in a queer voice, looking the Judge straight in the eye. An odd smile played over his lips, but there was no answering smile in his cold, clear blue eyes.

Suddenly Lamar drew back. The cold imprint of terror was on his face. "Good God . . !" he ejaculated slowly. In a flash, his hand shot out and grasped the narrow gleaming stiletto which still lay where Alcott had tossed it down before him. In another instant he had thrown his compact weight against the table, knocking it, and along with it our cards, our cash, our candle to the floor in another pandemonium of darkness.

I shall never forget those ensuing minutes. Somewhere near me, I heard the two men wrestling in deadly earnest. Panting, lunging, scraping, falling, rearing, clutching, scuffling, gasping. Bodies interlocked, knocking over furniture, curses, cuffs, the stench of sweat and fresh blood. Two desperate men battling for dear life. Why? Wherefore? It was beyond me.

I tried to throw my weight between them. Instead, I knocked over Ford, I think. And instantly two other men hurled themselves upon us, thinking our quarrel was the deadly one, I suppose. It was all a mess. Chairs overturning, doors opening, calls of police from the outside, the hammering of their clubs upon the door, then as they came in the welcome white flash of their searchlights probing, here and there, everywhere through the darkness. There was a moment's blank silence. Then all at once, we realized in surprise there was *no sign of Judge Lamar or Pete Alcott.*

"Good God! . . . where have they gone?"

Someone jabbed his finger toward the still open door that led to the room that had once been Ford's. I remembered in dismay that Alcott had failed to shut that door during his graphic reconstruction of the crime.

Now, through it, we crowded pell mell, like a herd of stampeding cattle. Again the police lights pierced the blackness, their beams stabbing at the walls, the floor, the ceilings. But they revealed only emptiness, complete and undisturbed.

We stared at each other like fools. We gazed about us like lunatics. The hall door stood open. "Try the corridor!" "The baths!" "The other room!"

We rushed here and there about the suite like a pack of maniacs. Then from somewhere, outside in the hallway, came the short agonized cry of a man in pain.

I think I'll never forget that particular cry. To the end of my days, it will come back to disturb the quiet of campfires, and the peace of lonely grey dawns. It was a sound that stopped the heart. It curdled the blood. In its tone was peril and darkness and need.

But where? Where? We looked everywhere for that cry. We pounded doors. We searched passageways. To me, that quest seemed to last not for minutes, but weeks, months, years, through all eternity. Yes, through worlds without end. It was maddening.

Then suddenly, Miguel struck the right scent. The

large storeroom across the corridor from Ford's room! He had left the door wide open when he had gone to get the candle for me. Now the door was locked. He tried his passkey, to no avail. The cupboard key was obviously on the inside. At a word from the police captain, Miguel and the aide began removing the door from its hinges. And so at length, under the harsh glare of police lights, we found ourselves gazing down on the prostrate, unconscious form of Judge Sanfred Lamar. And I turned aside.

For the face of Lynn's uncle looked gruesome and terrible. Not like one who had died and gone simply to Hell, but rather like one who had reached its nethermost rung before death had ever intervened. The right hand, stained with blood, was clutched tightly against his heart. His left still lay clenched as though in pain.

The Captain bent forward and examined the body more closely. He spoke quickly, in Spanish, to his companion. In another instant, they were prying Lamar's blood-stained fingers loose from their grasp and revealing, to our amazed eyes, the handle of the little stiletto where he had thrust it into his flesh.

And still I couldn't grasp it. Lamar who had so calmly and defiantly accepted every situation? Lamar at the end of the strength? Lamar plunged into that abyss of stark desperation where man and his reason are together overthrown?

I heard the police captain saying in English:

"From the position of the Señor's hand, and the direction of that knife in the body, it would appear a clear case of suicide."

The scratching of a pencil. The police aide was making notations.

"Also that store-room door—locked on the inside."

But the evidence was obvious.

"Now gentlemen, what can you tell us?"

A babble of ready tongues. And still the essential fact took an endless time crawling through my brain. Suicide! Lynn's uncle!

I saw someone pick up Alcott's discarded cable-gram and read it aloud. The words sounded a mile off.

PETER ALCOTT
HAVANA POST
HAVANA.

M'S BODY EXHUMED BY COURT ORDER YESTERDAY STOP MEDICAL EXAMINATION SHOWS DISTINCT TRACES OF POISON IN STOMACH STOP INVESTIGATION KEPT QUIET FOR PRESENT STOP SO THERE WAS SOMETHING ROTTEN IN DENMARK

BILLY

How the chain of Lamar's evil-doing clanked even at the moment of his death.

Then someone was saying, "Where's the other fellow?"

The police captain nodded. "Si! Si! That would be well."

He gave orders to his aide to make a thorough search for Alcott. Everyone joined in that quest. That is, everyone except Ford, who, after satisfying the Captain's questions, excused himself abruptly on some airy pretext of an appointment.

That hunt was thorough. The lights were on by

now and we looked everywhere for my missing friend. Literally, high and low.

At last we found a night watchman who told us that a man following Pete's description had passed out the rear door sometime earlier. Dimly, as one in a dream, I perceived that Alcott must have taken his departure immediately following Lamar's suicide, before we had ever reached the store-room door or the service stairs.

The police captain shrugged temperamentally. "Ah, well . . . we need little more for our record than that locked door and a few of these gentlemen."

Yes, all very well for the police to be philosophical. But *where,* and *why the devil* had *Pete* gone?

Chapter XXVII

THE REAL BLOW

I SETTLED my account at the hotel desk, sent a cursory statement of Lamar's suicide back to Tim Gerraghty as a sort of peace offering, and left the Sevilla Biltmore in a kind of daze. As I swung down the Paseo de Marti, I asked myself a dozen times if I had by chance dreamed the whole series of events. It was not simply that the facts had developed so differently from what I'd expected. As a newspaperman I was used to surprises. But this!

An intolerable sense of fatigue weighed me down, a dull heavy feeling under the influence of which I forgot all the horror, consternation and gloom I'd felt for Lamar's end; I forgot the ripping story Alcott and I had at last succeeded in landing; I forgot everything except a deep regret that our coup should have ended by bringing this tragedy to Lynn's door.

I was aware I must see Lynn without delay. I knew it was up to me to do what little I could to take the edge off this blow for her. With that thought in mind, I pushed along the street, looking about for a cab.

The night was damp and torrid. The moon on the gulf in the distance seemed sinking beneath its own weight of silver. Mournfully my footsteps re-echoed through the silent streets. But of all this I was aware only as one in a dream. The sad rhythm of my thoughts held me. Lynn! What was I going to tell her? The only decent part of the rotten mess was that Lamar had had the decency to stick a knife into himself.

"Your uncle Fred . . . not quite what we've thought him . . . that Wyndham mess of last year. . . . Something to do with those Schmidt racketeers. . . . Anything in the world that I can do. . . . Darling, please don't worry."

But I knew she was too clever not to. In an instant she'd see the whole baleful cataclysm of scandal that would be let loose. And that I should have had a hand in plunging her into this crucible of trouble. That was the thought that stuck and pinched and tormented me.

In desperation I tried to occupy my thoughts. Mechanically, I counted the masts of the fishing boats which I could see in the harbor. I counted lamp posts. I watched my shadow shorten abruptly, then lengthen to monstrous size as I passed each successive street lamp. But none of this soothed or lulled me. Lynn! Lynn! Damn my luck! Fate plays us scurvy tricks now and then!

At length I succeeded in finding a taxi. I gave the sleepy driver the number of Lamar's residence. "Drive like hell," I said to him. Now that the moment was at hand, I wanted to get it over with as swiftly as possible.

The moon had disappeared by the time we turned up the now familiar Vedado driveway. In front of me, the Lamar house loomed dark and silent! Paying the driver off, I sprang across to the entrance and rang the bell.

After what seemed an interminable time the door was opened by a sleepy butler, his white uniform only half buttoned over his still protruding night shirt.

"I would like to see Miss Lynn Dawson at once."

He looked at me in surprise and rubbed his eyes.

"Miss Dawson!" I repeated more sharply. "It's very important. You'll have to wake her."

"But she's gone, Señor!" he said stupidly.

"Gone where?"

"I don't know. She go away yesterday morning. She do not say where."

"Oh, that's impossible," I said foolishly.

But the fellow was obdurate.

"Yes, Señor. She come down sudden with all her baggage. She tell me to call a cab. That is all I know, Señor."

"Was anyone ill?"

The man shook his head. It was obvious he was as much at sea as I.

In sudden desperation I asked him to get me a drink. I felt in bad need of one.

And while he fumbled with the decanters and glasses, I walked to the mantel and pressed my forehead against its cool marble surface. "Think, old boy," I said patronizingly to myself. "It's the best thing you can do now!"

But my head refused to work. The past weary days were too much with me. Instead, I stared stupidly before me.

How long I'd been staring thus I hardly know.

But suddenly I was aware of an envelope at the other end of the mantel. At first it seemed more of a phantom than a reality. "Mr. John D. Ellis." Then I recognized the handwriting as Lynn's.

"You didn't mention a letter!" I said brusquely, as the fellow crossed to me, a tray with a glass and Bacardi in his outstretched hand.

"Miss Dawson say I should deliver it to the gentleman in the morning."

"Well, I'll take it now."

The fellow watched me with sudden interest.

I tore the note open.

Johnny dear,

This is goodbye! Something's come up unexpectedly. Perhaps we stayed out dancing too long last night—but anyhow, those hours were wonderful and I'll think back on them many times, I know.

As to what came later, I can say nothing. Only Johnny, believe me, it's a ghastly mess.

I'm getting away, as quickly and as far as I can.

The chances are we won't meet again, at any rate not for a long, long time. Think of me kindly once in a while.

Lynn

So this was the end. I gulped down my Bacardi in a wave of pity for myself, for Lynn, for half the mad world.

But mostly for Lynn, poor girl!

That she had suspected her uncle's guilt I could plainly see. But how? Could it have been that she found the clue in that well-thumbed volume of Macchiavelli's Prince that I'd remarked on just yesterday? I wondered. Could it have been that she had come upon her uncle the night before stealing back into the house after his miserable attempt upon Watts, his manner as suave as ever, his smile as broad, his still warm revolver concealed in his pocket?

Well. God alone knew, though maybe Alcott would have another good hunch. Yes, Peter Alcott, of course! He had enough to explain to me anyhow. I poured myself another glass of Bacardi and sick at heart, I turned out into the night to find him.

Chapter XXVIII

EXIT—A SLEUTH

I TRAMPED back to my hotel through the sultry night. I'd hoped exercise and exhausting fatigue would lay the ghost of the night's tragedy. But to my dismay, I found ghosts aren't shaken so readily. Step by step, Lamar and Lynn stuck to me, haunting, mocking or wistful. There was no eluding them. After a while, heavy-hearted and weary, I gave up the attempt. I grew used to my strange companions; Lynn, I decided I'd keep by me always, as a lone sentimental indulgence. As for Lamar?

The tangled facts were slowly taking form. Realistic and clear headed again, I knew we had the scoop of a life time. The newspaperman in me was boiling up, spilling over. Well, we'd covered our story and we'd covered it goddamn right. And what a story! An outstanding Judge with a life enmeshed in crooked underworld dealings! The wanton sacrifice of one of America's young sporting idols! The murder of a backstage political boss! The stern but visible justice of Lamar's end. And over and behind it all the long shadow of the Schmidt corruption. The dark menace of the racketeer in our very courts. There'd be a hullaballoo. It made me almost homesick for the old news factory. I could hear Gerraghty barking out orders. "Tear out the front page! Some-

thing big!" I could see the banner headlines and the
rumpus. And to think the old *Globe* would break
with the story and break exclusively. Jesus, I could
almost sniff the clean inky smell of that first edition.

And still there were questions, dozens of them
that kept rearing their heads, demanding notice. A
mass of things, churning in my consciousness, driving
me forward with wild impatience.

By the time I reached our tumble-down hotel I'd
come to the pitch where I wanted nothing so much
in the world as the sight of Alcott's battered old mug,
and the sound of him saying, "Y'know, I just had a
hunch . . . !" And the second thing I wanted was
a clear open wire to the *New York Globe*. My spirit
seemed bottled within me. I cleared the garden in a
half dozen strides, hastened irresistibly by the streak
of yellow light I saw shining from under the drawn
shade of our room. I pushed at the door, but it did
not give. Then in what for me was an unparalleled
surge of decent feeling, I remembered that Alcott
hadn't slept for a couple of days himself, and taking
my key from my pocket, I unlocked the door as
quietly as I could and tiptoed into the room.

But I could have saved myself the trouble. There
was no prone figure of Alcott snoring peacefully in
his bed. There was no sound of Alcott splashing
contentedly in his bath. In fact, there was no evidence of Alcott anywhere at all. Somewhat taken
back, ridiculously disappointed, I stared around me.

The room was in wild disorder. Bureau drawers
stood open. The closet door yawned cavernous and
wide. In the upset, I recognized a few of my own
things strewn casually over the floor and the furni-

ture. Mentally I swore at Pete for his cheerful impudence.

Then suddenly something struck me with peculiar force, riveting my attention, shaking me out of all minor annoyance. It was the absence of Pete's shaving set from its accustomed place on the bureau. Good Lord! And his grip from where it used to stand under the bed. I dashed to the closet and stared in. Gone were the now familiar, but still hideous orange pajamas. Gone the array of cheap haberdashery and worse suits and shirts. I yanked out bureau drawers, I peered into the bath. Gone was every shoe, every sock, every sign, every vestige of Peter Alcott.

Dazed and unbelieving, I sat down by the side of the bed. This was the last straw. Confronted by the final riddle of this abandoned room my spirits sank, bedraggled, exhausted. On the table nearby my old black memo book caught my eye, a doleful reminder of more sanguine hours. Dully I wondered how the blamed thing ever got there and then I realized that in the day's mad rush I had forgotten to put it into my pocket. Now it seemed, along with myself, a sad relic of all this insane adventure.

Mechanically I reached over for it and with my movement, a long envelope, hitherto unnoticed, was brushed to the floor. I stooped and picked it up. From the corner I noticed a packet of greenbacks protruding. Incapable now of any further surprise, I took them out and counted them slowly. Fifteen, one hundred dollar bills, crisp and new. A line from Alcott, in his familiar large scrawl, fluttered to the floor. It lay there staring up at me.

This, I think, should cover our expenses. Forgive me, Johnny, for taking French leave. I told you to pay attention to Porkie Smith's letter and that little gold medallion.

Pete

But I didn't bother to pick the note up. I didn't trouble to speculate how Alcott had managed to get his hands on that much cash. I didn't even question where Alcott had gone, though privately I hoped to . . . Hell! I was blazing mad.

Gloomily I stared down at my old black memo book, thinking of the myriads of questions therein, wondering like a schoolboy on examination how the devil I'd manage to get them answered.

I turned to the first page absently, then immediately I sat up. At a glance, I saw that the old precision and order had departed from my pages. My questions were still there, to be sure, standing stiffly at attention, but sprawling down the margins, across headings, between lines was a jumble of hasty writing that I could hardly decipher.

I drew my old book closer, peering intently at its pages. Then I gave a whoop of joy.

Under my first question: What is the mystery of the Wyndham will? Alcott had scribbled:

Simply Miss Isabella. She destroyed her father's real will, bringing forward an older one, whereby she would inherit jointly with her brother. Stephen was aware of her guilt, having seen her at the safe on the night of Wyndham, Sr.'s death. He did not mind the division of the estate, but as he grew older, the knowledge of Isabella's guilty act increased the strain between them. Keep this under your hat.

The reason for Charles Stone's visit to the Sevilla Biltmore? Pete's hunch was that Stone wanted to borrow money. And my hunch was Pete was right.

So my eye raced on, from one page to the next. Yes. There the answers all were. For Pete's strange questions to the night man at the hotel! Of Ford's use of his power of attorney actually to help Mrs. Dunlap. (Well, I had done the fellow an injustice, I had to admit it.) That mangled cigarette! The visit of Stone's to the Orient? Ah! So Pete had translated the Chinese letter which Stone had carelessly dropped in our room, and learned in that way that "Parson" Charles had secretly married his Chinese sweetheart. As for that wheel which had so mysteriously come off our taxi at Lolita's hacienda, Alcott still leaned toward the theory of accident. And he stuck to the same theory to explain the near casualty on the street corner and the delapidated ceiling that had fallen on our beds.

I read on, absorbed and fascinated. Once I even smiled to myself. Under my query about the mysterious room which Ford had engaged at the Sevilla Biltmore, Alcott had scrawled:

Have a heart. I've a hunch we shouldn't say any more to Mr. and Mrs. Ford about that.

But by the time I'd come to the end of the book, I was no better satisfied than I'd been at the beginning. Ironically I now wondered why I'd ever thought I would be. I saw clearly that most of those questions, enigmatic as they'd seemed when I had jotted them down, not so many days ago, had been answered already by the night's strange events, or, what was more to the point, completely overshadowed by the strange and more baffling problems to which this same night had given rise. Yes. But about everything pertaining to this last phase, Pete was curiously silent. Damn him! If he thought he was going to get away with this.

I got out my old portable and with vindicative energy, I commenced pounding away. Alcott or no Alcott, the facts had to be gotten into some sort of shape for the paper and promptly. But with all the loose ends dangling it was a harder job than I'd supposed. Dawn broke. Sunlight crept into the garden. And still I worked away.

I think it must have been long after seven, when I looked up from my typewriter, certain I had heard a knock.

Hoping, dreading, I knew not what, I crossed and opened the door. Outside stood my old friend the day porter with a letter in his hand. At a glance, I saw it bore a Havana postmark.

"Thanks," I said listlessly, handing him some change. I noticed the handwriting on the envelope was Alcott's and that the letter had been posted the night before.

I went back to the table and slowly opened it. Then, at once, I sat forward, perceiving the high speed and terrific strain under which that letter had been written.

I reprint that communication here in full because it was one of the strangest documents I ever read.

"Johnny," it began abruptly.

Chapter XXIX

AN OVERDUE EXPLANATION

YES. "Johnny," that letter began:

I don't know whether I'll ever get to see you again.
In fact, I don't know that I'll even be alive by the time
our session at the Sevilla Biltmore is over tonight. For
which reason, this letter, that justice may somehow be
done.

Should anything happen to me as I half anticipate,
my advice is to communicate with Calvin Watts as soon
as possible. By the way it was his chance recollection of
Judge Lamar having begged or borrowed matches and
lighters from everyone present on the fatal 13th that
clinched this mystery for me at last. Though to be
honest, I had a pretty good hunch that was the way the
wind blew even before I saw Watts last night. Watts is
better and he's going to pull through. And he'll help
you fight this thing tooth and nail.

The letter broke off abruptly. Half way down the
page, it continued in pencil.

There's something more I'd like to tell you, even if
it makes me late for our 10 o'clock appointment. It's
about that letter of Porkie Smith's. You thought it
unimportant. There you missed your guess. Do you
remember the 'bad customer' he described having found
on his boat on the night of February 13th? The one

who was so peculiarly silent and never even gave his name?

You should have looked into that matter. That fellow didn't give his name because he didn't know it. He didn't talk because he didn't know what on God's earth to say. His memory of every single thing that had happened to him before he opened his eyes on that fishing boat was gone. Wiped clean. A dead blank.

You would have found out that when Porkie Smith let him off in the States, the only thing he knew for certain was that for some unknown reason he wanted to get back to New York and badly. Why? He couldn't have told you. He didn't have a paper of identification about him. What was even worse for his plan, he didn't have a red cent to his name. Just his clothes and a few impersonal knick-knacks that must have been overlooked when he was dropped by chance on Porkie's boat.

Well, he knocked around at odd jobs at first. Then, by degrees, he found that he had a good bit of education and for some queer reason, he seemed to know a hell of a lot about sports. He traded on the last to good advantage, but despite his local success, there was always a constant inexplicable pull that he felt toward New York. Why? He hardly knew. Only for some vague reason that city seemed closer to his past.

At last when he had sufficient money saved up, he yielded to the impulse and took a train for New York. Once there, he found himself a job, but no particular light. His entire identity and background remained as obscured as ever. Terribly discouraged, he settled to his grind, succeeding in work beyond his expectation; but, aside from that, keeping much to himself, uncertain of anything and everything that lay outside his particular field.

Then one day, by chance, he picked up a newspaper. This Wyndham case had broken wide open. There was a picture of Steve Wyndham on the first page. Aghast with amazement, dizzy with wonder, *he suddenly knew who he was!*

At first, the sheer joy of discovery held him enthralled. You should have known him in those days as I did. Then by slow degrees, another feeling overcame him. He thought back upon his plight. His awful condition when he was picked up on that fishing yawl. The nightmare of those months of *not knowing*. (Amnesia's the correct name for this trouble, I've since found out.) It all seemed wild and unbelievable. The last thing he could remember was that he had been playing poker with some friends.

But were they friends? Slowly, bitterly, he faced that thought. And if they were friends, how could this horror have ever come about? Why had there been no protest? No outcry? He who had been so happy-go-lucky in the past was now bitten through and through with a desire to find out which of those men had done him in. For one of them had. Of that he was certain. As his mind turned back upon events he even found he had very good grounds of suspicion against a few. But the actual criminal? Yes? Which of those eight men was the actual criminal? He must know.

Meanwhile, the papers were off on the wrong trail. Nothing was uncovered. There were a dozen false leads. He watched them all, biding his time, waiting the opportunity he craved. For by now, with every ounce of his strength, with every square inch of him, he wanted justice and revenge.

Well, Johnny, I've a hunch you know the rest of the story as well as I do.

As to how I found out about this—don't puzzle too much, old punk. But then perhaps you've already guessed. Yes. In spite of the grey hair that came almost overnight, in spite of the scars that have changed my face almost beyond recognition, in spite of the broken nose and the loss of weight and oh, yes, let's not forget the nifty clothes—in short, in spite of every damned thing, I *am Stephen Wyndham!*

Nervelessly that letter fell from my hand. I picked it up and slowly read it through a second time just to make sure I hadn't taken complete leave of my reason. A kind of mad incredulity had me in its grip. I simply couldn't get the full import of that last sentence through my head. Then a legion of things came storming back into my consciousness, bolstering up Pete's amazing disclosure.

The very python skin cigarette case that had been our first lead on this adventure. Of course! I could see it all now. That case had been one of those few "impersonal knick knacks" left in Wyndham's pocket at the time of the tragedy. No wonder Peter Alcott had been able to produce it so opportunely.

There was Lolita's instant attraction to Alcott. Good Lord! Sure! She must have intuitively sensed who he was, or anyhow felt a strong resemblance. I laughed aloud at the recollection of her words that night in the garden. "Your frien'—he do not seem like the ordinaire newspaper man to me." And then I gave another laugh as I remembered the Police Communication that had spoken of the particular insistence of Señora de Sanchez that her arrest was an outrage and her confidence that when she could face Alcott and me justice promptly would be done. Well, I had to admit it, the lady was smarter than I.

My thoughts raced back to my first encounter with Miss Isabella and there loomed a whole phalanx of supporting testimony. Alcott's neat bombshell about the Wyndham will. Why hadn't I then suspected? Why indeed? Yet more significant things had passed me by.

Carefully I now went over that scene at the Wyndham mansion. When Alcott had suggested that visit to Miss Isabella's, he must have felt convinced that the change that had taken place in his appearance precluded the remotest chance of recognition, especially from a sister whom he had seen so infrequently. Yet even so, I recalled Miss Isabella's startled manner and strange comment in the darkened hallway when first she had heard Alcott's voice; and how later in the drawing room, she had peered at him again and again with such curious interest. Doubtless, seeing the gaunt grey-haired figure before her, her suspicions had been lulled temporarily, but they had not remained so for long. Something familiar in Pete's voice or manner must have come back to trouble her when once she had time to consider the matter carefully. I smiled now when I thought back upon the peculiar letter that she sent to young Stone the next morning. No wonder she had written in so anxious a vein. She must have been greatly puzzled by Alcott's conduct. She must have wanted to investigate at once. And poor "Parson" Stone? Uncertain, not too sure of his ground, shadowing us on her orders, of course.

Now that I thought it all over carefully, it seemed almost funny. No wonder that day at the Post Office Pete had dodged that face to face encounter with Stone. No wonder he had left me to attend that Charity Fete by myself. No wonder he had felt tired and impelled to turn in that very first night when young "Parson" Stone had paid his late visit to his rooms. Yes, and buried himself in the Sports section that day when Dunlap had burst into the newspaper office. I smiled to myself when I thought of what I had said to him only two nights prior. "You lazy bum, don't you think it almost time you took a crack at a few of our leads directly? You haven't talked to a single damned one yet—excepting old Miss Isabella." Well, no wonder he had answered, "I'll see them all, but in my own good time."

My thoughts raced to the night before when at last Pete had confronted what was left of that strange poker party. In the dim candle light of that chamber, changed as he was beyond any casual recognition, it would have been expected that no one except Stone and Lola, and possibly Sanchez could have guessed at his identity. And yet as I thought back on that scene, I remembered Hugh Ford's expression when Alcott had turned on him, and how that smart redhead's jaw had dropped open in sheer amazement and he had sat staring at the scarred, gaunt man before him as though he was seeing a ghost.

Of course! Of course! In the end Judge Lamar must have guessed the secret too. It accounted for his brutal attack upon Alcott. Good God! No wonder, faced with the implacable fact of Wyndham's risen corpse he had realized the game was up.

My mind turned to the singular stroke of good fortune that had enabled Pete to "come back" from that cunningly contrived doom. What a near call. A dark night! A hurried job! Lamar and Meenan had intended him for the black gulf, of course. And instead the gangsters had bungled, and he had landed among the hooks and rigging of Porkie Smith's fishing smack. Holy God! It was rare luck. Yes, even if that fall had netted him a few bad scars, a broken nose and a temporary case of amnesia, at any rate he had come away with his life. Thinking it all over, now, it seemed as simple as two and two, and so wildly, madly preposterously right! Man alive! What a story!

In a flash, I crossed to the telephone and grabbed the receiver.

"Get me Long Distance. New York. Canal 6-5600!" I shouted to the English speaking operator. "I want to talk to Mr. Timothy Gerraghty, *New York Globe,* soon as you can get him."

"Si! Si! But it takes a few minutes, Señor!" she answered dulcetly.

I hung up, but nonetheless, remained rooted by the phone, agog with impatience.

In twenty-three seconds exactly the bell rang. I snatched at the receiver.

"Hello! Hello!"

The operator spoke up. "An outside call for you, Señor. I'll put it through until I can get New York. Si?"

Then I heard Pete's voice at the other end of the wire.

"Good morning, Johnny!"

A gasp of surprise registered my presence.

"Don't pass out on me, old punk. I just thought for once I'd explain my sudden walk-out."

"You'd better!"

"Well, this has something to do with those missions of mine around the island! Remember?"

"Quit stalling and come to the point, you big bum!"

"The point is . . . er . . . those trips . . . well . . . they didn't all come under the head of work. See?"

"Aw, cut the mystery! The police want to talk to you."

"Damn the police! You've got to fix things with them and without saying too much. Yeah, and with Tim Gerraghty, too. What I want to tell you is—er—"

"Well, get it out!"

"Carol Sutherland Dunlap and I were married last night."

"Holy God! That's great. My congratulations! Where are you?"

"Pulling out on a cruise and in a devilish short time. What I want to know is . . . what do you say to coming along? It would give you a couple of months to ask questions."

"That's awfully decent. But, aw—I've an interview, day after tomorrow with Tim Gerraghty—only he doesn't know it yet. Anyhow, two's company—"

"But we're more than two already. Hugh Ford is taking us off for a honeymoon."

"Hold on!" I interrupted, my brain working now like a forest fire. "Then that letter you handed Ford at the table last night . . . ?"

"Exactly. It contained instructions as to where and how he should meet me. That was, providing I ever got out of that place alive."

But still the forest fire was raging through my head.

"Not so fast, Pete . . ." (Whatever was I to call him?) . . . "You don't get off without explaining one more thing!"

"What next?"

"That missing gold medallion with the "C. S." engraved!"

"Oh, that! It was an old one of Carol's. I took it myself because I would have liked to have kept her name out of all this mess if I could have. But one thing sure, you can't say I didn't give you decent warning that in the disappearance of that medallion lay a very important clue!"

"You old son-of-a-gun! You just wait! I'll do you both up properly for the *New York Globe!*"

"Oh, no you don't, Johnny. If you remember neither party to our contract is to give out any newspaper publicity without the express consent of the other. I'm not consenting . . . just yet."

"But, Pete, you lousy stiff. . . ."

"The Captain's calling us. Can't argue. Sure you won't join us?"

"NO!"

"Then get this. Carol and I are off for points unknown and a few months of quiet and rest. Lord knows we need it. I'll make it up to you later, old punk. Meanwhile, goodbye and good luck, Johnny Ellis."

Mechanically I replaced the receiver but stood where I was, dazed and wondering why in the name of reason I'd ever let myself into anything so absurd.

"That ends your world-beating scoop, old man,"

I said, dolefully to myself. "When you, and you only, hold every trump in the situation, too. Jesus God! What a break."

I called back the operator.

"Cancel that call to New York."

There was nothing else to do. I'd given my word.

I walked across to my typewriter and sat down in deep dejection. The typed pages looked up at me sorrowingly, full of reproach. With infinite reluctance, I slid the last sheet from the carriage and tore it along with all the rest into a hundred hopeless pieces.

"No newspaper publicity without the express consent of the other!" What a fool thing ever to have signed. Then suddenly I looked up. "No *newspaper* publicity . . ." that damned pledge had specified. But Holy God in Heaven! We hadn't said a word of all the other means that exist for relating a queer yarn. I could change all the names! I could shape it into a semblance of fiction! I could record those facts exactly as they had unfolded before me.

I took a fresh piece of paper and slipped it into place. Swiftly my fingers touched the keyboard. And then softly and cheerily I began whistling my old pet tune.

> *"I've taken my fun where I've found it;*
> *I've rogued an' I've ranged in my time."*

Bon voyage, Peter Alcott. We'll be even yet!

THE END